Books by Mary Wasche

Resolute Heart
Escape to Alaska
Murder in Wasilla

Resolute Heart

Mary Wasche

◇◇◇◇◇◇◇◇◇◇

Mary Wasche

Mary Wasche
PO Box 238
Isle, Minnesota 56342

No part of this book may be reproduced or transmitted in any form, including information storage or retrieval systems electronic or mechanical or photocopying without the written permission of the author/publisher.

This is a work of fiction. All names, characters, and incidents depicted herein are the product of the author's imagination.

Any resemblance to persons living or dead or to actual events is coincidental.

The unauthorized reproduction or distribution of this copyrighted work is illegal.

Cover design by Ron Engstrom

Book design by Lizzie Newell

Author photo by Stan Jones

Copyright©2017 Mary Wasche

All rights reserved

ISBN 978-1-942996-05-7

Published by Mary Wasche

Acknowledgements

Jesica Sartell, Editor Extraordinaire, for her attention to detail, literary skills and enthusiasm.

Beta Readers: Tanya Grittmann, Dawn Kellen, Don Brill, Teresa Lueck, Joyce Kennedy, Keenan Powell, Patricia Watts, Chris Lundgren, Stan Jones, Jeannine Bruesewitz, and Mary Katzke, for their wisdom, imagination and attention to detail while this work was being polished.

Special friend, Ethann Oldham, for her unwavering support as the story developed.

To my family, Joslyn, Maren, Jena, Nick, Justin, Katrina, Jake, Mike, Natalie, Andrew, Matt, Cindy, Ken, Koren, and Marty—you enhance my life. I love you all.

IF there is ever a tomorrow when we are not together, there is something you must always remember: You are braver than you believe, and stronger than you seem, and smarter than you think, but most important of all, even if we are apart, I'll always be with you.

—A.A. Milne

CHAPTER ONE

MEG clutched the saddle horn, heart thundering in terror, the furious gallop making it impossible to hold herself forward. She lurched back against her captor, gasping as his solid shoulders, chest, thighs and arms molded around her. Just when she feared she could hold on no longer the rider reined the horse to a halt beneath a canopy of stately magnolia trees lining the road. Branches laden with satiny white blossoms drooped around them and one sweet-smelling petal fluttered delicately onto the horse's heaving brown neck.

A second horseman pulled up beside them, shoved a battered Union Army hat back from his forehead and over the panting of the horses asked, "Stu, what the...?" His eyes skittered over Meg.

The man holding her answered, "It'll be getting dark soon. Reckon we better rest the horses. We've been mighty lucky nobody came along yet and noticed us." He tipped his head to the left over his shoulder. "Let's head down there. I hear a creek. I'll come back up and brush out the tracks where we left the road. Then we'll follow that stream all night so our tracks won't show." He flipped the reins. "Think you can make it?"

The other rider glanced at Meg again, then back to the other man." I need to get down and rest my leg. It's throbbing real bad." He shook his head and his voice rose with frustration. "What the hell were you thinking to grab the girl like that? This is crazy. You know they'll come after her. Let's not get into trouble after finally being so close to home. For God's sake, Stu, let her go. Now!" He kneaded his leg and twisted in the saddle to look at the road ahead. "We should ride on in daylight so we can get home quick, just like we planned. What were you thinking, grabbing her like that?" He paused, his breathing ragged.

Meg felt the man's arms tighten around her. He ran a rough hand down her arm. "No. I won't let her go. It's like she's a piece of the real world again, where things were sweet and soft and nice." He exhaled a deep breath and went on. "All these years since I joined, I haven't had a pillow or a decent piece of pie. My boots don't even have soles anymore." His voice cracked, taking on a higher pitch. He clasped his arms harder around Meg and ranted on. "I can't stand any more mosquitoes or lice or flies or rats. I have to get back to the way things should be. I've been wet and cold and muddy too long." With a heavy sigh he continued, "Bill, I've seen too much blood and dying. And I've been scared to death so many times I can't even think straight anymore. I just need her to help me remember how life used to be. I have to be with normal people again. I'm keeping her."

His arms were now so tight that Meg could hardly breathe. "I didn't get to go home at all after the first furlough, you know. Not once. Never got another one. Susannah's probably hitched up with some lucky fool who got out early. She only wrote me that first year, or else I never got the letters." He shrugged. "I just need a piece of real life back so I can feel like myself by the time we get home. And this girl's it."

"Hey, Stu. It's gonna be alright," Bill said, worry etching his voice.

Stu went on, his voice low and stronger now, rumbling against Meg's back. "We can travel at night. And we're way ahead of anyone who'll come looking for her. I don't think there were any adults at that farm. By the time they get a search party together, they'll never catch us. It's not like she'll really slow us down any more than your leg will." He gave a dismissive flap of his hand. "I'll let her go when I'm good and ready."

He glared at the other man. They stared at each other for a long moment, their gazes locked. Meg listened, heart still pounding.

Finally, Bill dropped his eyes, shook his head, and with a frown nudged his horse off the road toward the stream. Stu followed down the ravine, bumping against Meg while the horse picked its way over rocks and through brush, branches and vines. Meg's relief at the man's words allowed her to relax a little. Her breathing calmed. *Maybe he won't hurt me. Maybe he'll let me go before long.*

The men dismounted at the edge of the stream. Stu reached up, grabbed Meg's waist roughly and set her on the ground. He gripped her shoulders and forced her to turn to him. "Don't try anything. If you run, I'll have to tie you up. Don't even try it. I don't wanna have to chase you."

She looked up into blazing blue eyes beneath scowling brows and nodded. Her throat was too dry to make a sound.

"I mean it. Stay here with the horse," he ordered.

He jerked away, broke a leafy branch off a nearby bush and climbed up toward the road, looking back over his shoulder every few seconds. Meg didn't dare move.

Bill led his horse to the stream, favoring one leg. He knelt, arranged the bad leg, then cupped his hands into the rushing water and drank deeply.

Meg suddenly became aware of the ache in her dry throat. *Should I run now that Stu's out of sight and Bill is bent to the stream?* Stu's threatening words came back to her. She glanced to where Stu had disappeared, then hurried the few steps to the stream, dropped to her knees, and cupped handfuls of cool water to her lips.

Thirst satisfied, she checked the bank behind her, but still saw no sign of Stu. She had to get away soon, before she got further away from home. But reason took over. *Maybe he'll let me go if I do what he says.*

Bill rearranged his leg with great care as he moved back from the water's edge. He glanced her way, then averted his eyes and slumped into a heap in the sand beside his horse. He bent his head and began massaging the leg stretched out before him.

Sensing movement, Meg turned to find that Stu's horse had moved in to drink a few feet downstream. It raised its head to look at her and she noticed what a fine, strong animal it was. Meg wiped her hands on her dress and stepped over to the animal to pat its neck. It nuzzled her shoulder. She leaned into the sharp horsey smell and rough texture of its coat, overcome by poignant memories of Sugar. Sugar had been hers since the day the colt was born on the farm, and for many summers she'd ridden Sugar back and forth to her best friend Jeb's house almost every day.

She burrowed her face into this horse's neck, taking comfort from the familiar animal smell. She was sure it had been loved by someone, too, when it gave her shoulder another gentle nuzzle. Her hand ran across a rough scar in its hide, most likely a battle wound. She wondered if Sugar had survived the war and where she was now. Most of the returning soldiers had brought horses back with them. Maybe Sugar was among them.

Tears sprang to Meg's eyes. She wrapped her arms around the horse's neck and gulped back the sobs that clogged her throat. Feeling afraid and alone, she remembered Louie curled up on the porch floor, clutching his head. *How could this soldier have hurt a little boy? Louie's only six. What kind of man is Stu? He hurt my little brother. He could be lying about letting me go. Maybe my best chance is to get on this horse right now and gallop back up to the road, make a run for home.*

Sudden determination burned. She grabbed the horse's bridle and prepared to mount, but before she could act, she heard Stu scrambling back down the bank. He regained his footing and looked in her direction. Meg stepped away from the horse, shrinking from Stu's speculative glare. She dropped her eyes, backing away as he strode over, snatched the horse's bridle, and led it away to the grassy bank.

Meg sank into the sand, resigned for the moment, and watched the men unload the horses. Both wore shabby Union uniforms, faded from navy to dusty blue. Their worn boots were water stained and spattered with dried mud. Thin and haggard, they moved with obvious weariness.

Stu tossed a saddle bag to the ground and began unloading it.

"Come on over here, there's food," one of the men called in her direction.

She gave in to her hunger and cautiously walked over to where the men were crouched over Elsie's apron on the ground in the growing darkness tearing chunks of bread off the loaves and scooping blobs of jam onto the pieces. Seeing Elsie's familiar bread and jam being devoured by strangers unnerved Meg, but hunger prevailed and she reached in for a few chunks herself. The men moved aside without acknowledging her presence. Soon only one loaf and some pickles remained among the crumbs on Elsie's apron. When Stu stood up, Meg rose and hurriedly backed away toward the stream.

Stu reached down to give Bill a hand up. "Let's go, Bill. Can you keep riding farther?" he asked.

"Yeah, I'm good for now. Let's go on as long as we can. I'll holler if the leg gets bad," Bill replied in a resigned tone. "But, the girl... let her go now, Stu, before we take her farther away."

"No," Stu replied, his voice rising. He shook his head before continuing. "This food tasted so good. Real homemade bread, still soft and fresh. Those Sutler's wagon hoecakes they gave us were poor excuses for bread compared to this. And what they called corn cakes were always so hard and dry, we could hardly swallow 'em even soaked in coffee. I don't wanna see another piece of hardtack in my life. And coffee made from acorns—never again. I am just so hungry for fresh buttermilk and

Ma's warm biscuits with honey dripping down the sides. And a good beef roast with gravy. This food reminds me of home. So does the girl." He jumped up and brushed crumbs from his shirt. "Let's get going."

Within minutes, Elsie's apron had been packed again into Bill's saddlebag. Stu motioned Meg over to his horse and thrust her up into the saddle ahead of him without a word. The horses moved into the stream with Bill in the lead.

An enormous crimson sun began a slow melt into rose and yellow streaks over the tree tops on the horizon to the left. Then deep purple twilight lingered until a luminous full moon slid smoothly into the blackness overhead.

The rest of the long night became dreamlike to Meg. Moonlight glimmered like silver threads on the ripples made in the water by the hypnotic splash, splash, splash of the horses' hooves. Despite Meg's anxiety, her head drooped with exhaustion to the rhythm of the animal's walk and the mesmerizing chorus of crickets and frogs. Dozing and awakening, Meg grew too weary to resist the intimacy of Stu's body cradling her, and became grateful for the warmth of his arms protecting her from the cool night air. She tucked her bare feet into the curve between the stirrups and the horse's warm side. Stu's smell wrapped around her, too, unfamiliar and sharp, like gunpowder and wood smoke and the air after a rain.

Several times she awoke to feel Stu's head buried in her hair, his slow regular breathing telling her he was half asleep, too. Whenever she stirred, he shook slightly awake and tightened his arms around her.

The night's sounds began to change gradually. Once, Meg awoke to the piercing call of a bird. Soon, several more twittered, interrupting the dwindling chorus of frogs and crickets. A hint of pink appeared in the sky to the right. In the weak gray light, Bill's silhouette turned back toward them, then shifted forward again, and he guided his horse up the bank with Meg and Stu following.

The horses climbed toward a dense forest of tall evergreens bordering the river and Meg realized she was farther from home than she'd ever been. She stared at the changed landscape and drew in the sharp scent of pine. *It won't be so easy now to get home since I don't know where we are.*

Bill and Stu swung down from their saddles and stretched.

"Can you get a fire going?" Stu called to Bill.

"Yup."

Stu reached up for Meg and yanked her off the horse without meeting her eyes. "Don't run. I mean it. I'll come after you," he muttered in a low, cold voice over his shoulder. He remounted and rode off across the stream.

Meg shivered in the chill morning air and hugged her arms to her chest. She stood barefoot in the cool sand, searching her surroundings for a place to hide. She could run into the nearby woods right now. As soon as Bill wasn't looking, she'd bolt.

She turned to check on Bill and found him watching her. "Don't try it," he called softly, pleading. "Just wait a bit longer. He's not himself."

She responded with a brief nod. Maybe Bill would help her. Better listen to him.

At her acknowledgement, Bill turned away and began scooping a small pit in the sandy river bank. He threw rocks into it with practiced ease, then gathered twigs and leaves, tossing them into the pit before lighting them with a match from the battered tin case he drew from his shirt pocket. While the sky continued to lighten, he limped off and began gathering firewood. Meg watched his painful movements and a wave of compassion washed over her. Unexpectedly touched, she joined him, gathering and carrying several armfuls of firewood to the pit.

When she dropped her second armful of branches, Bill caught her eye and surprised her with a brief half-smile. "Thanks. Just wait a bit more. He'll come to his senses," he murmured, with a cautious look across the stream.

She noticed that he looked remarkably like Stu, as if they were brothers. Bill's deep blue eyes, shadowed by the wide-brimmed, stained hat, which looked slightly too big for him, were dimmed with pain. His rumpled uniform hung loosely on his tall, thin body, as if made for a larger man. Shaggy dark hair straggled over his collar.

Bill, busy with the fire, looked over and asked in a hushed voice, "Are you alright, Miss?"

"Yes," Meg answered in surprise.

"Try to do as he says for now," he added, and limped over to unsaddle his horse.

Seconds later, three sharp shots rang out in the distance. Bill started, then shrugged and continued dragging his saddle and coarse, striped horse blanket under a towering pine that provided a canopy of branches high enough for him to stand under. His compact black horse stayed close, greedily munching fresh, moist grass in the open area between the trees. Bill crumpled onto his blanket under the tree and stretched out on his back.

Meg remained close to the fire, gathering its warmth. She studied Bill's horse. Maybe she could run fast enough to untie it and leap onto it before Bill could reach her. *But he'd sounded kind when he warned me not to run. Maybe I should take his advice and just wait.*

But Stu had hurt Louie back home on the porch. Knocked him down, even though Louie was only a little boy. Maybe Stu didn't mean what he said about letting her go. *I shouldn't trust anything he says.*

A moment later, Stu and his horse splashed back across the stream. He looked her way, scowling, checking on her, tossed two rabbits to the water's edge, and dismounted. He pulled a knife from his boot, crouched into the sand, and with practiced strokes skinned and washed the rabbits and carried the meat to the fire pit. Ignoring Meg as she rose and backed away, he brushed the hot embers to the edges of the pit and tossed the meat onto the hot rocks at the bottom. He strode over to Bill's horse and dug some yams out of the saddlebag, tossed them on top of the rabbits, covered it all with embers and more rocks, and then pushed sand around the edges of the pit until it was nearly invisible.

He gave another threatening look at Meg, before stooping to drag his saddle and blanket under a large pine at the edge of the woods near Bill. He unwrapped Elsie's apron, tore off part of the last loaf of bread, and strode over to where Bill lay. Meg could just make out their conversation.

"Leg pretty bad, huh?" Stu asked.

"Yeah," Bill replied. "I have to rest it. But we made good miles, didn't we?"

"Real good. I expect we'll be past the Cumberland and near the Kentucky border tomorrow morning if we make good time again tonight. Then, it'll just be another couple more nights through Illinois. Will this bread hold you 'til the rabbit's done?"

"Yeah, thanks," Bill replied, and took a bite of bread as he settled himself back down.

Stu tethered the horses in a clearing between the pines, and returned to where Meg stood near the stream. He pointed to his saddle and blanket and motioned to her, voice low. "Get over there. We have to get out of sight."

Meg headed for the tree, now desperately wishing she'd run when she had the chance. Stu kicked sand behind him to erase their footprints as he followed. More alarmed and reluctant with every step, Meg crouched to enter the space beneath the pine, surprised at the thick carpet of needles and the feeling of enclosure. Stu followed, thrusting a chunk of bread at her as he passed. Meg remained standing and chewed the bread, unsure what would happen next. Stu spread his horse blanket close to the tree trunk, removed his threadbare jacket and laid it over the saddle as a pillow before motioning Meg over.

"Get over here," he barked.

Meg could no longer see Bill or the river, and became conscious of the intimacy of the space. She realized that he expected her to join him on the blanket. She took a step back.

"Lay down here. We have to get some sleep," he ordered. He slid down onto the blanket.

Meg squeezed her eyes shut and shook her head.

"Get over here!" he commanded. He punched the blanket and settled himself onto it. He wiggled back against the tree trunk, glaring at her.

Jolted by the force in his voice, Meg obeyed. Without meeting his gaze, she edged herself down onto the outside edge of the blanket, squirming far enough away to avoid touching him. She faced away toward the canopy of evergreen branches that hung to the ground around them. Her heart raced. The keen smell of pine permeated the air and bit at her nostrils.

As soon as she settled, Stu slid over close enough to lay an arm across her shoulder.

Meg jerked away and froze, stunned, hardly daring to breathe. Stu replaced his arm over her shoulder, pulled her back, then made no further movement or sound. His breathing slowed.

Shaken by Stu's boldness, wary and anxious, Meg lay wide-eyed, wondering if it would be possible to sneak out when both men were asleep. *I don't know where we are. I don't have food or shoes or a coat. I'll have to take a horse, but they'll surely hear me if I untie one. There might be bears or wolves around here. They made pillows out of their jackets, so I won't be able to take anything to keep warm. My feet are already cold.*

She wriggled beneath the weight of Stu's arm to draw her arms close across her chest, shivering with fear and cold. *Maybe I should just wait like Bill told me to, and hope Stu will let me go. Trying to escape'll make Stu mad and I don't know what he might do then. Maybe it's best to just wait a little longer. Pa would want me to think things through like this. I know he's already searching for me.*

Her heart ached at how worried they must all be. Jeb would be right there beside Pa for sure. She had to take care of herself and get back to them safely. Reassured by thoughts of loved ones and home, she let herself relax into the soft, fragrant bed of pine needles beneath the blanket. There was no movement or sound behind her except the sound of Stu's steady breathing. His arm lay heavy and warm across her shoulder, trapping her.

CHAPTER TWO

JIM and Miriam Benson were in good spirits as the mules pulled the wagon steadily toward home through the early evening shadows stealing across the dirt road. They looked forward to their arrival back at the farm with this treasured load of goods from Memphis. Now that the war was over and the blockades lifted, they were finally able to buy buttons, yard goods, leather, nails, seeds, coffee, and sugar. The animals, sensing home, moved with more energy than they'd shown all day.

"Should we stop at the Miller's or just keep going?" Jim asked his wife when they approached their neighbor's lane.

Miriam thought for a moment. "I suppose we should stop and invite 'em. We've made all those other stops about Meg's birthday party Saturday night, so it would be a shame if they didn't hear." She paused, "We might be too tired to come back and tell 'em after we've unloaded all this. They've been good neighbors in these hard times, and, Lord knows, everyone can use a party. I bet they'd appreciate some fresh coffee, too. I think we can spare a little, don't you?"

"Sure," Jim answered.

He looked fondly at his wife beside him on the wagon seat. She had to be just as tired as he was from the five days of travel, but she glanced up at him from beneath her bonnet with a soft smile. Her shoulders sagged a bit in the worn gray dress, and loose tendrils of light hair straggled down her cheeks. Although her face was shadowed by fatigue and her blue eyes dark with weariness, she hadn't complained once during the trip. They'd ridden in companionable silence through the long days on the dusty, rutted roads, enjoying being alone together after the long struggle of the war years. The night before, when they rolled along under the early stars, Miriam had softly sung "*Come Where My Love Lies Dreaming*". Hearing the song they'd fallen in love to, Jim had felt his heart melt like it had been frozen for years.

Miriam had to be just as anxious as he was to get home, so when he turned the mules onto the winding, lilac-bordered lane to the Miller's, he said, "Let's keep this visit short. I'm hungry and I'm sure they're waiting supper for us at home. Just think, we'll have fresh coffee tonight." After a moment, he added, "I hope Meg and Louie did fine with us being gone this long. It's the first time we've ever left him, you know."

"Yes, I sure do. I thought about him many times every day. But with Meg there, and Elsie and Moses, too, he probably hardly missed us."

A boy in ragged overalls appeared on the front porch as they pulled into the yard. "Pa! Pa!" he shouted. "Somebody's coming!" He darted inside.

Thomas Miller swung into the doorway, a long hunting rifle pointed directly at Jim and Miriam.

"My God, Thomas! Put the gun down. It's just us, Jim and Miriam!" Jim shouted.

Thomas lowered the gun and sagged against the door frame. His grave face lacked color, his rumpled clothing looked like he'd worn it for days, and his customary hearty greeting was replaced by a grimace of anxiety. Uncombed hair straggled above the beard which shadowed his pale cheeks.

"Thomas! What's wrong? What's going on?" Jim hollered, reining in the mules.

"Thank God it's only you," Thomas called back, his voice weary, and waved them toward the porch. "Y'all come on in. We've had a bad time of it. Come on in." He disappeared inside.

Sally Miller dashed into Miriam's arms as soon as they entered and burst into tears. Her husband shrugged at Jim, then gathered his wife into his arms while the children scrambled to hang onto their parents' legs.

After a moment, Thomas untangled himself and asked, "Could y'all do with a drink of fresh spring water? I kin send Tommy."

"Sure, that would be good," Jim replied. "We've been on the road since daybreak."

Motioning to his son to get the water, Thomas began to explain. "Sorry for the state of things here. It's only been a few hours since two Yankee bummers left. They showed up 'bout a week ago, grabbed Tommy, and holed up in our barn. Looked like one of 'em had a bum leg, maybe couldn't travel. They kep' one of our young 'uns with 'em all the time they was here. Never hurt 'em none, jest kep' 'em in the barn as a guarantee we wouldn't let on to anybody that they was here."

He reached down and lifted a toddler to his hip. "When I went out in the mornings, they let me change one young 'un for another. Sally had to cook 'em three meals a day. It coulda been tough what with all of us, but durned if the one didn't go out huntin' at night. He left rabbits or squirrels or possum by the barn door every morning for Sally to cook up. We didn't go nowhere, all that time. 'Fraid to let nobody find out they was here, ya know?"

He paused for breath and continued, "We couldn't hardly sleep, or even think, all the while they was here. I seen 'em go down to the river at night to fill their canteens and wash, but they always kept a young 'un with 'em. The one helped the other hobble down there. Then, this morning, they came ridin' out of the barn, jest like that. They had Jamie."

At those words, his wife cried out, "They had Jamie! They were taking Jamie!"

Her husband drew her tighter against his side. "The ailin' one looked a little peaked, but he sat his horse all right. The other one had Jamie in his saddle with him and said he'd let him down out on the road if'n he looked back and didn't see no rifle in my hands. Sally near went to pieces when they rode off with Jamie, but I'll be durned if he didn't swing him down jest like he said he would. Jamie ran pell-mell for us, and those two took off headin' north."

"North? Did they take the main road up toward our place?" Jim asked.

Thomas' panicked expression told it all. The four adults looked at each other in alarm.

Tommy, clutching a wooden pail of water, stumbled out of Jim and Miriam's way as they rushed past him for the wagon. Miriam scrambled in, gathered her skirts onto the seat, and Jim whipped the team into motion. The wagon careened down the road at desperate speed in the falling darkness. Never had the mile from the Miller's place to theirs seemed so long.

When Jim and Miriam turned the mules into the lane, they saw at once that something was wrong. Elsie and Moses stood silhouetted in the light of the open front door with Louie between them. Oil lamps glowed from the porch rails, throwing long streams of yellow light into the darkness. They recognized the neighbor boy, Jeb, and his father, Charles, pacing at the foot of the steps.

"My God! What's happened?" Miriam screamed, half throwing herself from the wagon.

"Just hold on! Hold on until we stop!" Jim shouted, jerking the mules to a halt.

They leaped from the wagon and ran toward the hushed group.

Moses stepped forward, hat clutched in both hands. Anguish creased his broad face. "It's... it's Miss Meg, Massah Jim. Union bummers. They done took her 'bout four hours ago. Me and Elsie was down at the cabin restin' so's we could help unload when y'all got here.

Shur'nuf, we shudda been here. Shur'nuf, we shudda. We's so sorry!" He bowed his head.

"No! No! Meg!" Miriam shrieked and lurched toward her husband. Jim grabbed her, his face frozen with shock.

At the sound of his mother's voice, Louie broke away from Elsie's hand and ran screaming down the steps. "Mama! Mama! They took Meg! They took her!"

"No! No! Oh the good Lord above!" Miriam moaned, her face a mask of agony. She reached for her husband and crumpled against him. Husband and wife clung to each other, Louie crushed between them.

CHAPTER THREE

Lulled by the soft light and stillness beneath the fragrant pine, Meg's thoughts drifted to yesterday. She'd been in the kitchen spreading apple butter on a piece of bread to carry out to the front steps for Louie while they watched for Ma and Pa to come up the lane. The bread was a treat to help him pass the time since her little brother had felt the absence of Ma and Pa more than she did. Three more loaves of Elsie's bread cooled on the table and a ham chilled in a crock down in the creek so supper could be served no matter how late Ma and Pa got home. Meg remembered telling Louie how glad she was that Jeb was on his way, bringing Sam and Cassie, to wait with them and help pass the time 'til Ma and Pa got back.

When the kitchen door had opened, she expected to see Louie, or Jeb with Sam and Cassie in tow. Instead, a shabby Yankee soldier with unkempt dark hair hanging to his shoulders had locked eyes with her. His gaze moved to the waves of honey blond hair framing blue eyes under feathery golden brows. When his eyes dropped to linger on her chest, she'd drawn her arms close across the front of her thin, worn dress with string twisted through buttonholes to hold it together, wishing her shimmy hadn't worn out last year. The soldier's gaze followed the curve of her hips down to her bare ankles and slowly back up.

She'd looked away, unsettled by the expression in his eyes. "What do you want?" she finally managed, her voice a croak.

He shook his head, as if to clear it. "Food," he answered,

then grabbed Elsie's apron from the door knob and tossed it toward her. "All those loaves of bread. In here," he ordered with a slap on the table.

He walked along the cupboards, wrenched open every door, grabbed pickles and jelly from the nearly empty shelves. "Where do you keep the meat?"

"There isn't any," Meg lied instinctively, remembering the hungry days after other bummers had come through and helped themselves.

She'd never forget the helpless rage on Pa's face when Union soldiers heading north had twice before roamed the house, taking what they wanted, or how Ma had trembled, white-faced and sobbing, after they left. They'd been lucky both times compared to what other families had endured and lost at the hands of bummers. But this time, Meg would not give away the ham Ma and Pa would need after their long trip. And the smoked trout in the wooden box under the kitchen trap door would stay there. Last Sunday at church everyone had talked about how relieved they were that the last of the bummers had finally passed through. Where had this one come from? If only Elsie and Moses hadn't gone down to their cabin, leaving her to handle this situation by herself.

The soldier finished ransacking the cupboards, slammed the last door shut and tossed everything onto Elsie's apron with the loaves of bread. He tied the apron corners into a thick knot and pointed to a bag of yams on the floor.

"Carry those out," he commanded, hoisting the apron onto his shoulder.

Meg followed the soldier out the door and spotted Louie whimpering on the porch floor. She dropped the yams and ran to kneel beside him, "Louie, Louie! Are you all right?" she cried.

He managed a wail, "I want Ma! My head hurts! I want Ma!"

Meg cradled him to her, murmuring, "It's all right. It'll

be better in a minute. Ma's coming soon."

Her relief that Louie wasn't badly hurt had been followed by the realization that the soldier must have done this to him. The soldier had hurt a little boy. She scrambled up and faced the man.

"Bring those yams over here," he ordered over his shoulder while tying the apron onto his saddlebag.

Filled with rage, her fear momentarily forgotten, Meg grabbed the yams where she'd dropped them, met the man on the steps, and fiercely shoved them at him. Surprised by the force, he stumbled backward, nearly lost his balance, then turned and stuffed the yams into his saddlebags with brisk movements. He paused for only a second, then whirled back and grabbed Meg roughly around the waist. He tossed her up onto his saddle with one powerful thrust, leaped up behind her, and kicked his horse into motion.

The other rider, hunched over his saddle as if in pain, roused and yelled, "My God, Stu! What are you doing? Put her down! You can't do this!"

Stu turned and shouted back over his shoulder, "She's coming with us! Let's go!"

The other rider spurred his horse alongside and with an incredulous expression, yelled, "No! You can't do this! It's kidnapping! No, Stu!"

But Stu charged ahead around the corner of the lane and out onto the road north. Behind them, Louie scrambled to his feet, wailing. "Meg! Meg! They took Meg!"

LOST in these memories, comforted by the certainty that Pa and Moses and Jeb had to be close behind by now, Meg's eyelids grew heavy. The warm, silent world beneath the pine soothed her, and she gave in to sleep.

Deep afternoon shadows outside the evergreen branches when she awoke told her that hours had passed. Stu's arm was still around her and he was pressed against her back just like he had been in the saddle. Dismayed, afraid to move, Meg's heart began to flutter. Stu stirred and shifted as if sensing her tension. His breathing quickened close to her ear. She shivered with sudden alarm.

He tightened his arms around her, and murmured, "You're so soft and warm. You feel so good in my arms. You smell like home." His voice turned husky. He moaned, "God," and she felt him tighten against her.

Meg kicked herself free and scrambled away from him on hands and knees. She turned to face him, struggling to draw a breath, terrified, not feeling the pine needles that bit into her knees and palms.

Stu rose and bolted out from beneath the branches, leaving her trembling. Meg crumpled to the ground, dazed, more frightened than ever. She longed for Pa and Jeb to show up, and wished she'd run when she had the chance.

CHAPTER FOUR

JIM, Moses, Jeb, and his father, Charles, endured the endless hours waiting for it to get light enough to travel. Jim, quiet and despondent, made frequent trips to the bedroom where his wife lay weeping softly into her pillow.

"We'll find her. I'll bring our daughter back to you, I swear. We'll bring her back!" His shaggy eyebrows knotted in concern over eyes that mirrored the pain in Miriam's. "She'll be okay, Dearest. She'll be back soon just fine. You know she's tough. We taught her to think and take care of herself."

"But she's only seventeen. She's just an innocent girl. What if they hurt her? What if... Oh, Dear God! Meg!" Miriam wailed. Tears streaked her face and wet strands of hair clung to her cheeks as she turned limply into his arms. They clutched each other on the patchwork quilt, trying to comfort one another through the long dark hours.

Outside, Jeb grew ever more impatient with the blackness beyond the circles of lamplight. Restless, frantic, eager to get on the road, he ran his hands again and again through his unruly red hair, pacing endlessly from one end of the porch to the other. He had to get to his Meg. Had to find her. He'd kill those bastards with his bare hands when he found them.

Moses and Charles paced along with him, collapsing on the steps only long enough to rest before jumping up again. Elsie worked by candlelight in the kitchen, packing saddlebags with smoked fish, sliced ham, apples, and biscuits. She wiped away tears as she worked, her thick black eyebrows knotted with agony.

The first streaks of light finally appeared on the eastern horizon and Jeb called out in a voice cracking with fatigue and dismay, "It's light! We can go now! Let's go!"

He and the three men sprinted off the porch and spurred their waiting horses down the lane north onto the main road. After a few minutes of hard riding, Jim raised his arm, signaling the others to stop.

"We have to start watching for signs of them. Two horses, one with a heavier load." His voice broke. He looked ahead. "They'll probably leave the road to avoid being tracked, so watch along the edges. Take it slow. We don't want to miss anything. Holler if you even suspect you see something that doesn't look right."

The group divided, two along each edge of the road, riding with eyes downcast, watching intently for hoof prints leading off onto the edges. The morning passed with only the clop of the horses' hooves breaking the silence. When the sun was directly overhead, Jim called for a rest for the horses. The men dismounted and shared smoked fish and hard rolls. They led the horses to a wide stream that gurgled through a ravine a short way down from the road, where men and horses alike drank thirstily. Only necessary words were spoken.

Soon all were back in the saddle studying the roadside. When the afternoon sun began to drop behind the treetops, Charles called out, "Jim. I can't see much anymore. I'm afeared I'll miss seeing somethin', and my bad hip is gettin' sore. Maybe we should stop?"

Unaware of fatigue himself, Jim noticed the others' weary faces for the first time, and reluctantly agreed that they needed to stop. "Sure. Let's pull into the stream down there and water the horses."

The group crouched on the banks of the stream, munching apples and pieces of jerky from their saddlebags. Men and horses alike gulped the cool, rushing water.

"Did anybody see anything? Any sign at all?" Jim asked again, desperation turning his voice hoarse.

"There shoulda been something!" Jeb declared. "I can't believe we didn't see anything!" He rose and stomped his foot. "There shoulda been tracks or some sign of them."

Only quiet head shakes answered him. In silence, they wrestled bedrolls from behind their saddles and soon all was quiet except for the sounds of crickets, frogs, and rushing water as darkness dropped around them.

Jim lay wide-eyed most of the night, tossing and turning, unable to stop thinking of his daughter and what might be happening to her.

He didn't see that Jeb lay awake, too, eyes hard and bright in the darkness, face contorted as he stared up at the night sky. Jeb saw no stars, only his beloved Meg's face. He squeezed away burning tears, turning onto his side so they trickled into his bedroll. Rage and misery chased each other across his features. His teeth and fists remained clenched in frustration. He, along with Jim, stirred at the first hint of light and roused the others.

The second day passed much like the first, their only strategy being to head north, the most obvious way bummers would go, and to ask everyone they met along the road. They met only four riders, both coming from the north and having encountered no Union troops or a young woman.

A tavern provided a hot meal and the shelter of a barn when darkness again forced them to halt. Even less was said between the four this night as they realized the desperateness of the situation. Nobody at the tavern had noticed bummers passing by. Nobody had word of a girl with long golden hair. Only exhaustion allowed fitful sleep for Jim and Jeb as the long night hours again crept by.

CHAPTER FIVE

MEG stirred from the ground beneath the pine when she heard one of the men call, "Come and get it! Come and get it!"

Jolted by his shout and suddenly aware of intense hunger, she swiped at her tears, struggled to her feet, and brushed the pine needles from her dress. Her mind raced. *I'm so afraid now. I have to get away as soon as I can. I'll run first chance I get.*

She stooped under the branches and stepped out into the dusk, legs quivering beneath her, and stumbled. She regained her balance and saw Bill emerging at the same time from beneath his tree, wiping the sleep from his eyes. Stu was bent over the open fire pit carving steaming meat and yams on a flat rock. He gave a fleeting glance her way, dropped his eyes, and motioned her over. The fragrant smell was irresistible to Meg's painfully empty stomach. She swallowed hard, fought back her anxiety, and joined Bill, who was hobbling toward the fire pit.

Soon all three crouched around the fire pit, sharing the food. Meg busied herself with the food, avoiding Stu's eyes although she felt them on her. Surprised by an unexpected feeling of compassion at how expertly the men had obtained and prepared this food, she realized they'd had to do it many times before. Meg summoned the courage to look up at Stu.

He was watching, seeming to drink in the sight of her. The intensity of his gaze made it hard to pull her eyes away and she became self-conscious. His eyes, the deepest blue she had ever seen, locked hers in a grip she couldn't break. His look was no longer menacing, but instead challenging, questioning, as if daring her to react. The dark stubble on his chin accentuated its square contour and the corners of his mouth had relaxed, no longer set in the menacing frown he'd worn before.

Confused, feeling heat rising in her cheeks, Meg finally tore her gaze away. She looked over at Bill, who was studying them, brows contracted in puzzlement. Meg felt her face growing warmer and dropped her eyes. When she looked up again, Stu and Bill were staring at each other as if in silent contest.

Stu gave an abrupt leap up and began preparing to leave. "How're you doin', Bill? Ready to head out?" he called with forced casualness.

"Good enough," Bill answered, his tone cold. "Let's get started." He turned away and strode toward his horse, favoring his leg.

Stu brushed all signs of their presence into the stream and saddled the horses. He hefted Meg up into his saddle, more gently this time, and swung up behind her to follow Bill's horse into the water. He held her firm and close.

Meg's apprehension at this intimacy gradually disappeared while twilight faded into darkness and the air cooled. Soon she found herself relaxing into the warmth of Stu's embrace. He hadn't hurt her back there under the pine. *Maybe he isn't as bad as I thought.* She allowed herself to savor the sweet, clean smell of the night air and the sound of the rushing water, losing herself to the moonlit world, letting it shut out all troublesome thoughts while black night claimed the sky.

"Cold?" Stu asked, his voice quiet, when a light breeze whispered across the water, stirring her hair.

"A little," Meg answered in surprise, giving an involuntary shiver.

Stu gathered her even closer to him and pressed her into his warmth. "I'm sorry about touching you there under the tree. I never did that before in my life, touched a woman without her saying I could." He nestled her closer to him and murmured, "But having you here with me is like a dream, like the war was a nightmare I'm just coming out of." After a brief pause, he asked, "What's your name?"

"Meg. Meg Benson."

"Meg?"

"For Margaret."

"I'm Stuart Logan. Stu." he replied.

Stunned by the unexpected turn of the conversation, Meg felt unable to respond. She repeated the name to herself. Stuart Logan.

Stu continued after a moment, "I just can't believe I'm almost back to real life. Ma's gonna be so happy to see Bill and me come riding up. I doubt that any word about either of us has reached 'em at home for a long time now."

Meg remained silent, not sure how to react to what was becoming a conversation.

Stu went on, "There wasn't any mail going out of the hospital camp by the time we left. We were delayed by Bill's leg so most everybody else had already left or been transferred out of the camp to real hospitals."

Meg turned in the saddle to look over her shoulder.

Stu glanced at her, then stared ahead into the distance. "God, it's good to be thinking of getting home. And to be actually holding somebody..." his voice trailed off.

Meg look back again at him, bewildered by his gentle words.

He met her gaze, his eyes a softer blue now in the moonlight beneath the shadow of his hat brim. The hint of a smile crossed his lips. She turned forward and waited uneasily, surprised at this change in him.

Soon, Stu began again. "I wonder how our Pa's been managing and how many horses we have left. I wonder if Lad—that's my dog—will remember me. He was the craziest little thing. Thought he should get a piece of anything I ever had on my plate. He'd lean his head on my knee and look at me with those pitiful eyes. And I'd always end up sharing a little. I can't wait to see him. I can't wait to sleep in my own bed and not wake up until I want to. I just can't wait to get home. It's been so long..." his voice faltered.

After another silence, he asked, "How was the war for you and your family? I know your area of Tennessee wasn't right in the thick of things, but we heard the fighting got pretty bad in the eastern part of the state."

"We didn't have it as bad as most f... f... folks..." Meg began, stammering a little. She paused, confounded at the turn of the conversation, bewildered that this conversation was even taking place. She heard vulnerability in this man's voice, weariness, eagerness to reach home, an apparent need to talk about ordinary life.

Giving a perplexed shrug, she spoke over her shoulder. "Pa got sent home after his first two weeks in the militia because he could read and write so well. He kept the records at our county courthouse for the rest of the war. He didn't talk about it much, but sometimes, women came right out to our farm, begging for any scrap of information he might be able to find out about their menfolk. Pa was the one who wrote out the lists of the missing and the dead and the wounded."

"Go on," Stu said.

"Well, we were real lucky to have him home. A lot of my friends didn't see their fathers for years. My friend Lucy's Pa never came home—they say he was killed at Vicksburg, but nobody knows for sure. Her mother took her and her brothers back to Massachusetts. A boy from our church, he was sixteen, ran off and joined. He died during the Seven Days, only a month after he left home."

Meg swallowed hard at her next memory. "My horse, Sugar, was the last one given from our farm when the Home Guards Committee came around collecting mounts for the troops. Sugar was mine since she was born. I learned to ride her and rode nearly every day. I was so sad watching her being led away down the lane..." Meg's voice faltered at the memory of her beloved horse.

She regained her composure and continued, "When we heard that three thousand horses were killed at Gettysburg, Ma told me to give up hope of ever getting Sugar back. If Sugar made it through the war, I hope she's with a family somewhere on a farm with lots of sun and grass. And other horses, too." She gulped. "I hope to have a horse again someday...," she said her voice wistful.

"I was at Vicksburg, too." Stu's voice was low.

Meg took a steadying breath and went on, "Pa and Moses, our hired man, buried our valuables as soon as the news of the first battles—like at Bull Run—came in. We still have it all, except some silver Pa just took down to Memphis to trade for supplies."

Her throat caught at the mention of Pa. "Pa and Moses kept our mules hidden in a hut they made out of big branches down by the swamp because Pa said we couldn't survive after the war without mules. He's gonna buy another cow, too, as soon as he can. Pa and Moses hunted and fished, and worked real hard all the time to get food, so it wasn't as bad as in the cities. We heard that children there were so ragged and skinny that their mothers went right to General Lee, begging for food. We had apples, and plums, and a peach orchard, and catfish and trout that Moses caught. But, sometimes all we had was muskrat or coon to eat, because all of our pigs except one went for the troops. And we had to give both cows and most of the crops from our garden. We could only keep four chickens, for the eggs. Everything else had to go to them."

"But you had enough to eat?" Stu asked.

When Meg nodded, he asked, "What else?"

"Well, the Baptist school I went to had to shut down two years ago. I miss going to school, but I read a lot. People bring books to the church and trade 'em back and forth. I read nearly everything I could get, especially while I was on watch out on the road with my friend, Jeb. We'd run home if anyone came down the road so our mothers could hide the food. And Ma always sent my little brother Louie out to the fields to warn Moses so he could hide the mules. We got along, but we ran out of nearly everything. Toward the end, we had to send all our curtains and most of Ma's dresses to be reworked into blankets and bandages. Mostly, we heard news of the war at church on Sundays."

After a silence, Stu spoke. "We talked about how it must have been for the citizens—to have the war fought right there on Southern soil. There was usually rain and drizzle when we bivouacked, so all we had to do, sometimes for days, was huddle around the campfires and talk. I had it better than most because I made major in my regiment by the end of the first year, so I didn't have to live in the worst tents that were always in mud."

After a long pause, Stu asked, "How did you hear about Lincoln?"

"The neighbor came over and told us. Everybody went right to the church. Even the men were crying. Nobody could believe it!"

"We couldn't either," Stu said. "I was waiting at the hospital camp at Knoxville for Bill to get well enough to be discharged. I was amazed that I'd actually found him."

"How did you?"

"Some officer recognized my last name, and told me he knew of a William Logan from his regiment who was at Knoxville so I went there instead of heading home. It was a miracle to find my brother alive. We were so glad to see each other! It'd been over a year since I'd had word of him and I didn't know if he was dead or alive."

His voice rose with emotion as he went on. "We were waiting for the doctor to say Bill could be discharged when the news about President Lincoln just swept the entire place. There was dead silence, except for the sound of men weeping, the whole day and night. Nobody even ate. I still can't believe it!"

Meg was astonished at what she was hearing from a stranger. The thoughts they were sharing were things she'd never talked about with anyone else. It was as if she and Stu completely understood each other. She felt caught up in a fantasy that shut out the rest of the world from this mystical night. She slid into that world with abandon, surprised at the unlikely recklessness that had overcome her.

They became one in the saddle as the night passed, molded, moving together, voices mingling. When Stu rested his bristly cheek against hers and then nuzzled into her neck, Meg turned back toward him, eagerly seeking his warmth. A delicious heat like she'd never felt before smoldered deep within her. Before long, the hands holding the reins rested atop her thighs, and she entangled her own with his rough, strong fingers. Later, when he pulled her closer than ever against him, she didn't pull away. A languor like she'd never known soon melted all concern. Contentment settled over her and she wished she could remain in Stu's arms forever. Now completely at ease, they rode through the surreal summer night beneath a scattering of sparkling stars.

When Bill signaled to pull out of the stream, Meg was startled at the quickness with which the night had passed. Stu helped her down from the saddle this time with gentle hands that lingered on her hips. She grew cold when he pulled away, shamelessly longing to be back in his embrace.

Meg gathered wood and helped Bill prepare another fire pit while Stu hunted. She felt no anxiety this time and had only fleeting thoughts about escaping. The sudden loss of fear was bewildering but she felt oddly content. Bill remained quiet this morning and avoided her eyes.

While sitting beside the fire waiting for Stu to return, Meg realized she'd never before been out in the woods at dawn. She watched in awe while the sun slipped steadily up the horizon like a golden fire, melting away the gray of the night. Noisy mockingbirds called to each other and flew busily back and forth. Robins chirped and twittered and bounced along the grass, heads cocked for worms. A prim, brown killdeer scooted across the dirt, searching for something. Small animals rustled in the undergrowth amid sharp-leafed laurels laden with shiny, black berries. The dew smelled fresh, lightly steaming away in the first strong rays of the sun.

Stu soon brought back three grouse to cook with the last of the yams. While she watched him prepare the food in the fire pit, Meg realized that she no longer felt afraid. She lost herself to the moment, giving no thought to the future, feeling uncharacteristically detached and uncaring.

She joined Stu on the horse blanket beneath a pine when they finished eating, this time without fear. When he reached for her and cuddled her close against him, she nestled easily into his now familiar body. Worn out and weary, neither spoke. Stu murmured a quiet "Mmmm," and snuggled his face into her hair. Meg quickly fell asleep, comforted by the sound of his even breathing, warmed by his arms.

She awoke to twilight outside the branches and found herself alone. Hungry, chilled in her thin dress, she wrapped the horse blanket around her shoulders and crept from beneath the branches. The men were sitting side-by-side on a log by the fire pit in the last of the daylight. Both men acknowledged her with brief nods when she perched on the other end of the log. They went on talking.

During a pause, Bill asked, "What about the girl? We should get to the Illinois border about sun-up. You said you'd let her go. You better do it now, before she gets farther away from home.

Stu hesitated for a long minute, then forced out a strained answer. "Yeah, you're right. I have to. I have to see her safely to a farm, though. I can't just leave her out here."

Stu kept his eyes averted from both Bill and Meg during the awkward silence that followed his words. They finished what food was left, broke camp and saddled up without further conversation. Stu avoided eye contact, silently helped her mount, swung into the saddle behind her with stiff movements.

As the horses carried them up the riverbank and onto the road, Meg felt confusion at the sudden prospect of being set free. She was torn between relief at being let go safely and unexpected distress at leaving Stu. She struggled with her emotions until a large, weathered farm house and barn appeared behind the fence line ahead. Stu had said not a word on this ride, and barely touched her, holding the reins awkwardly around her.

As the distance to the farm decreased, Meg heard a muffled sound behind her. She twisted around in the saddle to find Stu blinking furiously, his face contorted with anguish.

"I'm sorry. I'm so sorry, Meg. For what I've done. To take you from your home like that. And then to touch you. You're just a girl. God, I don't know what got into me," he whispered in a broken voice.

He kicked the horse into a mad gallop, bypassed Bill, and thundered into the farm yard. A plump woman appeared at the open farmhouse door, wiping her hands on her apron, her ruddy face alarmed.

Stu jerked his horse to a stop in the yard, leaped off, pulled Meg down, threw himself back up into the saddle, and disappeared in a cloud of dust.

In a daze, Meg turned to meet the startled eyes of the woman. "I'm Meg Benson from Crockett County and I want to go home!" she blurted out and burst into tears.

CHAPTER SIX

JEB and the men resumed the ride north at dawn. A few hours later a boy riding bareback on a mule appeared in the distance.

Jeb galloped ahead to meet him. "Have you seen a girl? A girl with long blond hair?" he called, as soon as he was close enough to be heard.

The boy jerked his mule's rope halter and squeaked with excitement. "Yup. They got a girl at the Lorenz farm. They's our neighbors. I'm headin' to the store with the news. We gotta get word to her kinfolk."

"A girl?" Jeb yelped. "Does she have long blond hair?"

"Well, yup. I seen her. She got long yeller hair, all right." the boy answered. "They say she got dropped off by a Yankee soldier last night. She's..."

Jim interrupted, "Where is she? Is she all right?"

Taken aback by the ferocity in Jim's voice, the boy's eyes grew wide and he began to stutter, "Ah, Ah, she's at the L... Lorenz's up the road. T... That a way. 'Bout a mile. I... I'm sposed to go tell at the store..." The riders left him still stammering in a cloud of dust.

Jeb rode in the lead at reckless speed, eyes sweeping the road ahead, frantic for the sight of a farm. Jim galloped close behind him, relief and hope shining from his face. Moses and Charles brought up the rear, pushing their horses with new-found energy. Jeb reined in his horse when he spotted a farmhouse ahead and looked back at Jim, a question in his eyes. Moses and Charles thundered up, then pulled back, too, to let Jim gallop on ahead.

Jim slid off his horse in a cloud of dust as a woman appeared at the door. "My daughter? Meg? Is she here? Is this the place?" he shouted.

The woman nodded, eyes bright. "Yup. She's here. Said her name's Meg, alright. She's plumb tuckered out. Right in here. Said she was from Crockett County. Long ways. What happened? She sure didn't say much. Just fell into bed soon as..."

Jim tore up the steps and brushed past her through the open door. He spotted golden hair spilling from beneath a red and gray quilt on a bed in the far corner of the large room and rushed over. He bolted to a stop, then perched on the edge of the bed as he drank in the sight of his sleeping daughter. His shoulders heaved with relief and he gulped back a sob. Everyone else gathered at the door.

Jim reached down and gathered Meg into his arms. He clutched her to his chest and murmured, "Pa's here, Angel. Pa's here."

Meg's eyes fluttered, then opened wide. "Oh, Pa! Oh, Pa! You're here! You found me!"

She returned his hug, holding on with all her might. Jim finally pushed her back a little and smoothed her hair from her forehead, blinking back tears before he finally released her.

Nobody noticed Jeb duck back outside the door or heard him try to choke back sobs of relief. He slipped back into the room while Meg and Jim were thanking the woman, moved over next to Meg, and gave her arm a light touch.

When she looked at him, he asked, "You all right?"

Meg nodded and reached to grab his hand. She was glad to see him, not at all surprised that he was here. She'd been certain Jeb would come looking for her with her father, and clutched his familiar hand.

After watering the horses and guzzling dippers of well water, everyone again thanked the farm woman. They rode away with light hearts, Meg tucked in the saddle in front of her father.

Just before the last of the daylight sank behind the trees, they came upon a weathered log hut. The barn in its yard looked big enough to shelter them all for the night. A dour, hunched old man appeared at the door of the hut at the sound of their horses in his yard. Light spilled across the dirt path in front of him.

"Can we shelter for the night in your barn? We've got a girl with us. We won't trouble you at all," Jim called out.

"Move on," the man replied, his voice sullen. "Don't want the likes of him on my property. Move on." With a hostile, pointed look at Moses, he disappeared back into the hut, slamming the door behind him. The riders milled about, uneasy.

Moses spoke up. Black curls bobbed beneath his hat as the words rattled off his tongue. "I kin ride on ahead all night. I ain't that tired. This horse kin make it if'n I rest him now an' agin. I wanna get word to the womenfolk that Miss Meg be safe. They be worryin' theyselves sick by now. You'all surenuf be findin' a place easier if'n I go."

He sat tall on his horse, shoulders stiff, head held high with brittle pride as he spoke. Before anyone could respond, Moses spurred his horse and disappeared down the dark road with a clatter of hooves.

Subdued and silent, overcome by weariness, the group continued on until they spotted a long, low, stone house at the road's edge. Light shone from six identical oblong windows onto a lean, white-haired man rocking in a high-backed wooden chair on the front porch. He didn't notice them until he heard Charles call out to him a second time.

He pulled himself upright and shouted back, "Where you'all headed this late at night?"

"We're looking for lodging. Headed to Crockett County tomorrow," Jim replied with a touch of uncertainty.

The old man surveyed the group. "Well, you're welcome to stay here. The wife and I been havin' heaps of travelers stopping lately. I'll let her know there's company for the night. Hitch the horses along that there rail for now. We'll git 'em unsaddled right soon and into the stable. First I gotta let Tillie know about travelers lookin' to be fed."

A woman turned from the stove as the group entered the house. She lifted a wooden spoon from the steaming pot she was stirring and turned her attention to them. A long polished pine table with matching benches stood before her. Dancing light reflecting from the fireplace played across her face.

"Tillie. Company for the night. Can we handle four?" the old man asked.

The woman's curious dark eyes surveyed them from deep wrinkles that covered her face like a detailed map. A cloud of fluffy white hair spilled from the braided chignon that wrapped her head. She smiled with a friendly grin, displaying worn, yellow teeth leaning against each other like old fence posts.

She turned her attention back to the stove, settled the spoon back into the pot, and nodded. "Spose so. Hello, y'all. Have to add to the soup here, now, if I'm gonna feed the lot o' ya. Maybe leave the two young'uns here to help me, while you tend to the horses?"

"Sure. Follow me, men." With that, the old man led Jim and Charles back out onto the porch.

The woman's eyes nearly disappeared into the crinkled maze of wrinkles on her face as she smiled at Jeb and Meg. "Come on over here, you two. Need some help stretching this for six now," she said in a surprisingly bright, firm voice.

Within minutes, Meg found herself peeling potatoes, while Jeb set spoons and pewter bowls along the table. The soup's fragrant smell and the warm, homey atmosphere put them at ease while they listened to the woman's chatter.

"Yup. We get more and more travelers stopping here these days. We put 'em up in the two bedrooms we added on jest before our boys left for the army. Both was plannin' to marry that fall and stay on here, makin' the apple orchard business bigger with us. We lost 'em both the next summer. Billy Bob at Antietam and Joe at Murfreesboro just three months later. Their young women stopped coming around by that winter, and we had this big place, all empty 'stead of filled with our boys and their families."

Her voice faltered. She paused for a moment, gathering herself, then continued. "Well, we're lucky, though. Both of 'em got decent burials here at the church cemetery. Lotsa folks around here never got to bury their men folk at all, but we got both of 'em back. Tilmans—over by the river—their ten year old young 'un ran off. Wanted to be a bugle boy, told his friend. They never did yet, to this day, find out why he didn't come back or where he is. My boys' diaries got brought back by people passin' through, too. I treasure those. Prob'ly, I'll wear 'em out, readin' 'em over and over. It's been hard, missin' em. Joseph's been good about it, but sometimes I see him jest starin' off, and I know he's pinin' for his boys. So we're glad for the folks who stop. Keeps our mind off it all, ya know? What's yer story? Where you'all headed?"

She ceased her chatter, and looked at Meg and Jeb.

After Jeb explained with brief, curt words, the woman turned to Meg, her face creased with concern. "Are you all right, child? Was it bad? Did they hurt you?"

"No, not really," Meg replied and dropped her eyes.

Jeb turned abruptly away, as if the words had stung him.

The woman studied Meg for another long moment. "You're a brave girl," she said, before turning back to the stove.

After a supper of savory soup with potato and sausage chunks floating in buttery broth, cornbread, and coffee, the group moved to the chairs in front of the fireplace. Meg grew sleepy at once, overcome by deep fatigue. Tillie led her to a small bedroom, but Meg was too tired to notice the charm of the matching blue patchwork quilts that covered the beds, the colorful hooked rugs, or the ruffled white curtains held back with big bows.

"You snuggle right in there and have a good sleep. Do you need anything? The privy is right out the back door there. Sleep well, Dearie."

Tillie patted Meg's arm with a gentle touch as she left. Meg ran out to the privy through the cool damp grass, then wiggled beneath the heavy quilt and fell into instant sleep. She slept deeply, exhausted, oblivious to the rage and anguish that flashed across Jeb's face in the moonlight while he tossed on a bed in the next room. She didn't hear him smash his fists into his pillow or see the agonized tears that slid from his eyes in the deepest hours of the night.

The trilling call of a brown thrasher just outside the window awakened Meg. She tiptoed out of her room to the privy and noticed Jeb sleeping as she passed the open door of the room next to hers. She paused, smiling fondly at the sight of the curly tendrils of her best friend's hair mashed into the pillow like some sort of crazy hat. She studied his familiar face in the repose of sleep, surprised at how different he looked. His eyebrows looked bushier and rust-colored rather than the reddish blond they used to be. The freckles that had always speckled his nose were hard to see this morning. He was long on the bed, taller than she remembered. The arm that hung outside the blanket had muscles that seemed to belong to a man instead of a boy.

Meg helped Tillie serve grits, eggs, and coffee, and clean up the kitchen while the men went to feed and water and saddle the horses. Tillie chattered constantly, as if starved for someone to talk to.

"If you ever pass this way again, do stop. It was a pleasure havin' young people around the house again, an' I truly hope I see you again. There's hardly any women or girls, ever. Go on, now, go to yer Ma."

She accompanied Meg out the door when the riders pulled the horses up to the porch rail. Jim passed a handful of coins to the old couple, and the group trotted south again.

Familiar landscape began to appear at midday and the horses, sensing home, broke into a gallop. The group thundered joyously down the lane to the house in a cloud of dust. Ma and Louie and Elsie tumbled out the front door and down the steps at the sound of the horses and engulfed Meg in a wild mass of hugs and tears.

Louie danced around her and squealed in delight, "Meg came home! She's home!"

CHAPTER SEVEN

Meg awakened in her own bed to the warmth of the sun streaming through the open window. She'd slept late and smiled at the familiar sight of Louie across the room, his skinny arms and legs sticking out of his nightshirt as he sprawled on his bed in the deep slumber of childhood. She lay for a moment remembering her arrival home, the relief on everyone's faces, and the warmth of the hugs. She thought, too, of the unspoken questions that had flickered in Ma's eyes.

Her mother's question-filled eyes had searched Meg's for a moment after the first long hug, before the others moved in on them. Jeb had hovered around, agitated, as if he didn't know what to say or do, until his father insisted they go home. Louie danced around in excitement, grabbing Meg's hand and chattering. Elsie enveloped her in that huge, soft, familiar hug, murmuring words of comfort and welcome. Pa and Moses came in from unsaddling the horses and joined everyone in the kitchen for Elsie's hot-cross buns. Meg sensed that everyone took great comfort in being there in the kitchen, as if nothing had happened, as if life was normal.

Later, Ma tucked Louie into bed, then came over and sat on the edge of Meg's bed. Her voice caught when she asked, "Margaret Ann, are you all right?" Uneasiness at what was unspoken burned the air between them. "Did... did they...?"

Meg cut her mother off, murmuring an awkward, "No, Ma. They didn't hurt me." Her tone was evasive. She dropped her eyes, glad for the dimness of the room.

They shared a long uncomfortable silence before Ma sighed and said, "Go to sleep, Honey. I'll see you in the morning."

Meg, grateful for the security of her own home this morning, lay quietly for long moments while memories flooded over her. She could almost smell the fragrance of the pines, and blushed at the memory of how she had willingly molded so close against Stu. And at the contentment she'd felt during those long hours pressed against him in the saddle. Stu's face was vivid before her, his blue eyes and straight black brows, his strong lips and hands, his long, lean body. She shivered at the memory and burrowed deeper into her quilt.

She slid the covers off a few moments later and tiptoed out of the room past Louie. Still in her nightgown, she walked into the kitchen where Elsie and Ma were kneading bread dough on the table.

"Good mornin', Chile," Elsie greeted her. She brushed crumbs of flour from her plump hands and stepped out the back door. Puzzled at this abrupt and unusual departure, Meg looked at Ma, her eyebrows lifted in question.

"Elsie is going down to see if any greens are ready to pick. Here, take her place," Ma said.

Obediently, Meg pushed up her sleeves and began following Ma's motions. They worked side by side, slapping the dough in rhythm, until Ma finally broke the silence, "What happened, Meg? Pa and I need to know. Did they do... do anything to you?" Her voice was strained. She kept her eyes on the dough.

"Not really," Meg answered quickly, pushing hard at the ball of dough in her hands.

"Did they, did they...?" Ma asked, without looking up. "Are you sure you're not hurt?"

Meg shook her head, feeling her face flame. She cringed. "No, Ma. It was only the one, and he didn't really hurt me. They were two Union soldiers, brothers, going home to Illinois. Bill had the hurt leg. Stu was the other one. The one... the one who... who took me."

"Did he touch you?" Ma asked. She gave a sideways look but Meg pretended not to notice.

"Well... kind of... he..." Meg stammered, couldn't continue. It was impossible to tell her mother that a man had slept close beside her, had held her intimately pressed against him in the saddle for hours, that she'd welcomed the hands that caressed her. She had no words to explain the feelings that had overcome her during the long hours of murmured conversation in the moonlight. She couldn't describe her mesmerized state of mind during the time she spent with Stu. She couldn't tell her mother how strong Stu's presence was even this morning, or how warm she felt at the memory of being cradled in his arms.

She kept her head bent, and felt her face burning with shame at what Ma was asking. Words wouldn't come. She kept her face lowered, working on the dough. Ma had never before talked to her about things like this.

"Meg?" Her mother's voice was stern. "Tell me."

Finally, Meg was able to murmur, "Well... he... but..."

Miriam abruptly stopped kneading, her fingers clenched into the dough. Meg glanced at her and winced at the stark pain, which flashed across her mother's face. Miriam's hands remained buried in her ball of dough during the silence of the next few seconds. She didn't make a sound. Meg kept kneading methodically, not knowing what to do, not daring to look at her mother, not able to explain more. She could hardly breathe.

They were that way when Elsie burst through the back door, a floppy bunch of greens dangling from her hand. She halted and took in the frozen silence. A deep sigh escaped before she stepped forward, dropped the greens on the table, and gathered Meg into the comfort of her big soft arms.

"Here, Chile. Y'all come with your Elsie. Let yer Ma be for now. Come with me, Meg."

Meg allowed herself to be led away, just like when she was a little girl. Her heart felt heavy, her legs wooden, as she left her mother standing there. The sunshine of the morning held a faint chill now as she hitched her nightgown up past her knees and helped Elsie feed the chickens and gather eggs like they always did.

Elsie softly sang "Swing Low, Sweet Chariot" in her soft low voice while they worked, as usual. Meg took comfort from the familiar task of placing warm eggs in the basket and stepping around the scuffling hens at their feet. Elsie shuffled on stout legs as she worked alongside Meg, puffing lightly from the effort of singing. Her black eyes flashed comfort to Meg from beneath the tangle of salt and pepper frizz that sprouted from the edges of her red bandanna.

"It's gonna be fine, Chile. It's gonna be jest fine. You wait an' see," she murmured several times, as if she needed to reassure them both.

When they finished with the chickens, Meg started back through the kitchen to change out of her nightgown. The bread dough lay in lumps on the table. Ma was nowhere to be seen.

Meg spent the day helping Elsie do the washing in the big tin tub in the wash shed and hanging clothes on the line. Louie dawdled underfoot, trying to help, wanting to be near his big sister.

Jim's mouth was set in an uncharacteristic hard line during the subdued and awkward supper, and he snapped at Louie harshly several times during the meal. Miriam picked at her food and kept her head bent low. Everyone avoided looking at each other, few words were spoken. Puzzled by the strange atmosphere, Louie became fussy. Meg found it hard to eat, even though the venison in gravy, creamed greens, and gingerbread was one of her favorite meals.

Well before anyone else was finished, Miriam excused

herself, murmuring about not feeling well and escaped to her bedroom. Elsie kept up a comforting chatter after the meal while she and Meg cleaned up. Meg tried to reassure herself that maybe things would get back to normal in a few days. *Nobody knows everything that happened. And they'll never have to know.*

There were three firm knocks on the back door before the dishes were quite finished, and Jeb let himself in. He stood holding the door open, dressed in one of his father's blue-checked muslin shirts, his unruly curls slicked back, his face grim. He blurted out, "Can you come out? For a walk, I mean? Before it gets too dark?"

Surprised at seeing him in the evening, Meg looked at Elsie.

"Sure, Chile. I'll let the folks know you'all be with Jeb. Be sho' to git back soon, though. We don't need no more worrying 'bout ya."

Jeb followed Meg out the door, then moved ahead of her and led a silent, fast walk down the path toward the swamp. He stopped and faced Meg as soon as the house was out of sight.

His face twisted with pain as he asked, "What happened to you while you were gone? Did they hurt you? Did they touch you? I'll kill them if they hurt you. Tell me what happened."

Jeb looked and sounded like someone Meg had never seen before. She hardly recognized the harsh voice or the face knotted with bitterness. His hazel eyes smoldered dark with anger under scowling brows. He pounded his fists together as he spit out the words. Meg hesitated, too surprised to answer right away, afraid of the effect her words might have.

"What? Answer me! Tell me!" Jeb demanded.

Meg only managed to stammer, "Jeb... wait a minute." She took a deep breath and spread her hands. "Well, I... he... but..." She gulped and looked at him, trying to hide the emotion that flooded over her remembering Stu's voice, his hands, her response.

They stared at each other in the semi-darkness for an awkward, too long moment. Meg tried to gather the words to answer him, not knowing what to tell him or how much or what to say. Suddenly, she realized that words would be unnecessary. They knew each other so well that she didn't need to say the words out loud. Jeb's face darkened even more before he jerked away. He grimaced, then let loose an agonized shout, and gave a violent kick at the rocks along the edge of the trail. His arms flailed the air.

Words poured from his lips. "You're mine! Everybody knows you've always been mine. He had no right. I'll kill the bastard! You're spoiled. He'll pay for this! God damn it. He touched you, didn't he?"

Jeb raged on. Meg stood helplessly, her heart sinking, shocked at this Jeb she'd never seen before. He finally calmed down, seeming to see her for the first time in many minutes. He gave a shake, grabbed her arm with a too tight grip and led her back up to the kitchen door. He slipped away into the darkness without a word

CHAPTER EIGHT

THERE was no sign of Jeb for the next three days while everyone busily prepared for Meg's birthday party. Meg tried not to think about Jeb's words, but they haunted her thoughts. *He said our life was ruined.* Ma and Pa seemed to sense that something had happened with Jeb, but they didn't bring it up. Nobody mentioned the kidnapping, either.

Daily activities and the excitement of the party preparations eventually lifted everyone's spirits so life had nearly returned to normal by the time the neighbors began arriving for Meg's party. Meg felt relieved by then that the kidnapping was behind them, and was quite sure that Jeb would show up. *Maybe he just needs some time to himself to think about things.* They'd spent so many years as best friends and sweethearts that she couldn't imagine this coming between them forever. It had been hard not to go over to his place during the past few days, but she knew it was probably best to just wait a little for him to settle down. She watched for him among the arrivals to the party.

Women carried pots of steaming roast pork wrapped in dish towels, sweet potato pie, smoked turkey, blueberry muffins, and fluffy biscuits to the long plank tables. Children chased and squealed in the fragrant straw of the freshly cleaned barn as the fiddlers warmed up. The yard began to fill with horses and wagons and the sound of voices calling out as people greeted each other under happy circumstances for the first time in four years. Girls and women wore hastily sewn new dresses that flowed to the ground like giant flowers of every color. Ribbons, bows, and ruffles trimmed necklines and sleeves and bonnets. Men and boys wore crisp, new, shirts tucked into clean linen pants. Freshly trimmed lamb chop sideburns, beards and moustaches showed beneath their carefully combed hair.

Meg's party dress was a deep, shimmering blue with white lace along the scooped neckline and trimming the sleeves. Ma's choice of fabric brought out the brilliance of Meg's sapphire eyes, and set off her smooth shoulders. Elsie and Miriam and Meg had sewed on the dress for two nights, and then made a flowered one for Ma, too, taking great comfort in each other's company on such a long awaited and pleasant task. They'd refolded the new paper patterns with great care for reuse and to share with others. Elsie saved all the scraps and gratefully accepted the leftover fabric Miriam turned over to her for her own use.

Guests arriving for the party sought out Meg, wishing her a happy birthday, as if glad for the cheerful topic. The kidnapping wasn't mentioned. Men who previously hadn't noticed her lingered a bit longer than necessary, seemingly transfixed by the luxurious, honey-colored waves that flowed halfway down her back and the sparkle in her diamond-like blue eyes. She was surprised at the length of time they held her gaze, even men Pa's age. Frequently, she felt someone watching her, only to turn and find several men staring at her.

Meg had no idea that during the bleak long years of war she'd blossomed into a stunning young woman whose innocent charm captivated every man who saw her. Her lush hair was kissed to a glossy, shining gold by the Southern sun. Her slender curves and delicate face with sapphire eyes beneath arched brows drew every man's attention.

Jeb finally showed up. He didn't say a word about his absence. He seemed to be over his outburst, and he and Meg returned to their usual, easy camaraderie as soon as they saw each other. He looked different tonight in a new black flannel shirt with his hair slicked back like the older men. When he crossed the barn toward her, Meg was struck by how much he suddenly looked more like a man than ever. He looked taller now, and sturdier. His shoulders and neck had thickened to match his long arms and broad, strong hands. His face, no longer boyish, held a slight shadow of whiskers where it used to be smooth. He strode purposefully toward her, his eyes locking into hers with grave intensity. Meg smiled a welcome at him and he smiled back as he approached, then moved to stand beside her, grabbing her hand. She squeezed his hand and felt tremendous relief as he squeezed back three times—their signal.

Soon the fiddles started and her father grabbed Meg's hand for the Virginia Reel that traditionally began festivities. Meg whirled through the following dances, with partners changing so quickly she could hardly catch her breath. She noticed that Ma and Pa were dancing, but wondered why Jeb hadn't been her partner yet. Several times, she caught sight of his black shirt in the far corner with a group of men who were gathered around the whiskey barrel that the Sawyers had rolled in. The men seemed to be talking and laughing heartily as they passed the tin dipper around, and Jeb was right in the middle of it all. Meg was glad to see him having fun.

The fiddles cascaded through melody after melody, while men and boys of all ages sought out the exquisite young girl in the glimmering blue dress. They vied for the chance to be near the beauty with the hair like sunlight tumbling nearly to her waist over creamy shoulders, cheeks pink with excitement, and jewel-like eyes sparkling in her angel face.

The fiddlers stopped for a break and voices drifted

across the darkness from the hollow down at Elsie and Moses' cabin. The haunting strains of "Go Tell It on the Mountain" and "Steal Away" wafted to the barn, sung with harmony and deep emotion by the choir of voices belonging to those who had come from neighboring plantations and farms to join Elsie and Moses. Their bonfire sparkled in the distance like a grounded star.

Meg sat down on a bench along the barn wall to catch her breath. Jeb appeared and settled next to her, draping a possessive arm around her shoulders. Zona and Zelda Winston settled their big skirts on the other side of them, with smiles of greeting on their identical faces.

"How's my girl?" Jeb asked in a hearty voice, giving Meg's shoulders a squeeze.

Several other young people joined the group. All chattered and teased and laughed, happy to begin catching up on the missed time of the war years.

Suddenly Jeb scowled, and hissed at John Brinks, who was standing in front of them. "Hey. What're ya doin' lookin' at my girl like that?" His words sounded a little slurred to Meg, his voice ragged.

"What?" Brinks asked, blinking rapidly and taking a step back. His tall frame shifted toward Jeb and his wide, friendly face reddened. He held his hands up. "What, Jeb?"

"You know. Lookin' at Meg like that. She's mine. Keep your damn eyes off her!" Jeb retorted. He rose from the bench and raised his fists.

Another young man stepped forward into the awkward silence that followed and grabbed Jeb's arm, his face knotted with concern. "Hey, Jeb. He wasn't doing nothin' wrong. Nobody was lookin' at Meg wrong."

"Yeah. I wasn't looking at her funny," Brinks added, and began to back toward the door.

The young man dropped Jeb's arm. "Hey, Jeb. What's wrong with you?"

Jeb backed away, then dropped back to the bench beside Meg in sullen silence. Moments later, everyone had drifted away, and Meg and Jeb found themselves sitting alone.

Jeb turned a ruddy, angry face to Meg. "You stay here with me now. That's enough dancing with other men. Dance with me now. Just with me."

He pulled her out onto the floor, but his feet were clumsy and his manner ill-humored as he led her around.

"Jeb, I need to sit down for a while and get some water. Let's go get some water," Meg suggested.

"Whatsa matter? Don't ya wanna dance with me? Is that it?" Jeb demanded.

With a puzzled frown, Meg pulled him toward the bench. Jeb grabbed her elbow, shoving her ahead of him and out the barn door into the darkness outside. He pushed her hard against the rough boards, propped his arms on either side of her head, and hissed, "Don't ever pull me at again. Got it?"

His breath reeked of whiskey. As she absorbed this, he gripped his fingers hard into her arms and gave her a shake. Meg tried to pull away, startled by the pain and his actions.

"Jeb! You're hurting me. Let go!"

Jeb finally let go with a last, long vicious squeeze. "Fine. I'll let go of your arms. But I'll never let go of you. You belong with me. You're mine. We belong together. None of those other men have any right to look at you. Nobody else will ever touch you again!"

He staggered backward before grabbing her around the waist and guiding her back into the dance. The rest of the night was a blur to Meg as they stumbled through the dances and she tried to absorb what had just happened.

The next morning when Meg rolled awake, her arms hurt. She turned her elbows out and discovered dark bruising. She quickly pulled on an old dress with long sleeves, then sat through church, not hearing a word, wondering what to do. Jeb was not in his usual place in the pew with his family.

He didn't appear until early afternoon as Meg sat on the porch steps at home while Ma and Pa napped. Subdued and pale, Jeb walked up the front lane and plunked down beside her on the steps as if nothing had happened the night before. Meg waited for him to speak, while Sam and Cassie and Louie played hide and seek in the trees in front of them. But Jeb made only occasional casual comments, and later they all walked down the road to the halfway point between the two farms, just like they always did at the end of an afternoon together. If not for the bruises, Meg would have wondered if she had dreamed Jeb's roughness.

CHAPTER NINE

MEG had just stepped out the back door a week later to gather some sheets off the line when a movement at the edge of the yard caught her eye. She saw the figure of a man standing half hidden in the trees and recognized Stu before shock could register.

She stared, frozen, until he took a step forward and called softly, "Meg?"

Meg stood staring, heart hammering, too stunned to react.

"Meg. Come here. Come here out of sight. Please, Meg," he called again.

Meg glanced over her shoulder at the kitchen door, then walked toward Stu as if drawn by an invisible force. Her eyes never left his face. She felt transfixed by Stu's steely blue eyes, now highlighted under a wide leather hat. He was ruggedly handsome, the gaunt spareness nearly gone, appearing taller and more powerfully built than Meg remembered. He stood half shadowed while she approached, then stepped backward as she got close, drawing her into the woods. Her heart pounded harder with each step toward him.

The instant they were protected from sight, Stu reached out and drew Meg tight against him. His strong arms felt so familiar that she melted into them without thinking. They clung to each other until Stu pushed away. He held Meg at arms' length, studying her face as she looked back in wonder.

"Stu?" she stammered, "What... what are you doing here? Where did you come from?" She searched his face for answers. She absorbed the sound of his voice, his smell, the familiar lines of his face, as she tried to regain control of her thoughts.

"I had to come back and find you. I can't stop thinking of you. I just had to come back to you," Stu replied.

Meg knew his words were sincere. His eyes held her spellbound.

He drew her again to his chest. "You are so beautiful! Just like I remembered."

His lips found hers in a hungry kiss of such passion that it carried her at once back to the blanket beneath the pine. She trembled with emotion, and Stu crushed her to him to steady her, his lips never leaving hers. The kiss was long and intense and they melted into it like they'd never been apart. Meg abandoned herself to the pleasure, forgetting everything in the acute sensation of feeling that she was where she belonged.

At last Stu pulled back, breathing hard, his eyes dusky. "I've dreamed of kissing you like that every day and night. I just had to see you again. I had to see that you made it home safely."

At Meg's smile and nod, he went on. "I remembered exactly where your farm was. I got here early this morning and decided to wait for some sign of you. It was easy to watch the house here and see you come out. I can't believe I have you in my arms again. Are you all right?"

"Yes, I'm fine," Meg replied.

He went on, "Did your people find you right away after I left you? I hope you didn't have a hard time getting home. I've worried about you ever since. And I've thought of you every day since I left you at that farm. I never should have left you like that. I'm so sorry. So sorry."

Stu's face burned with intensity and he pulled her to him again. Meg folded herself into his embrace as they sank to the ground. He took her face in his hands, asking again, his voice gentle. "Are you all right? What's happened?"

"I'm fine. Pa found me right away the same day. He was close, searching. So, I got right home."

"Thank God. I worried. I knew you were tough, but I worried."

He took a deep breath. "You look so pretty and so sweet, just like I remembered. Just like you are in my dreams. I can't believe I've found you. I thought about you so much. Every day! Every day!" His voice caught.

He turned eager, admiring eyes to her, pulling her back into a strong embrace. Meg didn't resist. She felt helpless, drawn into his spell, and abandoned herself to it. He began to breathe heavily and moved his hands down to caress the dip of her waist and cradle her hips. Meg melted into him. His lips nibbled hers with hungry kisses. She was amazed at the response of her body and shook her head to try to clear it. Her movement caused him to become still.

He raised his head and groaned, "Look at me."

Meg opened her eyes. Stu's smoky blue eyes searched hers. When Meg nodded without hesitation, he drew a ragged breath and began to kiss her again. His lips teased hers with feathery touches until their breaths mingled as one and she felt overwhelming heat building within her. She welcomed the firm yet surprisingly gentle hands that cradled her face, brushed her hair back, and caressed her cheeks. He nuzzled deep into her neck and she reacted with a muffled moan.

When Stu moved his hands to her hips and began slipping her dress up, she moved her hands to help him without reservation. He reached down to smooth the leaves beneath them, then fumbled with his clothing while Meg settled onto the ground. Then his lips claimed hers again. She lay dazed by the sensations, stunned to be back in his embrace, wondering what was to come. She was surprised at the intensity and wantonness of her own reaction to his lips and hands.

Stu moved over her until his strong solid body pinned her beneath him. She liked the weight, the maleness of him and how he pressed her into the smooth, cool grass. The surrounding brush and bushes formed an enclosure, hiding them. His kisses grew stronger and deeper, their breathing faster, and she responded, matching his passion. He sank his lips into her throat, buried his face. The sensation of his whiskers on her skin and the power of his tongue on her neck sent tingles through Meg's body. When he moved up, hungrily kissing her ears, her eyelids, her cheeks, her forehead, ripples of intense and surprising desire claimed Meg. She felt response and desire like she had never imagined and gave in to it until nothing existed but their breathing and their bodies.

He murmured against her shoulder. "Oh, Meg, you are so beautiful. You're everything I ever dreamed of. Even sweeter than I remember."

Meg shivered before giving herself over to the power of his embrace and murmured words. He moved against her and she felt his hardness against her stomach. Filled with wonder, curiosity and an astonishing, burning need deep within, Meg gasped, but Stu's mouth consumed her breath. When she felt him position himself firmly between her legs, she felt a flash of fear. Before she could react, his unexpected, sharp entry caused a squeal of surprise and pain to escape her lips.

At that, Stu abruptly became still. He held himself still and pulled his head back from her shoulder. "Does it hurt?"

Taking a deep steadying breath, Meg realized the pain had been only momentary. She opened her eyes, looked up at him and whispered, "No. No."

"Sure?" Stu asked, his voice soft with concern.

When Meg nodded, he nestled against her and resumed his movement. Meg felt transported by the motion, and lost herself to the pleasures he brought. Before long, he shuddered, let out a moan and collapsed against her. He rolled sideways, pulled her close to him and brushed her eyelids with soft kisses until their breathing returned to normal. They lay against each other, exhausted by the passion and excitement they'd shared. He kissed her again and again, and murmured "Meg, oh Meg."

She languidly gave herself to the comforting warmth of Stu's arms. All too soon, she felt Stu pull away from her and begin to shrug into his clothing.

Meg recovered her senses, shame and embarrassment overcoming her. She sat up and hurriedly fumbled into her clothing. She brushed away a trickle of blood from her inner thigh and pulled her dress back down with trembling hands, then sat for a moment, stunned and shaken, rocking with her arms wrapped around her knees. What had happened was amazing, and she knew her life had been forever changed. She wondered how she would be able to meet Stu's eyes. At that thought, she saw Ma's face, and Pa's, and then Jeb's, and was overcome with shame. Hot tears began to slide down her cheeks.

"Meg. Meg," Stu began. "What... what is it... did I hurt you?" He noticed the blood on her hand. "My God! It was your first time, wasn't it?

Meg ducked her head and curled her arms around her knees. "Go," she said. "Go." Her voice shook.

"But... but..." Stu began.

Meg realized what she had to say. She had promised to marry Jeb. *The wedding is only four weeks away. This wasn't supposed to happen. Stu doesn't belong in this world. What have I just done!*

"Go!" she repeated in an agonized voice. "Get out of here. I'm promised to someone else. I'm marrying him next month, like we've always planned. This shouldn't have happened. Leave. Just go. Please."

She looked up at Stu, tears now pouring down her cheeks. He reached to pull her up, but she swatted his hand away and scrambled to her feet. Hurt and confusion chased each other across Stu's face. His eyes sought hers, but Meg turned away.

"You have to go. Now. Just go. Please."

Pain tore through her heart, tears streaked her cheeks. She refused to meet Stu's eyes, and took a step back toward the house. Suddenly, in a rustle of brush Stu was gone. Meg walked out of the woods in a daze, reached for the clothesline, and woodenly tossed a pillowcase down into the basket.

CHAPTER TEN

MEG was determined to push away memories of what had happened with Stu, fought the shame and guilt, and wondered how she could have done such a thing. It had been as if Stu held some power over her, changing her into a different person when she was in his presence. She tried not to dwell on it. Stu had to be a part of the past.

Two days later, Meg, Miriam and Elsie stood side-by-side in the kitchen, kneading bread dough and making pie crust. Meg noticed the shadow at the door first and turned at the muffled sound of a footstep. Miriam and Elsie followed her gaze, then froze. Miriam took a protective step toward Meg, but Elsie gave out with a small cry and moved toward the door.

The man was dark skinned, six feet tall, muscular. A deep, guarded voice called, "Mama?"

Elsie rushed toward the door, arms outstretched, giving strangled, broken sobs.

The man moved back, pulled the door open toward him and reached out for Elsie. They met and clutched each other, both bursting into tears.

Miriam gave a puzzled, fearful look at Meg and slipped a protective arm around her daughter's shoulders.

"Fetch Moses," Elsie cried, breaking from the hug. "Chile, go fetch Moses, fast as ya kin. It's Cato! Cato!" She sank back into the young man's arms. He drew her back tightly to him, buried his head in her hair, murmuring "Mama. Mama."

Miriam pulled away from Meg, her eyes wide with astonishment. "Go get Pa and Moses. Hurry!"

Meg sprinted for the field, waving and calling. "Moses! Pa! Come quick!"

As soon as the men noticed her, they rushed toward her, alarm growing on their faces.

"Come quick! It's Cato!" Meg yelled.

Moses stumbled, his face a mask of shock, then rushed past Meg and Jim.

Jim stopped, grabbed Meg. "Wait. I have to tell you. Cato. He's their son."

"What?" Meg asked, incredulous. "They have a son?"

"He was sold the year before we bought the farm. He was only ten. Moses and Elsie asked us not to talk about him because Elsie was just getting over the grief. I guess Cato called for his mother from the caged wagon until his voice grew too faint to hear."

"Pa! Why didn't you ever tell me this?"

"We decided to honor their wishes. They wanted to stay on the farm when we bought it, and after the emancipation, too, in case Cato ever made his way back. And now it seems he has."

Meg and Jim took their time walking back to the house. Miriam met them outside. "Let's give them some time alone. Can you believe it, Jim? Cato came back! I'm so happy for them!"

That evening, after cornbread, greens and ham, all stayed late at the kitchen table, listening to Cato. Elsie sat close to him, always touching. A still stunned Moses seemed to drink in the sight of his son, shaking his head often in disbelief, a smile teasing his lips.

Cato told of his run for the North the day after the emancipation was announced. He was conscripted into Sherman's army as soon as he reached Virginia, soon promoted to driving the mules of a supply wagon, and then transferred to the colored cavalry regiment. He served with honor and now planned to head for St. Louis where he could join a wagon train heading west.

"Now I seen dat my folks are good, I gonna move on. I stay a while, but I gonna move on. Need fresh air, freedom," Cato said. He turned to Jim and Miriam. "My thanks for keepin' 'em on here. They's jus' fine. You'all good people."

Cato drove Elsie to town in the wagon the next day, returning with two store-bought wooden rocking chairs for their porch. He left a week later, after putting a new roof on Moses' and Elsie's cabin. The goodbyes included his promise to return within two years. His parents moved now with lightened steps and contented faces.

Meg thought things were back to normal until the morning two weeks later when she woke up trembling and ran for the back steps, overcome by nausea. When she dashed through the kitchen, Elsie and Ma looked up in alarm. Ma hurried out to where Meg sat shuddering on the step, and comforted her with an arm around her shoulders. When the same thing happened the next morning, Miriam and Elsie exchanged looks of dismay before Miriam hurried out to her daughter.

"Meg, do you realize what this means? Do you know what's happening to you? Morning sickness like this means there'll be a baby. Was it the soldier?" Ma asked brokenly, wringing her hands, not meeting Meg's eyes.

Meg nodded through her surprise and confusion, dazed at this information. Ma rose abruptly and went back inside without another word.

Meg remained sitting on the steps, too shocked to move. *A baby. Stu's child.* Thoughts of Stu suddenly consumed her. She remembered the vivid blue of his eyes in the afternoon shadows, his strong, lean arms and legs, and his weight on her. She remembered the sensation of his breath on her cheek and the roughness of his whiskers when he nestled his face against her neck. She saw again the crinkle of his eyes when he smiled, and the way the slashes of his dark eyebrows almost met. The image of his sensual lips and rugged smile came to her unbidden. She longed for the sound of his voice. She could feel the smooth grass beneath her again, and shivered at the memory of the passion they'd shared. She felt alone without him.

It was as if her childhood had been suddenly ended and the only one who could understand was Stu. She longed to tell Stu of this child. She yearned to see him again, but knew these feelings were unreasonable. *What's this power he has over me? Is it because he sees me as a beautiful, desirable, interesting woman instead of little Meg Benson?* With him, she had felt alive, adult, vibrant, loved and cherished. *Is it because he was my first lover? What is this strange obsession?* She spent the following days in a daze, feeling lost, changed, and afraid.

That next morning, the nausea came again and her mother disappeared into her room right after Meg ran through the kitchen. That night at supper, the lines around Jim's mouth were deep and grim. He spoke not a single word while Elsie served the meal, kept his eyes turned down and his head bowed low over his plate. He choked down only a few bites before abruptly shoving back his chair and leaving the table. Ma poked at her food in silence and then glided off to her room without even taking a bite. Louie perched on his chair, uncharacteristically subdued, looking from one to another, as if he sensed that something was very wrong. Meg was devastated by the reaction of her parents and very alarmed at what this pregnancy would mean to them all.

And Meg realized that Jeb would have to be told. He had begun showing up every evening to sit with her or walk with her while they discussed the wedding and the life together that lay ahead. Just last night, he'd kissed her awkwardly before he left for home, a brief kiss that was almost childlike compared to Stu's. He'd had no more outbursts like at the dance, so Meg tried to push it to the back of her mind as the bruises on her arms faded.

Only Elsie had noticed the bruises while they were weeding the garden together. She'd pointed to the barely visible yellow markings, which Meg thought no longer showed and asked what happened. Knowing her secret would be safe with Elsie, Meg explained. Elsie shook her head and muttered to herself, but let the subject drop. The next day in the chicken yard she assured Meg that Moses would talk to Jeb if Meg wanted him to. Meg declined, but had to promise to tell Elsie if it ever happened again. Meg decided not to worry about it. She convinced herself that Jeb had been drunk and it wasn't like him to hurt her. She pushed it from her mind.

She knew Jeb was carrying most of the load on his family's farm because his father's hip injury from the war never seemed to heal before flaring up again. Jeb's mother had been ailing for nearly a year, too, so the care of Sam and Cassie often fell to Jeb. His mother spent her days crumpled in her rocking chair by the window, listless and often unable to get up. Doc Lambert, only recently back from the war hospitals, tried to give a name to what was ailing her, but had been unable to figure it out.

Meg realized that Jeb escaped to her every night for comfort, and for a connection to earlier, easier days. She knew he counted on her for companionship and relief from the burdens at home and how much he looked forward to starting their life together like they'd always planned. She dreaded having to tell him about the baby. So she put it off night after night, not knowing how to do it. She knew that the longer she waited, the worse it would be. Her mother and father never mentioned it, almost as if not acknowledging it would make it go away.

On an especially sultry night a week before the wedding, Jeb suggested a swim at the pond. Meg readily agreed, remembering with fondness all the summer afternoons they'd splashed and laughed in the cool water. They stayed in the water late this night, until the water was a smooth black pool speckled by reflected starlight. When Jeb glided up beside her and slid his body against hers, she felt his hardness for the first time, and knew there was no more time to wait to tell him. She jerked away from him, splashed her way out of the pond, and scampered up the bank.

As she pulled her dress over her wet shimmy, Jeb ran up after her, calling, "Meg! Wait! I didn't mean anything by it. I couldn't help it. Don't be mad. You know how much I want you and I'm a man now. Don't be mad."

He reached for her but Meg pulled away. She took a deep breath, faced him and blurted out, "I'm not mad, Jeb. It's just that... It's just... I'm having a baby, Jeb."

Jeb stopped in his tracks. He stared at Meg in disbelief. "What! Was it him? That bummer? The one who...?"

Meg couldn't answer. They stared at each other in the darkness. Suddenly, he snatched his clothing and bolted away. Meg walked home alone with slow steps, her heart heavy. She slipped into bed and waited a long time for sleep to claim her.

There was no visit from Jeb the next night, or the one after. Meg went through her daily activities despondent, at last feeling the full burden of the pregnancy. She felt dragged down by worry about Jeb and her parents, as well as a persistent and puzzling longing for Stu. The days dragged.

While Meg helped Elsie put away the last of the dishes on the fourth night, they turned at the sound of someone pushing open the kitchen door. Jeb stood there, looking haggard. "Meg. Can I see you? Outside?" he asked in a tight controlled voice.

Meg stepped out and Jeb gathered her into his arms, pulling her into the shadows. "I hate that bastard Yankee devil for what he did to you. But I don't hate you. I'll say the baby's mine. I'll take care of you. We'll get married Saturday as planned."

He took a deep breath. "Let's fix up Grandma's old log cabin. I've gone to look at it. The wood stove still works good and the walls are solid. The well is still working. I want us to have our own home."

His eyes sought hers with an eagerness that surprised her. His words tumbled out. "You know we belong together. That Yankee bastard can't take away the life we always planned. You're mine and you know it. So let's get the wedding done!"

The love and hope on his face were so welcome to Meg that she broke out in a sob of relief. "Oh, Jeb. I've been so worried." She stepped into his embrace.

She felt him shudder a little and heard tears in his voice as he moaned, "Why did that have to happen to you? I can't stand that another man had you. You were mine. Only mine."

Meg bristled, jerked away, and wiped her tears at his words. The thoughts that had consumed her during the past few days sprung from her lips. "If you want us to be married, Jeb, you have to know that it didn't just happen to me. It happened to us. This baby will be the start of our family. It will be our first child forever. You'll have to accept that. We have to move on with the life we planned. We can have our life together but we have to be able to get over this."

"I know. I know," he replied. "I can't live without you. You're right. I'll try. What... What was it like? Was he rough? If he hurt you, I'll find him and kill him, I swear." His eyes blazed.

Meg looked at the ground. "No, he didn't, didn't really hurt me." She gulped. "I can't talk about it. Can we try to forget it?" Even as she spoke, Meg was shaken by memories of the passion of that afternoon in the grass.

Jeb reached over and lifted her chin, forcing her to look at him. "He didn't hurt you?"

Meg met his gaze and shook her head.

"Then I guess I can try to put it behind me if you can. I'll try my best." Jeb leaped ahead of her on the path, flinging his arms in wild glee. "C'mon! Let's go. We're getting married! Getting married!" he sang out as he danced along the path.

Meg felt the first smile in a long time break over her

face as she watched him. Soon she was dashing up the path beside him. At last, she felt like herself.

MEG tried to stop the yearning for Stu while wedding plans consumed every minute of the following days, but he remained strong on her mind. While people chattered gaily around her, her thoughts drifted to the way Stu had made love to her. Sometimes, someone would speak to her, but she couldn't comprehend what was being said and had to force her mind back from the memory of Stu's lips on her throat. Everyone laughed at her, blaming wedding jitters. Meg knew this was a turning point in her life that didn't feel exactly right but she felt powerless, swept along in the festivities as if a rushing river was whirling her away under water and she couldn't break the surface.

Jeb's romantic advances seemed childlike. The quick, almost rough hugs, the clumsy way he held her against his body, his cool lips that didn't explore her mouth with thrilling heat that made her stomach melt.

He became enthralled with the idea of being married, and worked late into the nights making his grandmother's abandoned cabin into a home for them. Meg worked alongside him, washing the dusty log walls, sewing curtains, stuffing dried moss and cotton into ticking for a new mattress for the old bed frame. Ma brought them a new red and white checkered oilcloth to cover the scarred wooden table.

As Meg was sewing the last seam into the mattress early one evening, Jeb grabbed it from her hands, threw it onto the bed frame and pushed her onto it beneath him with a frisky smile. "Yup. This will work," he grinned and gave her a brief kiss before rolling away and leaping up to continue hammering a piece of shutter.

She lay for a moment, fighting memories, and guilt. She'd lain willingly beneath another, giving in to the thrilling heat and intense passion of her body's response to Stu's lips and hands. Jeb didn't know how often she felt drawn to those memories or how pain knifed through her heart when she thought of Stu.

Jeb walked her home from the cabin every night, chattering about the life that lay ahead of them. He didn't seem to notice her distraction. Neither one ever mentioned the pregnancy. He grew bolder with his kisses now and held her long and hard against him outside the kitchen door in the darkness before he left for home. Meg knew his commitment was total, and struggled with guilt that hers wasn't the same.

CHAPTER ELEVEN

MEG wore her mother's lace-covered wedding dress. The day was perfectly sunny, the ceremony just as she'd always dreamed her wedding would be. Ma and Pa's faces shone with happiness. Her friends circled her in excited wonder and envy. But Meg moved through it all as if in a trance, drawn away by an unseen force.

Then she was a married woman. When her pregnancy began to show, knowing smiles met her everywhere she went. Meg knew this course was the best for her parents and for Jeb and for the baby. She lay awake at night beside Jeb and responded to him as best she could when he reached for her. She longed to feel the passion she'd known with another. But it wasn't there. Stu's child grew within her, and his memory stayed strong within her heart. Sometimes she felt him calling to her as if from afar, and her heart would fill with pain. Then she would turn and bury her face in the pillow beside her husband in the little cabin in Crockett County.

A strong, healthy boy was born in March. His straight, dark little eyebrows almost met, just like his father's, delighting her. Her heart filled with love as she clutched her son, her own piece of Stu, to her breast. Love for him and for his father filled her heart. She decided to name him Stephen, a son his father knew nothing of.

Jeb came to her bedside as soon as he was allowed after the birth, concern etched on his face. He bent over her bed. "Are you all right?" he asked, worry creasing his face.

"Sure. Did you see him?"

"Yeah," answered Jeb and averted his eyes for a moment. "You sure you're fine?" He patted her hand on the covers.

"Mmmm hmmm. I'm tired, that's all. See you tomorrow," Meg murmured, overcome by fatigue.

Jeb leaned down and gave her a quick, dry kiss before leaving with quiet steps. Meg could tell he was uneasy. She knew how difficult this all must be for him and felt grateful to him for accepting what had happened. A strong and familiar feeling of affection for him took her by surprise and she burst into tears of relief. *Maybe it will all work out. He's such a good man, such a dear friend.*

She greeted him with a warm smile the next night, and at this, his tentative look became one of relief. He stayed at the bedside, holding her hand and talking until late while the baby slept. Meg sensed that he felt more comfortable than he had since the wedding.

A few days later, as they walked slowly back to their little cabin with Stephen cradled in her arms, Meg noticed Jeb's step was light and his face brighter than she'd seen for a long time. *He must be relieved that the pregnancy's over.* Now if only little Stephen would fit into their lives.

She decided that night to return Jeb's devotion as best she could. He'd been her closest and dearest friend ever since she could remember, and was unselfishly providing a home and a life for her and for a child who wasn't his. *I'll appreciate the life that lays before me, push thoughts of Stu away, concentrate on making a home for Jeb and raising Stephen, and be the best wife possible. It isn't right or fair to Jeb to be holding onto thoughts of another man.*

THAT first year wasn't easy. Jeb left their little house early every morning to spend his days helping his father with the farm. His mother continued to waste away in her rocking chair by the window, so Meg found herself spending much of her time up at their big house. She helped with cooking and laundry and cleaning, cared for the invalid woman, and watched Sam and Cassie. She walked the children over to her parents' house in the afternoons where they played with Louie and she helped Ma and Elsie. Stephen grew accustomed to days spent that way and thrived on the attention from both families.

After supper at one house or the other, Meg and Jeb walked home with Stephen drowsing in Meg's arms while the sky lingered between day and night. They fell into bed in the gathering darkness of their little cabin and as Jeb came to her, Meg fought the memories that wouldn't go away.

Once, in the darkness just before they were falling asleep, Jeb rolled toward her and asked quietly, "You still think about him, don't you?"

Meg had been unable to respond. In the morning, neither acknowledged the unanswered question. It was the only time Jeb asked. They both knew the answer.

On a rainy afternoon in the middle of October, Jeb's mother didn't wake from her rocking chair. She was buried on the hill behind the church on a windy Sunday. After that, Meg found herself spending more and more time at Jeb's father's house. She and Jeb had time together only at night in their own little cabin.

STEPHEN at six months was a healthy baby who nursed hungrily and grew steadily. To Meg's disappointment, Jeb showed only mild interest in him, but she hoped that would change as time passed. Stephen's eyes were the same vivid blue as his father's under miniature slashes of dark brows. His hair grew in thick golden waves exactly like Meg's. It was a striking combination, and the handsome little boy received much attention wherever they went. Meg loved caring for him and never felt more satisfied than when he snuggled into her, nestling down in great contentment. She couldn't look long enough into his eyes while he nursed, and cherished her role as his mother.

It was at the Winston's Halloween party that Meg finally admitted to herself that all wasn't well with Jeb. He left her side as soon as they arrived, joining the other young men outside by the whiskey barrel. Meg spent the first few hours of the party laughing and gossiping with the other young women, fighting a feeling of uneasiness.

The men began trickling into the hall as darkness fell. Jeb came in last, looking somewhat disheveled and with a lopsided grin. A few of the other young men appeared to be in the same shape and received boisterous teasing from the group. Soon, the banjo player picked up a lively tune and the couples headed for the dance floor.

Except Jeb. He grabbed Meg's arm and spun her to him. "Let's go home."

Meg retorted in surprise, "But, why? Everything's just starting. Don't you want to dance?"

"I don't want you here with every guy staring at you every minute like they always do. I'm takin' you home where you belong. Right now!"

He jerked her toward the door. A few of the dancers looked quizzically in their direction.

"Hey! Where ya goin?" one boy called.

Jeb ignored him and pulled Meg out into the night. She couldn't keep her tears from spilling over, and clutched the edges of the wooden seat as the wagon careened along the dirt road in the moonlight. Jeb drove the mules harder than necessary, controlling them with sharp pulls of the reins.

Once home, Meg bitterly hung her dress on a peg in the bedroom and reached for her nightgown. But Jeb roughly grabbed her and shoved her onto the bed before she could get it on. His lovemaking was coarse and forceful, and he reeked of whiskey. Meg lay passively until he rolled off. She slipped out of bed after he fell asleep, and went to Stephen's empty crib, wishing he was not at Ma's for the night. She desperately needed to hold him close. Without reservation or guilt this time, she allowed herself to think of Stephen's father.

She remembered Stu's tenderness as he brushed the hair from her face and kissed her with lips as soft as the wings of a butterfly. His face and voice were distinct in her memory tonight. She felt as though she could almost talk to him, and wondered if he was thinking of her, too. The wistful pull of the memory was so strong that she sat in her rocking chair by the window for hours letting the moonlight and memories settle over her like a comforting cloud.

Silent tears slipped out as she realized that the life she was committed to with Jeb would be forever clouded by the kidnapping. Any man would be affected by such a thing happening to the woman he married. But she'd hoped they could overcome it together, drawing on the strength of their years together. As the months passed, she'd become hopeful that Jeb was accepting her and Stephen and their life together. She'd been doing her best to let go of Stu's memory. Every time she found herself thinking of him, she forced the memory away. She'd been trying to be a good wife to Jeb and took full responsibility for Stephen's care so the baby wouldn't be a hardship for Jeb. She tried to figure it out. *I thought we were happy. So why does Jeb need to get drunk? Why does he treat me this way when he drinks? Is that when he can't hide his true feelings? Will he never get over the feelings left over from the kidnapping? Why hasn't he been able to tell me he's still struggling with it?*

For the first time, Meg felt resentment toward Stu. This was his fault. If he hadn't taken her, none of this would be happening. What it was about him that had captivated her so? After all, Louie had been on the porch floor that morning, hurt and crying because of Stu. And Stu had just thrown her down from the horse in the farm yard when he left her. *Maybe he's a deceitful liar. Maybe none of what he told me was even true. Maybe he's just a selfish, mean Yankee getting in his last licks at someone from the South. Had he just been pretending and using me? Does he ever think about what he's done to my life?*

At dawn, Meg still sat in the rocking chair by the window, alone and cold in her nightgown. *Was my dream of Stu just a nightmare? How could I have felt love for him? What's wrong with me? How can I keep a part of myself from my husband and cause him this anguish?* She knew Jeb sensed it. She knew he must be reminded of it every time he looked at Stephen.

By the time the morning sun first shown over the windowsill, Meg knew what she had to do. She climbed into bed beside Jeb, snuggling close to his warmth beneath the quilt, and murmured, "Jeb. Jeb. I love you. I truly love you with all my heart."

He stirred, wrapped an arm around her in his sleep, then fell back into deep slumber. Meg let herself slide into sleep, too, exhausted by the night.

THE green of the Tennessee countryside slipped into autumn's reds, oranges and golds while Meg devoted herself to her marriage and motherhood. She focused on making Jeb happy, keeping the cabin neat and clean, spending her days taking care of Sam and Cassie at the big house. She folded willingly into Jeb's arms at night. She brushed her hair until it shown, and sewed clothing and quilts for her little family. For Christmas, she sent away for a new gray hat in the latest style for Jeb with money she secretly scrimped from the fund for the general store.

Stephen thrived in the warm atmosphere of his mother's newly found peace, growing steadily, sleeping through the nights with a soft baby snore in his wooden crib by the stove. It was cozy in their little home on the cold winter evenings where they spent more time now that the crops were in. Jeb chopped wood beneath bare branches in the weak light of December afternoons, hunted and trapped, and enjoyed Meg's growing skills in the kitchen. He carved a checkerboard and pieces, and they bantered and played until the firelight faded. When he sometimes brooded for no apparent reason, Meg teased and talked and distracted him until he pulled out of it.

Meg felt successful with her full, busy, and productive life as the months passed. She grew satisfied and proud of her dedication to Jeb and her marriage. Thoughts of Stu became less frequent and intense as she fought away the temptation to indulge herself in them. *What happened is over and must be forgotten. I have to let it go.* She hoped that Stephen would become theirs in Jeb's eyes before long so they could become a real family.

It was usually at night, in the quiet before she fell asleep, that Meg was unable to resist the thoughts that she was able to keep at bay all day. She couldn't fully be free from the connection to Stu that lingered stubbornly, couldn't completely accept that his intensity had been false. In the moments before sleep overtook her, she weakened and indulged in memories of what had happened beneath the pines, and on that day in the woods. In the seclusion which darkness allowed, she let herself search for an explanation for these feelings, as if her thoughts could be hidden by the night. In the mornings, she firmly buried all association with this part of herself, and refused to allow it to be real. But a deep instinct simmered, and she knew Stu would never be gone from her life. She was certain they would meet again, although she fought the feeling.

Sometimes, she caught Jeb looking at her quizzically, and she would launch into conversation or activity to distract him. He seemed to study her often, searching, brooding, but never said anything. Meg told herself that she was most likely imagining it, and proceeded with life as normally as she could.

CHAPTER TWELVE

THE church harvest dance offered an opportunity for the young people of Crockett County to gather again. The Winston's barn windows threw long, rectangular beams of light onto the frosty landscape as Meg and Jeb approached in the wagon, and voices drifted across the fields in the brittle night air. Meg felt free because Stephen had been dropped off with Ma and Pa until morning, and was pleased at being able to wear the new red velvet dress that she had worked so hard on by lamp light. Jeb, lighthearted, drove the team of mules through the night, his hat set rakishly to one side. He was obviously pleased at the prospect of a night out. Meg was in good spirits, too, looking forward to the potluck food, the brightly lit lanterns, the music, and time with her friends.

Jeb helped her down from the wagon, then headed directly for the young men gathered in the shadow of the barn around the whiskey barrel. "See you in a few minutes. I'll be right in. Let's dance the first one," he smiled, and gave her a firm pat on the rear as she turned toward the open barn door.

With a light heart, Meg joined Zona and Zelda as they discussed the handsome new young preacher. All the girls twittered and blushed when he entered a few minutes later, conspicuous in his sober black suit and white collar. Meg felt distanced from her friends as a married woman, and found it difficult to giggle along with them.

The fiddlers struck up the first dance, and Meg looked around for Jeb, but to her disappointment, he hadn't come in yet. She declined many invitations to dance during the next hour while she watched the door for Jeb to come in. She grew irritated at his absence and became tired of sitting on the wooden bench on the sidelines while everyone else moved to the rhythms on the dance floor. She walked to the barn door and peered outside, but the crowd around the whiskey barrel prevented her from seeing Jeb. She knew he would be angry if she showed up there to "fetch him", as he would see it.

Finally, when a progressive dance drew more and more people onto the floor, Meg found herself the last one left not dancing. The new preacher landed at her feet fresh from a whirl and gallantly bowed, his face beaming. She had to agree with her friends that he was a very appealing man. His black hair fell thick and wavy above merry brown eyes. A neatly trimmed dark beard and moustache framed the straightest and whitest teeth Meg had ever seen.

He smiled broadly, sweating slightly from the exertion of dancing, and extended his hand to Meg. "Do me the honor! Can't let you sit here by yourself all night! Come on now!' he cried as he pulled her onto the floor.

Meg acquiesced, feeling it would be rude to decline the preacher and joined the crowd on the floor. It felt good to be out being whirled to the skillful, smooth steps of the young man, and the music ended much too soon. He accompanied her back to her bench, thanked her, then grasped her hand between both of his for a long moment as he looked into her eyes.

Meg pulled her hand away, flustered, and turned away from him. At that instant, she saw Jeb watching from just inside the barn door.

"Oh, here you are," Meg rushed over to meet him. "Ready to dance now?"

Jeb grabbed her arm without a word and pulled her outside. He led her to the wagon, stomping all the way, climbed in and waited for her to clamber into the seat. He startled the mules with a vicious whip before she had her skirts settled in the seat, nearly sending Meg sprawling.

Meg clutched the wooden edges of the wagon with both hands, surprised and angry, and demanded, "What are you doing?! You almost made me fall out! Why do we have to go?"

"Who was that?" Jeb asked, his voice icy with undisguised fury.

"You mean who I was dancing with? That's the new preacher. He's the only one I danced with. I didn't think it was polite to say no to him. I was the last one not dancing in the progressive. We only danced one dance." Anger pulsed in her neck. "Where were you all that time? You said you'd be right in and we'd dance the first dance. What took you so long?"

"I saw how he held your hand at the end. You did more than dance one dance, didn't you?" Jeb responded, ignoring her question, his voice harsh and too loud.

They lurched in the seat as he whipped the mules. With a sinking heart, Meg realized that Jeb was drunk again. She retreated into silence for the ride home, hoping he would calm down.

Jeb matched her silence, throwing himself to the ground as soon as they reached home. He turned away to tie the mules while she climbed down and pushed her way into the cabin.

He followed her in and slammed the door. "I told you before not to dance with other men! I told you!" he shouted.

Meg backed away from him, scooting along the wall toward the bedroom, feeling afraid of Jeb for the first time in her life. He strode toward her, scowling, face flushed with anger and drink. He stopped, looked at her for a long moment, then slammed his fist into the wall. Cursing, he made an abrupt turn and flung himself out the door. She heard him whip the mules again and the sound of the wagon as it clattered out of the yard.

She slipped out of her dress and hung it back where she had so eagerly removed it only hours before. She crawled into bed, numb with misery, and let hot tears slide down her cheeks. The look on Jeb's face was that of a miserable man. *I've been doing my best to be what he needs in a wife. What more do I need to do to make him happy?*

She heard Jeb stumble in the door many hours later. He thudded heavily onto the bed beside her as if unaware of her presence.

Weak morning light awakened her from fitful sleep, and she slipped out of bed and moved to sit in the rocking chair by the window. She clutched a quilt around her shoulders and gave in to a strong and sudden feeling of loneliness. It was as if Jeb had drifted away and become someone she didn't even know.

It was clear now that suppers at Ma and Pa's lately had been dominated by Jeb's moods. The warm love she'd felt at that table during her childhood had disappeared. She and Jeb never lingered after meals anymore, not there or at Charles' house. Jeb's moods seemed to have taken over her life. He directed how they spent all their time. She hardly ever saw her friends and had been looking forward so much to last night's festivities.

Gray daylight gradually lightened the window while Meg remembered another day she'd watched the world awaken. Even though she'd been frightened of Stu and where he might be taking her, her pleasure at the beauty of the sky, the sounds and smells of the morning, and the fascination with the living creatures who had welcomed the day with her as she sat on the riverbank came back clearly.

Now she sat watching another morning arrive, feeling cold and separated from the sounds of the birds, the freshness of the air, and the warmth that steamed from the leaves and grass as the sun's rays hit them.

Jeb finally rolled over awake and murmured in her direction, interrupting her reverie. "Come back to bed. Get back in here."

Slowly, Meg turned to face him.

"What's the matter?" he began. His words trailed off when he saw her face.

Meg continued to stare woodenly, not saying a word. Jeb's bleary eyes and matted hair showed clearly in the bright morning light, and she smelled the sour reek of stale whiskey. It came to her in a flash that Jeb was a drinker. *I'm married to a drinker.* Her heart sank. She stared bleakly back at him.

"Oh, Meg, I'm sorry. I didn't mean to leave you alone. I only shared a couple of dippers with the men. I get tired from working so much and it makes me relax. I don't know what got into me to go back there without you... it won't happen again. Come on over here," he pleaded from the bed.

"Go get Stephen," Meg replied, her words hard and cold.

Meekly, Jeb rolled out of bed, wincing as his feet hit the cold floor. He dressed with clumsy moves and left. He shuffled away down the path, looking back over his shoulder several times. Meg stood at the window watching him. She felt disdain and dislike for him for the first time in her life. *Why does he have to seek comfort in drink? Why can't he be happy with our life? I've been doing everything I can to be a good wife. What kind of a future lays ahead if I'm married to a drinker, someone who'll always hold the kidnapping against me?*

The older women talked about men like Seth Asmus who drank away every cent he got and left his wife and young ones hungry and ragged in that shack down by the railroad tracks. *Will that be Jeb pretty soon? Is that the life that lays ahead for me and Stephen? What am I supposed to do? It wasn't my fault about the kidnapping. Why can't Jeb get over it and be like he used to be? Why do I have to be the one to keep trying to make everything work?*

She was still at the window when Jeb returned carrying Stephen. As they approached, Meg realized that this was the first time she had seen Jeb hold the baby. She took

Stephen from Jeb's arms without making eye contact. Rigid and unfeeling silence hung between them. She hugged Stephen, desperate for the warmth and comfort she always drew from his sturdy little body.

"I told your Ma we wouldn't be comin' over for supper tonight. That we wanted to stay home for once. I'll go up to Pa's and get some pork chops. We can stay here," Jeb offered, his tone conciliatory and eager as he reached toward her.

Meg didn't answer him, and jerked away from his outstretched arm.

A contrite Jeb hung around the cabin all day after returning promptly from his father's farm with the meat. He tried to start conversations several times, but Meg was unwilling to respond. Finally, he went out to the yard and half-heartedly split some wood. Meg rocked Stephen and held him close against her breast for the hours he slept. She finally fried the pork chops in late afternoon when hunger became intense, but ate in silence in her chair by the window. Jeb wolfed his down, then drowsed on the front steps until dusk, and went to bed early.

Meg awoke the next morning feeling weighted down, almost unable to get out of bed. She listened to Stephen's cries from his crib, and with her back turned to Jeb, said dully, "I'm staying here today. I'm tired."

As Jeb dressed, he pleaded, "Meg, please. You know how sorry I am. I didn't mean it. I'll never drink again, I promise. I don't know what made me do it. Please. Meg, I'll never drink again if it makes you so unhappy."

"Well, why do you always have to drink like that? Can't you have fun without the whiskey? John Brinks and some of the other boys don't spend all their time out by the whiskey barrel. What's wrong? Don't you like our life? Aren't you happy?"

"Yeah, I'm happy. You know I love you and I always have. I don't drink that much and I can do without it anytime. From now on, I won't drink then. Now, are you happy?" Jeb asked.

A boyish grin stole across his face as he came closer and drew Meg into his arms. "Come on, now," he begged. "You know I love you. I promise I won't drink anymore if it bothers you that much."

His eyes looked like they used to, warm and familiar. Meg allowed herself a tentative smile, and felt an ember of hope flicker in her heart.

He hugged her hard to him. "I'll come back early today and get you. We can go back up and eat supper tonight with Pa and Sam and Cassie. I'll ask him to make those potato pancakes you like. And we'll have that sausage from the general store. You just stay home today. That's fine. You work too hard anyway." With a smile, Jeb kissed her lips lightly and walked out the door as if all was right with the world.

It remained right only until the Christmas hay ride. Then, his breath misted with whiskey from one of the flasks the young men carried, Jeb again became hostile and rough. This time, Meg found it harder to be forgiving the next day. This time, it was nearly impossible to hope. She grew sad remembering how the other girls had laughed and tumbled in the hay, carefree and gay, and couldn't remember how it felt.

CHAPTER THIRTEEN

MEG made up her mind at Stephen's first birthday party. Ma and Pa and Louie chuckled when Stephen grabbed a fistful of frosting and stuffed it into his mouth, leaving white smears on his cheeks and nose and chin. Elsie and Moses gave fond grins, their familiar faces cheerful and content. But the warmth and love that surrounded Meg couldn't overcome her distress at Jeb's absence.

That morning, Jeb had promised to come right over after he was done in the fields, but that should have been several hours ago. He'd missed supper last week once, too, claiming too much to do for his father. There'd been a faint odor of whiskey as he crawled into bed beside her later that night.

While Stephen's birthday cake was being cut, it became apparent that it was happening again with Jeb. Meg watched her handsome baby bask in the attention of those who loved him, felt her heart grow cold, and made up her mind what she'd do tomorrow. She memorized the happy faces—Ma's delicate smile at her grandson, her pale blue eyes set off by candlelight, the strands of light hair trailing from the soft bun at her neck. Pa's contentment showed in his eyes as he settled into his favorite chair by the fireplace and tamped down his polished wooden pipe. Meg studied the glints of silver highlighting his rusty hair and thick moustache and looked for a long time at his broad shoulders. She straightened her own in resolve, and vowed to be just as strong. Louie's impish grin as he swiped fingers of frosting tugged at her heart. Elsie and Moses stood near the door, their reassuring shapes like solid pieces of her life.

It would be hard to leave and cause worry to these loved ones. But she felt confident of her plan, strong and sure and able to handle what lay ahead. She looked around at the familiar kitchen, securing it in her memory while the loving sounds of her family surrounded her.

Jeb's return very late, with no words spoken as he slid clumsily into bed, deepened her resolve. He again smelled of drink and made space for himself in the bed with rough movements, as if nobody else was there. It made Meg more certain than ever that her destiny lay elsewhere, not in a cabin in Tennessee with a drunken husband.

She slept little that night, tossing fitfully. When first gray light began to drive darkness from the cabin windows, Meg ended her long wait and slipped out of bed.

Stephen's little mouth scowled in sleepy protest, although he didn't waken when Meg gently gathered him and his blankets from the crib. She carried him to the barn, shielding him from the dawn's crispness, and settled him in the straw while she saddled the horse. She picked up the parcel of clothing and belongings she'd secreted under the hay, tied it to the back of the saddle, then wound Stephen securely across her front with a shawl and mounted. She guided the horse out the door down the lane, away from her life.

Meg took a last look when they passed the house where her loved ones lay sleeping. Lingering mist steamed around the house like a puffy white skirt. She locked into her memory the high poplar trees that ringed the yard, the wide front porch, and the solid squareness of the white frame house. Then she turned her face north and urged the horse forward along the misty road.

Meg had been on the road for several hours by the time the morning sun grew hot and she felt thirsty. She worked the horse off the road through thickets and over the rocky ground down to the stream. Stephen awoke to the jostling movement of the horse, the sound of the water and the warmth of the sun on his face.

She dismounted to let the horse drink and then shared one of Elsie's rolls with Stephen. When she showed him how to crouch down and sip water at the stream's sandy edge, he splashed, squealing in delight when the cold drops landed on his arms and face.

They remounted and rode north in the stream for hours, letting the horse splash along at its own pace. It was easy to cuddle Stephen to her. He liked the rhythm of the animal's walk and dozed lightly in her arms. Meg drifted in and out of memories of another time when horse's hooves had splashed like this in the same stream.

By midafternoon she realized that Joseph and Tillie's place should be nearby up on the road. Pa and the others had ridden hard with her after sleeping at the old couple's house on the way home from the kidnapping, so she knew that today's pace would put her about there by now.

She guided the horse up the bank, then walked it along the road, searching for a glimpse of the long low house with six oblong windows. Apprehension overcame her for the first time when she realized she was alone on the road with a year-old baby, and not sure exactly where shelter lay ahead. But to her great relief, the road's next curve showed the familiar house.

While Meg dismounted at the hitching rail on the front porch, Tillie appeared at the door, her face puzzled as she wiped flour-covered hands on her apron.

"Tillie? Do you remember me? Meg?"

"Well, for land's sake! Is that you, Dearie? What are you doing here? Are you all by yourself? What's this you have? A baby?" She started down the steps, arms outstretched. "What in heaven's name are you doing alone way up here with a baby along? Here, I'll take him. Come on in."

Meg unwrapped Stephen from the sling she'd worn across her shoulders all day. She shrugged the stiffness from her back and handed Stephen down into Tillie's arms.

Once inside, she explained her situation to Tillie, surprised to find herself faltering a bit with the words. "I just had to do this. I feel in my heart that it's right for Stephen and me. I have to go to Stu. I know Ma and Pa will worry, but I can't stay there anymore."

Tillie listened, her eyes darkening more and more with worry, then shook her head. "Oh, Dearie. I don't know. Do you know Stu's last name? Are you sure you'll be able to find him? What if you get to the area you think they were headed for and nobody knows them?"

Meg looked down at Stephen snuggled in her lap and tightened her arms around him. "His name is Stuart Logan. I know I can find him." She met Tillie's eyes with a determined gaze. "I just couldn't change Jeb. I tried my best."

Tillie frowned. "Where will you stay tomorrow night and the next night? You have a baby along. Oh, I just don't know about this."

Fear snaked its way into Meg's heart while she listened to Tillie's words. She didn't know where Stu lived, only what he'd told her about the ranch just across the Illinois border, that his brother's name was Bill, and their last name was Logan.

"You don't have much to go on. Why don't you go back home and try to work it out?" Tillie asked, her face now knit with lines of worry that deepened her wrinkles. "Surely your husband will come around. He was such a quiet young feller, as I recollect. He has to be a good man for you to have married him. And he gave this baby his name."

Tillie gave a firm toss of her head. "Give that young man another chance. You can't head to Illinois by yourself with a baby. It's much too dangerous for a young woman to be on the road by herself."

"Well, I did try as hard as I could. I gave him lots of chances," Meg replied, feeling familiar anger and frustration rising. "I'm sure Jeb believes his life is messed up by having to think about me with another man and having that man's son in our house. I don't think he'll ever get over it. I did everything I could think of. I was the best wife I could be." She shrugged, eyebrows raised. "If I leave, maybe he'll find someone else or be happier because we're not there to always remind him. I'm not going back. And I'm not afraid."

Tillie's reply was interrupted by Joseph coming through the door. "Well! Well! Look who's here." Joseph asked, brushing sawdust from his knees. "And jest as purty as ever. What brings you up this way, young lady? Is your Pa coming right along, too?" He gave a cheerful grin and waited for an answer.

He looked from one to the other, face tightening with curiosity at the silence that greeted him. While Tillie explained, his eyebrows scrunched together and the lines bracketing his mouth deepened. "Let's have some supper and think on this," he said, his voice now somber, and headed for the table.

Tillie's fried ham, sliced thick and accompanied by creamed potatoes, warmed Meg as much as the kindly old couples' concern and their tender attention to Stephen. Tillie mashed potatoes and spoon fed Stephen, her mouth forming little o's along with him each time he opened his mouth. Joseph doted on the boy, bouncing him on his knee in the chair by the fireplace after the meal. Tillie cuddled the boy until his eyes drooped and finally remained closed. The warm glow of oil lamps in the windows, the crackling fire, candles flickering on the kitchen table, and the cozy surroundings comforted Meg.

She and Tillie and Joseph talked for a long time, while Stephen slept snuggled into Tillie's lap. By the time it was very late, Joseph and Tillie had accepted that Meg's mind was made up. Joseph insisted that he would accompany Meg for the next few days while she rode across the rest of Kentucky and into Illinois. He threatened to bundle her up and take her right home to her Pa if she protested. The half-hearted chuckle that accompanied his words didn't disguise serious concern on his part, and she didn't argue with him. He vowed to leave her side only when she'd located Stu.

Meg was secretly glad, recalling her apprehension that morning when she wondered if she would find Joseph and Tillie's house. Doubts about this whole thing had begun to creep into her mind during the conversation with Tillie and Joseph, but her commitment remained strong. The fire dwindled to glowing orange embers and Meg grew drowsy while Tillie chattered about the food to be packed in the morning.

She lay awake only long enough to admire the colorful rag rugs, crisp white curtains and simple charm of the cozy room she'd slept in once so long before. She refused to let herself dwell on the memory of how Jeb had slept in the next room last time they were here. Secure for this one night at least, comforted by Stephen's warm little body snuggled next to her, she pushed away worries about tomorrow. She felt surprising relief that Joseph had insisted on coming with her, and slipped into deep slumber.

Meg helped prepare a breakfast of grits and scrambled eggs in the morning, while Joseph saddled the horses and packed the saddlebags. Tillie had been up early, packing biscuits, jerky, a canteen of lemonade, and hard taffy wrapped in strips of cloth. She waved from the porch as they left, but her smile wasn't quite convincing, and concern showed in the hands that twisted her apron.

"Good luck, Dearie!" she called. "Come back this way whenever you can. You're always welcome. Come home safe, Joseph."

Meg held up Stephen's little hand and shook it back in a tiny wave toward Tillie, causing smiles all around. Then, she turned around and faced north toward Stu, toward her new life.

CHAPTER FOURTEEN

It was easy to follow Joseph's sturdy brown horse at its steady pace through the sunshine of the day. Stephen drowsed most of the time in one lap or the other, gazing wide-eyed at the new surroundings when awake. Joseph reined in at a carved wooden sign on the edge of the road as afternoon waned.

"We should water the horses," he called over his shoulder. "Let's go down to the river over there. We're into Kentucky now. We should pass through this panhandle in four or five hours and be crossing into Illinois by sunset." He paused and swiped a hand across his forehead, worry crinkling his eyes. "Are you still sure about this? How's the little fella doing? I haven't heard him makin' a fuss all day."

"Yes, Joseph, I'm sure. And Stephen's doing just fine."

With a resigned shake of his head, Joseph led the way to the river. They shared Tillie's biscuits, jerky and taffy while the horses drank and munched grass near the bank. Joseph tipped the canteen of lemonade to Stephen's lips, chuckling when the boy's eyes lit up with surprise at the unexpected taste. Meg joined him in the laugh, enjoying the distraction from her worries.

They remounted and headed north, Stephen now tucked in front of Joseph. Meg stretched, glad for the freedom to rearrange her posture as she rode. She smiled at the sound of Stephen's baby talk chatter that drifted back to her while Joseph pointed out birds and clouds. Her baby's eyes were bright with curiosity when he turned back for reassurance that she was still there and the breeze ruffled his golden hair in the afternoon sun. Meg waved to him each time, cherishing the sight of his tiny dark eyebrows and the sturdy little legs dangling off Joseph's saddle as he bobbed along.

Afternoon passed quickly until the sun slid behind the hills on the horizon, shadows stole over the road, and a cool breeze arose. A large whitewashed sign WELCOME TO ILLINOIS took them by surprise when they rounded a bend.

Joseph twisted back around in the saddle and called, "Well, we made it! Are you still sure about this?"

"I'm sure," Meg responded with a firm nod. Being away from home for these last few days had strengthened her resolve about starting a new life. Feeling free and light and hopeful now, she nudged her horse forward in front of Joseph. Ahead lay the life and love she knew was right for her.

Meg led the way into Illinois, heart beating hard with anticipation. She inhaled the smell of the pines and let the memories flood in. She'd made it. She would find her soldier.

Joseph called out to her after a few minutes. "Meg. Hold up. It's getting pretty dark. We better stop for the night. Find a tavern or an inn or somethin'. You've got an old man and a baby along, ya know."

Meg recognized the fatigue in his voice and was filled with sudden guilt. She pulled her horse up and waited for Joseph and Stephen to come alongside.

"Mama! Mama!" Stephen cried, reaching for her.

While they were transferring him onto Meg's horse, a black buggy approached from the north, with two riders on horseback following close behind. With a great jingling of bridles, amid a cloud of dust, the buggy and riders reined in beside Meg and Joseph. A finely dressed couple peered down from the buggy seat, brows raised in curiosity.

"Hallo there. Where you headed?" the man called out. He pulled hard on the reins, quieting his team as the woman held onto the edge of the seat to keep her balance.

The woman's face shown white beneath the largest ruffled yellow bonnet Meg had ever seen. The coats of the team of shining black horses gleamed beneath silver studded harnesses. The men who had reined in behind them milled and tried to settle their mounts.

"Lookin' for lodging for the night," Joseph answered.

"You're in luck. Just ahead there, see the building way up the road on the right? It's Griffin's Tavern. Good clean place. We just had a hot dinner there. They got beef stew tonight and cornbread. They have rooms, too. Didn't seem crowded so you should be able to get a place to stay," the man continued.

"Thanks," Joseph answered, "Griffins it will be."

"You moving on further north tomorrow?" the man asked. "Rain's comin' soon now, they say." He waited for an answer, eyes flickering over Meg and Joseph and Stephen. The woman leaned forward across the buggy seat to get a better look.

Obviously these people were wondering about them, Meg realized. How strange it must appear—an old man accompanied by a girl and a baby, out on the road on horseback with night approaching.

One of the men on the horses behind the buggy called out, "We're headin down to Kentucky for horse racin' tomorra at Union City. George and Bess here were headin' the same way, so we all left from Griffins at the same time. We'll be travelin' together for the first few hours 'til they get to their cutoff, 'specially with the storm comin' in."

The woman nodded, adding in a smooth, refined voice, "We decided to continue on heading for home and try to beat the rain. It's only two more hours until we'll be there."

It was clear that everyone expected a similar sharing of information from Meg and Joseph.

"We've been traveling for a couple a' days, up from Tennessee," Joseph provided. "We'll be trying to locate someone in this area. We plan to start searching tomorrow."

He glanced at Meg. Everyone followed his gaze. Meg found herself the center of attention and felt her face heating up. Stephen struggled upright in the saddle in front of her, looking from one face to another. A few throats were cleared.

The nearest man on horseback spoke again. "If ya don't mind my askin'. We all been living around these parts all our lives. We know most everybody. Who ya lookin' for?"

Joseph looked at Meg, a question in his eyes. She nodded.

"Well, we're looking for two brothers. They got back from the war together. One had a shot up leg. They've probly been back in these parts at their home place for well over a year now. Name's Stu and ah... ah..."

Faltering, he looked to Meg.

"Bill," Meg replied." Stuart and Bill Logan."

The couple in the wagon shared a quick glance before the man stole a sidelong look back at the riders behind the buggy. In the awkward silence, Meg sensed that the names had meant something to them. She could feel it in the air. Horses shifted, dust rose, no one spoke.

Suddenly, widely spaced heavy raindrops began to fall in big splats. In the distance thunder growled before the sky cracked open with a blaze of lightening, freezing the scene for an instant. Stephen jumped, cried out, and twisted back, clutching at Meg in terror. The man in the buggy reached behind him and tugged the top more securely onto its posts. The horses began to strain at their bridles and whinnied, eyes wide. Meg comforted Stephen with a hug and pulled the corners of her saddle blanket up over his legs.

Sure that this opportunity would be lost if the rain caused everyone to separate, Meg blurted out, "Please! If you know of the Logans, tell us! Do you?"

The riders pulled up alongside the buggy, ignoring Meg's question, not making eye contact with her or Joseph, almost as if embarrassed. "George, we gotta move on. Didn't expect this storm so soon," one called. They pulled their hats low and spurred their horses off into the rain.

George studied Meg and Joseph as rain drops plopped down with increasing frequency. The wind picked up, blowing shreds of ragged white clouds across the sky and whipping tendrils of Meg's hair across her face. Meg realized how it must look. *Us searching for two men. Me with a baby.*

She brushed the wind-whipped hair back off her face and appealed to the woman in the buggy in desperation. "Stuart Logan is the man I love. If you won't tell us if you know of him, would you please let him know Meg's here at that tavern ahead? He doesn't know I'm trying to find him. Would you at least tell him I'm here? Please?"

With a slight nod, the woman acknowledged Meg's plea, then pulled her cape more tightly around her and settled farther back into the wagon seat. Meg was certain that the woman knew who Stu and Bill were.

George noticed his wife's nod and added, "All right, then. Stay at Griffin's for two days. If nobody has showed up after that, go back where you came from. Get on now. You need to get that little feller out of this rain. And we gotta get this buggy on home. Head on up there, now. Wait two days."

With that, he flicked the reins and his team of horses charged off down the road, mud flying from their hooves.

Joseph spurred his horse toward the lights of the tavern ahead, with Meg close behind, rain soaking them. Not much was spoken between the two as they sat in their damp clothes over stew in the stuffy, noisy tavern. Then Joseph shuffled ahead of Meg, shoulders bent, face drawn with fatigue, leading the way to their rooms at the top of narrow, scuffed wooden stairs.

Meg's small room contained a single bed against the wall, a scarred wooden rocking chair and a dusty window covered by yellowed lace curtains that looked ready to fall apart. She rolled a sleepy Stephen out of her arms onto the bed as Joseph set her bundle down on the chair. The air smelled stale and vaguely of other people.

"Thank you, Joseph," she turned to him.

Fatigue creased the old man's face beneath the stubble of white whiskers. "Lock this door right after I leave. Don't open it 'til I knock and you hear my voice in the morning. They got chamber pots in the rooms so you don't need to go out for anything. My room is next here on this side. We'll get this all figgered out in the morning." He turned to go. "Now, be sure not to unlock this door, young lady. You hear?"

Meg tucked Stephen under the covers next to the wall and settled beside him, thoughts of home coming to mind. She wondered how Ma and Pa had taken her departure. They must be very worried by now, especially about Stephen. Guilt overcame her. *How could I have just left like that?* She'd been so intent on getting away to Illinois that she hadn't really considered the impact this would have on them. *Elsie and Moses will worry about us, too. Louie will miss me and Stephen, and wonder where we were.* She made up her mind to send a message south with anyone who passed through this place tomorrow, or to get a letter out if there was mail service.

Through her worry came the realization that she hadn't thought at all about Jeb. *How was he taking this?* She let go of thoughts of Jeb, surprised by a feeling of indifference, and allowed her thoughts to turn to tomorrow. She knew in her heart that word would get to Stu. She could tell that those people all knew who she was asking about. It had been clear on their faces. *Tomorrow, tomorrow, I'll be in Stu's arms.*

CHAPTER FIFTEEN

STEPHEN toddled back and forth across the worn board floor, laughing while chasing a tattered string ball from one end of the tavern porch to another. Meg and Joseph relaxed in well-used wicker rocking chairs and watched him play. It had been much quieter in the tavern this morning while they discussed what to do over sourdough hotcakes that soaked up the tangy maple syrup.

Meg penned a letter to her parents right after breakfast and was assured by the tavern owner that since the mail trains were running steadily again, her letter should reach Crockett County in a few days.

> *Dear Ma and Pa,*
>
> *I hope you aren't too worried about me and Stephen. We are in Illinois and safe. We spent our first night with Tillie and Joseph. Remember them, Pa? Where we stayed on the way home when you came to find me? Joseph has come with me the rest of the way into Illinois. We're waiting here at Griffin's Tavern on Hokum Road just inside the Illinois border for word on finding Stephen's father. He came and found me there at home last fall. I'm sure now that our place is with him. I tried everything I could to make a good life with Jeb, but he's not happy. I suppose you know that, too.*

Please don't let Jeb know where I am. I'll write again as soon as I have news. Try not to worry too much. I have almost twelve dollars that I saved from the general store money. I'm sorry for the way I did this. I promise to keep in touch and I'm being careful. Stephen is well. I miss you all very much.

Your loving daughter,

Meg

Meg agreed with Joseph that it was best to stay at the tavern for the next two days like the man in the buggy last night had advised. It was a relief to be out of the saddle. Joseph's wan complexion and slow-paced movements made it obvious how hard the few days in the saddle had been on him. Warm morning sun seeped into Meg's arms and face as she relaxed. She'd braided her hair, and her mother's faded hand-me-down cotton dress, though slightly too big, hung comfortably loose in the sultry heat of approaching midday. Far away from the worries that had plagued her back in Tennessee, she gave in to the soothing surroundings.

Suddenly, the shaggy brown and white dog that had been dozing in the sun at the bottom of the steps sprang to life. His ears pricked up, and he gave a sharp yelp in the direction of a rider just becoming visible down the road. Something about that rider caused Meg's heart to thud. The silhouette was vaguely familiar. She bounded from the chair and turned wide-eyed to Joseph.

He met her gaze, then stood up and moved to the top of the step, staring hard into the distance. "I don't see so good far away anymore. Do you think...?" he asked over his shoulder. He shaded his eyes with a hand, peering toward the rider.

Meg didn't answer. Her heart was hammering so hard she could hardly breathe. She rushed to stand beside Joseph. Stephen ran up and clutched her leg, following her gaze.

Meg gasped. Could it be? Already this morning?

The rider approached steadily, his face hidden in the shadow of a wide hat. He sat his horse in a posture familiar to Meg, but an odd feeling overcame her.

"I don't think it's him... it's not..." she said to Joseph. "But..."

Before she could continue, the approaching horse's clatter made conversation impossible. The tavern proprietor joined Meg and Joseph on the porch as the rider pulled up. He sat for a moment while the dust settled, stared down at them, then focused on Meg.

"Meg?" he asked. "Is that really you?"

At his voice, Meg realized who it was.

"Bill...? she stammered, shaken by the sight of Stu's brother. "Bill!"

Bill nodded, then began to dismount.

"Hey, Logan. What brings you in? It's not mail day," the proprietor boomed.

Bill stepped closer to the porch steps. ignoring the man's words. "Meg! They told me you were here. How did you get here?"

Meg stared, mouth going dry. Bill had grown a neatly trimmed beard that perfectly matched his distinct, straight dark brows. The blue eyes she remembered looked clearer now that the shadow of pain was missing. When he removed his hat, she felt a rush of recognition. The last time she'd seen that head of hair, it had been long and shaggy, bent over yams and grouse at a campfire. He now looked healthy and strong, no longer so frail. She dropped her eyes to the leg he'd favored.

He stepped forward and began up the steps. "My leg has pretty much healed," he responded to the unspoken question in her eyes.

The proprietor looked from Meg to Bill, brows knit, the tip of his tongue caught between his lips. "You two know each other? What's this all about? What's going on here, Logan?"

Bill turned briefly to the pudgy man in the stained apron. "Hey, Ruben. Yeah, we know each other. Go back a ways, in fact. We need to go in and talk a bit. Got any cold cider in there, or just your usual watered down whiskey?"

Ruben gave a big chuckle and rubbed his hand over his bald head. "You and that rascal brother of yours never miss a chance to give me a little hell, do ya? Ya know damn well I have the best drinks this side of the Mississippi! Now git in here, all a' ya. Y'all set right down there and git yer talkin' done."

He turned to Meg. "What's a pretty little lady like this doin' here havin' business with one a' them Logan rascals, anyway?" He turned with a lopsided grin and waddled through the swinging doors.

Meg, heart fluttering so hard she could hardly breathe, turned to Bill. "Where's Stu? Why did you come?"

"Let's go inside. I'll tell you everything."

Joseph leaned down, gathered Stephen up in his arms, and walked down the steps toward the dog. He looked back over his shoulder with a smile of understanding.

Once inside, Bill seated Meg at one of the round wooden tables in the empty tavern. They stared, each waiting for the other to begin.

Ruben appeared, banged chilled pewter mugs of cold cider down in front of them and wiped his hands on his bulging apron front. "Well... what..." Suddenly sensing the charged atmosphere, he halted in mid-sentence. He looked from one to the other, then turned away and ambled off toward the bar.

Bill curled his hands around his mug and began. "Meg, I can't believe you're here! It's good to see you. You look well." His smile reached his eyes. "Stu told me he'd been to see you."

Both turned at the sound of Stephen's happy squeal as he dashed through the tavern door with a merry giggle, looking back over his shoulder. Joseph rushed in and gathered the little boy up with an apologetic smile. "He likes to git me to chase him." He swept back out, a grinning Stephen propped over his shoulder.

Bill turned to Meg, face scrunched with curiosity. "That little fella looks mighty like Stu, from what I could see just now. Is...?" His eyes widened and he tipped his head toward Meg. "Is that boy...?"

Meg realized she'd been holding her breath. Words wouldn't come. She nodded.

Bill gave a wide grin. "Well, well! Does Stu know?"

Meg shook her head and Bill's eyes widened again. "Well! That beats all. Stu's son, huh? I have a nephew!" A grin spread across his face before he went on. "I couldn't believe it when George showed up at our gate first thing this morning and told me about meeting you on the road last night. Lucky I was out at the corral so Ma and Pa didn't even know he stopped by. I just couldn't believe it when George said a pretty young woman named Meg was at Griffin's looking for us..."

"Where is Stu? Why didn't he come?" Meg interrupted, impatience finally overcoming her shock.

"Well, Meg, he's not here. He left 'bout two months ago now. He was pinin' real bad for a long time after he came back from seeing you. He never did tell Ma and Pa about taking you like he did—ashamed, I guess. It wasn't something anyone would ever think he'd do. I still can't figure out what made him just grab you like that. It's not like him at all." Bill sighed and searched Meg's eyes for a reaction. "He felt real bad about it, that I know."

Meg drew in a deep breath, heart sinking. The room became too bright. Bill's words sounded hollow, coming from far away.

"He's not here?" she managed to croak through the tightness in her throat. "What do you mean, gone? Where? For how long? When will he be back?"

Bill winced. "Well, we don't know. He just saddled up one day, went in and hugged Ma and shook Pa's hand and said he had to go. They were sure surprised. I wasn't, though. He'd been pretty withdrawn for quite a while. He tried to hide it, but I knew it was because of having to leave you there when he went back to make sure you were home safely. He told me he'd been hoping he could bring you back with him, if you'd be willing. He said he'd realized you were everything he ever wanted."

Bill's words came fast. "He was really shocked that you were getting married. Took it real hard. I tried to tell him he should go back again and tell you how much you meant to him and ask you to come back here before you went and married somebody else. But he said he already messed up your life enough and it would be best if he just moved on. He said he'd to try to get over you, try to forget. But he couldn't. I could see despair in his eyes every day."

Bill paused, looked off into the distance, and took a swallow of his cider. "He tried to forget you. I think it was hard for him 'cuz I hitched up with Virginia Lennert right away when we got back. She was widowed with two young 'uns. We got married and now we all live with Ma and Pa at the ranch. Virginia's a good help for Ma, since Ma's pretty crippled up in her hands now. Virginia's due to have our young one soon, and I could see how hard that was on Stu."

Bill paused again, but when Meg didn't say anything, he went on. "He acted just plain lost most of the time. Got quieter and quieter. Sometimes I'd find him down in the corral at night, jest staring off into the distance. I knew it was you on his mind. Then he got so he wouldn't talk about it anymore. Told me to let it be. I thought he should tell Ma and Pa. They deserved to know about what was troubling him. But he wouldn't listen."

Bill waited for her to reply, and Meg asked again, agony filling her voice. "He's gone? He didn't say where or for how long? Your folks don't know about me?" She couldn't breathe through the crushing disappointment. *He isn't here! What will I do now?*

Bill looked at her, his eyes solemn. "You missed him by two months. He's gone. He was in a bad way. I don't know when he'll be back, or exactly where he is. He's stubborn, Meg. He could stay away a long time. He hasn't written or sent word. Nothing. Nothing at all."

He shook his head and spread his hands across the table. "I'm sorry, I just don't know when he'll be back. I know he loved you. I know he wished you could be with him. He pined for you, I'll tell you. He really pined for you."

Meg couldn't hold back the tears. She pushed back from the table and stood, weeping, shoulders shaking. Bill rose and came around, patting at her shoulders with awkward hands.

Bitter, heartrending sobs overcame her. "No! He can't be gone. I have to find him!" She shook Bill off. "I have to find him!"

Bill stepped back and spread his hands in understanding. "I'll help you, Meg. We'll figure out what to do." His eyes grew warm with compassion. "Why did you come now? What brought you here? Was it because of the young 'un?"

Meg gulped back sobs, then dried her eyes on the handkerchief he handed her. Ruben shuffled over, carrying the cider pitcher, but backed off when he saw the tears and the intensity between them.

"Here, now. Let's sit back down," Bill said, and helped Meg back into her chair. "Let's talk about what to do. Now, first, what brought you here?"

Meg forced out an answer through her constricted throat. "I'm sure my place, and Stephen's place, is with Stu. Stu needs to know he has a son. I did get married back home. But my husband turned from being my best friend into someone I don't even know. He doesn't like living with another man's child and he thinks what we always had between us was spoiled by the kidnapping."

Bill dipped his head. "Go on."

She wiped her eyes and went on. "My husband drinks too much and broods about the kidnapping. He can't seem to get over it. He isn't happy. I don't think he even likes me anymore. I did all I could to make it work with him, but I don't think it's ever going to be all right."

She took a sip of cider, licked her dry lips, and shrugged her shoulders. "I never stopped thinking of Stu, all this time. I tried and tried. I know we belong together. I can't believe he's gone. I just can't believe it. What will I do now?"

Bill's face filled with sympathy and distress. Suddenly, his eyes brightened. "You can come home with me," he offered, voice rising with eagerness.

He reached across the table and covered her hand with his. "We'll tell Ma and Pa all about it together. I don't know if that's what Stu would want, but I think it's the best thing to do. He might be mad, but we can tell him it was because we decided together that it was right."

He raised his chin toward Meg. "Yup. I'll stand with you if you want to bring Stephen out to the home place and meet Ma and Pa. I think they have a right to know about you, and that you're here, and to know about their grandson."

He pushed his chair back, eyes shining with hope. "Will you come with me? If they agree, maybe you can wait at home with us until Stu gets back. The ranch is doing well. There's plenty of room for you and the little feller. We can send word on the mail wagons that head out West and try to get a message to Stu. I heard they post unclaimed mail at all the trading posts and forts. We can do the same to the main post offices out East. There can't be many other Stuart Logans. Maybe he'll see letters if we send enough of them everywhere. Or someone might know of him. Want to try it?"

Bill's face had grown bright with hope, but Meg couldn't answer through the tightness in her throat. This was something she never dreamed would happen. All she'd thought about was that she would find Stu and then everything would work out.

She swallowed rising sobs and managed to blurt out, "I don't know, Bill!"

She bolted from the room, tore up the stairs, and flung herself through the door into her room. She dropped onto the bed and let the heaves of grief overcome her.

Late afternoon shadows lay across the wood floor of her room by the time Meg finally managed to dry the flood of tears and descend the stairs into the tavern. A murmur of male voices from the porch and Stephen's little running footsteps on the floorboards drew her attention. She pushed through the swinging doors and stepped out to see Joseph and Bill side by side in the wicker rockers.

Joseph rose and rushed to her. Without a word, he gathered her to his bony chest.

Meg sought comfort there for a moment before pulling away. "I'm fine, Joseph. I've decided what to do."

She turned to Bill. "I think you're right. We should introduce Stephen to his grandparents. I think Stu would understand and agree that it's time to let them know about us. Stu and I love each other and your parents have a grandson they don't even know about. We can be ready to go as soon as you want to. How far is it?" She paused, cautious now. "Do you still think it's the best thing to do?"

Bill rose, favoring his leg slightly, and it caught Meg's eye. *How tired he must be.*

"Bill, I'm so sorry for making you wait all day like this. It just took me this long to accept that Stu's gone. Thank you for coming to let me know, and for offering to take me back with you. I realize that I'll just have to wait until word gets to him and he comes back."

Bill took a step toward her. "I agree with you. I think I should take you and the boy home with me. It's only an hour's ride north of here. We'll get your horse saddled right away. We should leave before dark."

He turned to Joseph. "Joseph, what do you think? If we go now, will you be heading on back home in the morning, then? "

Joseph turned to Meg. "We talked it pretty near clear through, Meg and I agree. It seems best for you to go back with Bill. Best to git it out in the open."

He leaned toward her, eyes earnest. "If your kinfolk come my way, though, I have to tell them where you are. They gotta be near sick with worry by now. You need to send another letter to them about all this and where you'll be. You're just a young girl, and with the baby and all, they gotta be plenty worried."

Meg recognized the same determination in Joseph's eyes that she'd seen when he decided to ride with her to Illinois.

"You're right, Joseph. I want my folks to know I'm safe. They should get my letter soon. And I'll send another right away as soon as we get settled."

She drew a deep breath and threw her shoulders back. "But if Jeb comes looking for me, please don't tell him where I am. He'll either be angry and mean, or beg me to come back to him. I'm not ready to face him. I need to make it on my own and try to make a better life. Please promise me, Joseph?"

"No promises, Missy. I reckon I don't know how I'll act if I have to face your husband. I know I won't lie. Never have, never will. If your Pa shows up he'll need to know where his daughter is. He seemed like a mighty fine man, and you takin' off like you did must be taking a toll on him. You better send word to him real regular. Me 'an Tillie need one of your letters now and again, too. Just send it to Joseph Sawtell, Coopers Mill, Tennessee. You hear me, young lady?"

Meg saw the steel in his eyes and knew he meant every word. "Yes, Joseph. I can't thank you enough for getting me here." She smiled her thanks. "I'll be fine going with Bill. At least I can be at Stu's home place and with his kinfolk until we find him. I promise to write home, and to you. You and Tillie have been so very kind. I hope someday to find a way to repay the goodness you've shown me. I'll never forget you and when I pass that way, I'll always stop to see you."

Joseph unfolded himself from his rocker, stood and rustled his body up straight. "Well, then, I'll help you pack up. And I'll head for home first thing tomorrow. Tillie will be frettin' by now, I'm sure. You remember where we are, should you need anything. Anything at all."

Meg looked at Bill, who motioned to the door. "Go pack, then," he said. "I'll get your horse saddled up and bring it around to the rail. We can be home by dark if we get on the road right now."

CHAPTER SIXTEEN

MOMENTS later, after a quick hug for Joseph, Meg secured Stephen in the shawl across her chest, mounted up and set off following Bill. Joseph waved from the porch steps, his kindly face shadowed by the growing twilight, until they were out of sight. Stephen fell into instant slumber in the saddle in front of Meg, lulled by the rhythm of the horse's steady walk. Meg's heart warmed as she followed Bill, remembering other nights on horseback, following his silhouette. Comforted by his presence, she felt eager to meet his parents and wife and to see where Stu called home.

Daylight had faded into rose and gold on the horizon when Bill turned off the main road onto a wide, hard-packed dirt lane bordered by low, red brick fences. Stately oaks, their branches a crackled black maze against the now deep purple twilight sky, stood in majestic rows behind the fences. Meg caught sight of an imposing two-story red brick house in the distance. Her eyes widened at the many rows of windows bordered by white shutters, the long veranda flanked by profusions of pink rhododendrons glowing in the dusk, and a tidy cobbled drive making a wide curve across the front.

"Hello!" Bill called loudly. "Hello, in there!"

Figures spilled onto the porch. Meg reined in behind Bill, then sat without moving, feeling suddenly shy, while Bill dismounted. A young woman with a mass of dark curls tumbling over her shoulders, a small boy and girl at her heels, hurried down the steps and into his arms. Behind her, a tall, white-haired man with a woman at his side appeared at the top of the steps, lit from behind by the open door. It was impossible to see their shadowed faces, but Meg sensed they were staring at her. Bill returned his wife's embrace, and leaned down to ruffle the hair of each of the children who clung to his legs. Then everyone turned to look at Meg.

Bill stepped toward the veranda and halted halfway. "This is Meg," he said, his voice strong. "I rode to Griffin's this afternoon, not to town like I said. There's something Meg and I need to tell you. We better go inside."

He turned back to Meg. "Come on, Meg. Hand the boy down to me and let's go in. Georgie, please take both horses. They'll need water and food. Thanks." Bill walked over, lifted Stephen down from Meg's arms, and started up the steps.

The stable boy held the bridle and offered his arm. Meg dismounted, smoothed her dress, nervously tucked her hair back into its braid and followed Bill. The others remained where they stood, surprise and curiosity filling their faces as she passed them. With a quick look at each of them, Meg climbed the steps behind Bill. She glimpsed curious, guarded faces in the dim light. There were no smiles.

The size of the room they entered astounded Meg. Intricately carved wood moldings trimmed the high ceilings, and heavy furniture covered in brown leather formed a clustered half circle before a massive stone fireplace. Its gleaming wood mantel held polished brass plates of varied sizes that glimmered and shone in the firelight. A large, thick circular wool rug woven into a brown and green leaf pattern further warmed the room. Thick brown velvet drapes tied with gold tassels framed the windows on the far wall. A cluster of multicolored Currier and Ives lithographs hanging on either side of the fireplace, depicting bowls of fruit and idyllic landscapes, caught her eye.

She was awed by the luxury and comfort, and realized that this wasn't an ordinary farm—it was a prosperous ranch. This was far beyond what she had imagined when Stu had talked of the "home place". As she stood, overcome by this first impression, the children ran to a checkerboard on a small table in the corner.

"My turn!" shouted the boy.

"No, mine!" squealed the girl, grabbing for a piece. They looked expectantly at Meg, hoping for a reaction to their scuffle.

The young woman spoke from behind Meg, her voice low and firm. "Robbie and Sissie, not now. We have a guest. You two can finish the game later if you want. But it would be rude not to first show hospitality to this woman your father has brought into our home."

The children scrambled away from the chess set and scampered over to stand in front of Meg, their faces upturned to hers in curiosity. Each had pale blue eyes in a freckled face, a snub nose, and fair hair sprouting from forehead cowlicks. Meg gave them a smile of acknowledgement before turning to Bill.

He turned to his wife and held a soundly sleeping Stephen out to her. "Here, Virginia. Can you find a place to tuck this little fella in? He hasn't even woke up, even with all this commotion. Then come on back and I'll introduce you all to Meg."

He handed Stephen to his wife. Virginia looked at Meg with a question in her brown eyes. "Is it all right if I tuck him in Sissie's bed for now? Her room's right up at the top of the stairs. I'll put pillows around him." She hesitated. "You can come along."

Meg followed Virginia up the wide polished wooden stairway. Virginia laid Stephen down with great care onto a colorful quilt that covered a low bed in what was obviously a little girl's room. A row of cornstalk dolls sat on the window sill and small articles of clothing lay scattered among other toys on the floor.

"She doesn't keep it picked up all the time," Virginia

apologized. "We weren't expecting Bill to bring company," she added with a friendly smile that crinkled the corners of her eyes.

Meg smiled back, then glanced at Stephen, who slept, blissfully unaware of his changed surroundings. The travel and the days at Griffin's must have tired him out more than she realized. She leaned down and tucked the quilt close around him while Virginia moved pillows between him and the outer edge of the bed.

"Thank you." She turned to Virginia, heartened by the young woman's friendliness.

"You're welcome," Virginia replied, her eyes sparkling with friendliness and her small white teeth forming a perfect welcoming smile.

She turned and led the way back down to the main room where Bill stood with one hand on the mantel, obviously waiting. The older man and woman had taken seats, but both rose when Meg and Virginia entered. The children looked up from where they'd been sitting cross legged watching the flames in the fireplace and scrambled up, faces expectant.

All eyes turned to Meg. She looked at Bill and gave a small shrug.

He dropped his arm from the mantel. "Meg, this is my mother and father, Ruth and William Logan. My wife, Virginia, and Robbie, and Sissie. Everyone, this is Meg..." An awkward pause followed his words.

"Shaw, Meg Shaw," Meg interjected, realizing that Bill didn't know her last name.

"Pleased, I'm sure," Ruth murmured, her voice cool, and sank back into her wing backed, red velvet chair. She was a petite woman, trim and neat in appearance. A rich, deep green dress fell to her ankles in generous folds. Meg could see that Stu got his dark hair from her, although the thick braid wrapped on top of her head showed threads of silver that sparkled in the light from the fireplace. Unreadable eyes beneath arched brows met Meg's glance briefly, then dropped to the hands in her lap. Her lashes lay on lustrous skin. Although her lips were thinned in a firm line, the elegance of her small, triangular face was striking. It was hard to believe this dainty woman could be Bill and Stu's mother.

Meg shifted her gaze to William, who remained standing beside his wife's chair. His straight, thick black brows contrasted sharply with the white hair that waved back from his forehead. It was plain to see where Bill and Stu got their eyebrows. He was a tall man, slightly heavy in the middle, imposing in his bearing. William studied Meg, returning her look with bold eyes.

"Well. I don't know where to start." Bill twisted away from the fireplace. "I wish to God Stu was here," he went on. His face contorted, eyes darting from one to another. Virginia moved to stand beside him and he grasped her hand.

At the mention of Stu's name, the puzzled looks on everyone's faces intensified.

"Well, there's no easy way to say this," Bill struggled on. "Ummm. Ummm..." His eyes locked onto Meg's, pleading, as he tried to continue.

Meg realized she had to participate. *Stu would expect me to be strong. So would Pa. They'd expect me to take responsibility. This will be one of the most difficult things I'll ever have to face. It isn't fair to leave this all up to Bill.*

"I'm Meg Benson... Shaw, from Crockett County, Tennessee..." she began, cringing at the mistake in saying her married name. "I know Bill from when he and Stu passed through my family's farm on their way home from the war. I'm in Illinois because I'm trying to find Stu. We've been in love these two years since they came through. The baby I have with me is Stu's son."

Ruth gasped, clutched her hands to her mouth. She jerked upward toward her husband. They stared at each other, eyes wide, color draining from their faces.

Virginia, eyebrows raised, looked into Bill's face for confirmation.

He gave a shrug. "Yeah. That's right. It's Stu's boy, but he doesn't know."

In the frozen silence that followed his words, Meg realized she was holding her breath.

Bill turned to face his parents. "It's true. The baby is your grandson." He took a deep breath. "Stu doesn't know about him."

"Why? Why couldn't he tell us about all this? If he had a wife and child, I know he would have told us!" Ruth cried out. She lurched forward, hands outstretched toward Bill, tone entreating. "Why didn't he tell us? Why didn't you tell us? Why did he leave? I don't understand! I don't understand this at all!"

"Bill...?" William turned toward his son, dropping a steadying hand to his wife's shoulder.

Bill's eyes sought Meg's. Their next words would be vital. It was suddenly clear that they would have to choose between showing Stu in a bad light while trying to explain the kidnapping and pregnancy, or that it would be Meg who would look bad, as if she had given herself to a passing soldier and was now trying to make a claim upon him with an illegitimate child. This reaction was unexpected. They'd assumed it would be easy—just explain, and everyone would be excited about new members of the family here to wait for Stu's return. They hadn't thought beyond a welcome and the excitement of introducing Stephen and Meg. The silence stretched while Bill and Meg stared at each other in consternation.

Suddenly, Ruth rose from her chair. "I don't know what this is all about. Bill, you have some explaining to do to your father and me. Virginia, please take the children to bed." Her tone was icy. She stood rigid, avoiding looking in Meg and Bill's direction.

Virginia motioned to her children, who solemnly followed her up the stairs. They peeked back over their shoulders, subdued by the tense atmosphere, and their eyes darted toward Meg in curiosity and confusion.

Ruth turned to face Meg and Bill, while William moved close to her side. Their faces were grim.

"Now, Bill. What's all this about? What's this about Stuart being married and a father?" William demanded. He put an arm around his wife's shoulder and glared at his son.

Bill cleared his throat, stole a sideways glance at Meg and began with a grimace, "Well... well... Like Meg said, it happened while we were on our way home. Umm..."

Meg took a deep breath and stepped forward. "Stu and I love each other. I expected to find him here. He came to see me again in Tennessee shortly after he and Bill first passed through. But when found out I was promised to another man, he did what he thought was best for me and left me to my life there. He's a good man and I love him with all my heart. He never knew about the baby."

She paused, feeling her knees begin to tremble. Her voice came out shaky. "I brought his son here so we could be together. I've realized our place is with him."

She turned to Bill, who looked at her with relief. The explanation Meg was giving to his parents would not be one that would discredit his brother. "That's right. If Stu was here, he'd be mighty glad to see them. Meg and I thought we'd send word with the mail heading to all points out West and back East and hope one of the letters reaches him. I know he'll come right back as soon as he knows Meg is here."

After a long, awkward pause, William spoke, his voice low. His words were directed to Bill. He avoided eye contact with Meg. "This is quite a shock for your mother and me. We'll need to talk this over. Have Virginia see to finding a place for Mrs. Shaw to sleep. Bill, I'll see you in the corral at daybreak."

The curtness in his voice held a cold dismissal. William turned away, held his arm out to Ruth, and escorted his wife from the room without another word. Neither looked back.

Bill turned to her, his face reddening. "Meg. I'm sorry. I never thought they'd react this way. I'll talk to Pa in the morning. I think I can get him to understand."

"No, Bill. Don't say anything against Stu. I didn't come to hurt him or his family. I don't know right now how to handle this. They probably think I was a loose woman and trapped Stu with a child. Better they think that than to paint a bad picture of Stu while he isn't here to defend himself. He made me into a woman, and showed me what it means to love with all my heart. I can't come here and do anything that will make him look bad."

She crossed her arms across her chest and gave a challenging look to Bill. "And that's what will happen if we try to tell them how it was. It'll just hurt him no matter what or how we try to say it. I won't have you telling them," Meg stated. "I love Stu. I can't damage the love his parents have for him. We cannot tell them until Stu's here to explain with us!" A feeling of strength and power overcame her and she felt a look of defiance cross her face.

Bill drew back. "But what will you do? They might not welcome you here if they don't understand how it all happened. They seem pretty upset." He grimaced. "I sure didn't expect this."

"I'll figure out what to do," Meg replied. "Let tomorrow bring what it may. Now, please, show me where I can sleep. Is it with Stephen?"

Bill sighed, shook his head and turned to Virginia with a helpless look.

"Come with me," Virginia murmured, took Meg's arm and led her up the stairs. "Here you are." She slipped away down the hall without another word.

Meg slid her dress off, hung it over the back of the only chair in the room and crawled in beside Stephen. She cuddled him, and spent an uneasy night turning the events over in her mind. *It isn't fair to ask Bill to fight my battle. He has a growing family, didn't contribute at all to this situation, and has always been very kind to me.*

Stu wasn't here. He hadn't told his family about her. It was up to her to figure out what to do.

Stephen stirred in her arms at daybreak, waking her from a fitful slumber. "Mama? Mama? Tirsty." he squeaked. His blond curls stuck to one side of a cheek reddened by the pillow. He looked around at the strange room and then back at her. His little black eyebrows knit. "Mama?"

Meg rose from the bed and carried him down the stairs, looking for a door to reach the privy outside. At the far end of the hall, she discovered a door that led to the back stairs down to the yard. She carried Stephen across the dewy grass toward the whitewashed wooden privy, amazed by the deep green fields and white fences that spread in all directions. Red barns and stables with white trim stood to one end of a large, round corral to the right of the house. She could just make out the shapes of two men leaning against the fence, and recognized them as Bill and his father. They were absorbed in intense conversation, and didn't look her way.

After using the privy, she tiptoed Stephen back into the hushed house and dressed him quietly. After changing into the best dress she had along, a gray muslin with a black lace collar, and brushing her hair thoroughly before tying it back with a black satin ribbon, she led Stephen down the steps toward what she thought would be the kitchen.

Behind the first door she tried, she found morning sunshine streaming into a large square kitchen. Brightly flowered curtains surrounded wide windows. Matching cushions bursting with color covered the seats of eight wooden chairs clustered around a large rectangular oak table. It was the prettiest kitchen Meg had ever seen. Her delight was quickly dashed by the memory of last night. How she wished it had been different.

She settled Stephen into a high wooden child's chair in a corner. She found a small tin cup, pumped water for him from a pump next to the sink, and sliced a piece of bread from a loaf that was sitting on a shelf nearby. The jam jar was right there, too, so she spread jam on his slice of bread.

Meg pulled a chair over to the highchair and sat as Stephen ate, helping him lift the cup to his lips. He grabbed at the cup with both hands, determined to hold it by himself. She sought comfort in his bright blue eyes, and studied again the straight black brows, which almost met, exactly like his father's. And like his grandfather's. She smiled at the golden tendrils, which curled behind his ears and imagined giving him his first haircut. He grinned back at her and patted at the jam on his bread, amused by its stickiness.

At the sound of the door, Meg turned to see Virginia entering the kitchen, followed by a barefoot Sissie, still in her red flannel nightgown. Meg noticed the bulge of the unborn child Virginia carried.

Virginia smiled. "Good morning. I see you found something for the little one. Do you need anything else for him? I'll be making some oatmeal for the children soon. He can have some of that, too. And you, too, if you like. I always make coffee. Will you have some, too? Did you sleep well?"

Meg sensed nervousness beneath the chatter and friendly smile. "Sure, thanks. Coffee would be nice. I can help with the oatmeal." She continued, feeling hesitant. "Virginia, I know it's difficult to have us here under the circumstances. I want you to know that I'm glad to have met you. Bill's a good man, and you're lucky to have him. I'm sorry about the trouble I've brought to this house, but whatever today brings, I'm glad I've found Bill happy."

Virginia looked at her for a long moment, then rushed over for a quick, impulsive hug.

She smiled as she backed away from Meg. "And I think Stu found himself a good woman. I wish he was here. It would make this all so much easier. Ruth and William have been nothing but kind and generous to me and my children since we joined the household. I'm very surprised at how they acted last night. It's as if they're angry at Stu for leaving, and for not telling them about all this. They seem to have trouble believing he could have kept this from them. I don't know if they'll be accepting of all this, even if Bill tries to explain. It's quite a shock for them."

She moved toward the stove and reached for a pan, speaking over her shoulder. "I've never seen that look on Ruth's face before. I can tell she's angry and upset, even suspicious. She's a strong woman. We do things her way around here. Her sons are her pride and joy. So this has to be quite a shock. And really hard for her."

Sissie clambered onto her mother's lap. "Mama. I'm hungry. When's oatmeal?"

Virginia pumped water into the pan, just as Ruth entered the kitchen.

"Good morning!" Virginia volunteered.

"Good morning," Meg echoed softly, with a hopeful look at Ruth.

Ruth's face was as tight and closed as the night before. A web of fine lines showed at the corners of her eyes in the morning light. Her movements aged her, as if it was difficult for her to move smoothly. She wrung her hands continuously as if they pained her. She bent stiffly to give Sissie a brief hug, then murmured a muffled "Good morning", without really looking in Meg's direction.

"Do you have the coffee going?" The question was directed to Virginia. "Father and Bill should be in from the corral soon. They've been down there since sunup. Do you know if Luella brought any eggs up yet this morning?"

Virginia turned to her mother-in-law. "Yes, the eggs are outside the door, I noticed. Looks like a nice batch of them today. I just got down, so the coffee's not going yet. Meg said she'll help with the oatmeal so we can get the little ones fed."

Ruth paused for a long moment. Her back stiffened and her voice turned frosty. "It seems you are managing fine. Excuse me. I seem to have a headache this morning. I'll be going to my room. Please have Luella bring me poached eggs and toast, and coffee when it's ready. I'll have it up there."

With that, Ruth marched out. The door closed hard behind her. There was dead silence in the kitchen. Meg and Virginia looked at each other, stricken. Meg felt her face begin to burn as Virginia's face filled with sympathy, then embarrassment.

Before either could figure out how to end the awkward silence, Bill stomped in the back door, followed by William, bringing the smell of horses and the sharpness of the morning air with them. A frisky brown and white dog accompanied them and ran to sniff Meg's knee.

"Is this Lad?" she asked, remembering Stu's hope that his dog would still remember him.

William's eyes widened.

Bill turned to Meg. "Yup. That's Lad." He gave a puzzled look. "Oh, Stu told you about him?" He pulled a chair over near Meg. "Got that little fella liking Virginia's raspberry jam, I see." He tousled Stephen's hair.

William turned away and walked to the opposite side of the kitchen and began pumping water into a tall tin coffee pot. His lack of greeting put a pall on all in the room. Meg suddenly wished she was anywhere but here. She felt snubbed by Ruth and now very uncomfortable in William's presence. She could see that Bill and Virginia were puzzled and uneasy, too, when she noticed them exchanging a questioning glance.

Meg's hurt quickly became angry determination. It was obvious that she and Stephen weren't welcome here. She sensed rejection that William and Ruth didn't even have to speak aloud. Meg felt like an outsider, an intruder into their comfortable lives. It was obvious that Bill hadn't been successful down at the corral.

"I'm going to leave." Meg turned to Bill, her voice low.

"No. Wait. We can all talk about this some more," he answered.

But Meg was determined to remove herself and Stephen from this awkward situation as soon as possible. She would go back to Griffin's and think about what to do. It had been a terrible mistake to come here. *Maybe I've already hurt Stu in the eyes of those he holds most dear. I never should have come.*

William remained at the pump, his back to them while he held the coffee pot under the flow of water. Virginia came to stand behind Bill, and turned sympathetic eyes to Meg.

"You don't have to go," Bill pled again. "Pa and I discussed it all. They need time to think this through. They…"

But Meg interrupted him. "No! It's clear I never should have come. I won't stay where we're not wanted. If they can't recognize that I brought them their grandson out of love, and that I left my life to be with Stu, then they don't deserve to have us here."

This time she declared her words loudly. Anger began to build deep within her. She rose from the table and lifted a sticky Stephen from the highchair.

William turned from the pump, holding the filled coffeepot. "I'm very sorry, young woman, that you find it necessary to leave before we settle this matter. You're invited to remain while we investigate these circumstances you've brought to our lives. If this is indeed our grandson, we will make a place for you both until Stu returns. My son's wishes are hard to predict at this time, with his disappearance and now the shock of your arrival and all. You understand that this is very unexpected? It isn't necessary for you to leave."

He balanced one hand under the coffee pot as he spoke. His look was almost challenging. His lips were firmly set and his jaw clamped, as he waited for her to respond.

Meg still smarted from Ruth's snub and felt distressed, disappointed, and insulted at William's questioning of her integrity and intentions. Caught off guard by William's strong, straight black brows over deep blue eyes so much like his son's, she buried a sudden rush of longing for Stu. Leather boots with silver tips shone beneath finely tailored black pants and his crisp white shirt. William's presence dominated the room, his appearance firm and strong. It was obvious that he was used to getting his way. He watched her with a steady gaze, awaiting a response, testing her.

Meg moved Stephen firmly onto her hip and stared William full in the face. "I'll be leaving at once. If we meet again, it will be only under circumstances in which my son and I are treated with courtesy and respect. That day will include Stu." Filled with resolve and simmering resentment, she turned to Bill. "If you would be so kind as to get my horse ready, please, Bill."

William's eyes widened momentarily. When he shifted his gaze to Bill, Meg turned quickly and marched out of the room. She was too upset to be sure if it was a glimmer of respect that flashed in William's eyes, but she was too angry to care.

Soon, her belongings were being secured into the saddle bag and she mounted to leave. Virginia and the children stood on the steps while Bill lifted Stephen up into her arms. William and Ruth were nowhere to be seen, although Meg thought she glimpsed a shadow at an upstairs window.

"Thank you for your kindness," Meg called out to Virginia, and received a sad smile and wave in return. With puzzled looks, Sissie and Robbie joined their mother, waving halfheartedly.

"I'm going with you," Bill announced, giving the horse's saddle strap one more firm yank.

"That's not necessary, but thank you. It's only an hour's ride and I remember the way. I'll be at Griffins Tavern until I decide what to do," Meg replied. "Thank you so much, Bill. If you hear from Stu, please tell him I was here. Will you?"

"Sure, I'll tell him. But I can't let you ride off alone. A woman with a young one. I'll ride with you until we spot the tavern. I'm going along." Bill's tone left no room for argument.

Meg tipped her head, acquiescing, and jiggled the reins.

Choking back tears now, not waiting for his reply, she yanked on the reins and spurred her horse to a gallop. She rushed down the lane between the brick walls, nearly blinded by the tears that streamed from her eyes. She wasn't wanted here. She didn't know where Stu was. She felt Stephen brace himself in alarm in her lap, and slowed the horse as her little son began to whimper in fright. Behind her, a trail of dust obliterated the world of the man she loved. It was a world she wanted to join. But that, as well as the world she had left behind in Tennessee, held no place for her. She ignored the clatter of Bill's horse trotting behind. The sound ceased as Griffin's came into sight. Meg didn't look back.

CHAPTER SEVENTEEN

As soon as they reached Griffins Tavern, Meg tied her horse to the hitching post, gathered Stephen to her chest and dashed through the dining room and up the stairs without so much as a glance at the people inside.

She tucked a sleepy Stephen into bed and paced the little room. While she watched her little son sprawled in sleep, she realized how hard this must be on him. The travel, the strange faces, the removal from the only world and the only people he knew back home in Tennessee.

But she was determined not to go back in defeat. *If I go back now, Jeb will never change. My life will never change either.* She grew certain that the shadow of the kidnapping and Stephen's father would forever cloud a home and relationship with Jeb. She was sure Stephen would also suffer. She allowed herself no tears of self-pity or weariness, but paced from wall to wall, thinking furiously. By the time Stephen awoke an hour later, rumpled and hungry, Meg had decided what to do.

She soothed her baby while she changed him into clean clothes, singing the same lullaby Elsie always sang to him. His eyes brightened at the familiar tune, and he tried to babble along. She hugged him long and hard when he reached up both arms for her. Whatever it took, she would make sure this child had a good life, that he was loved and had all he needed. Her heart warmed when he cuddled into her neck as she carried him down the steps. The dining room was now empty, but she could hear Ruben banging around in the kitchen.

"Hello, Ruben," she called to get his attention.

"Well, good day to you, too, young lady," he called back, and shuffled through the swinging doors. "Will you be havin' a cool lemonade with me? I was jes gonna pour myself some. She's a hot one today."

His small, deep-set eyes held curiosity, and his round face glistened with the heat of the day. With each breath, his chest and shoulders heaved in his damp white shirt. He tugged at the stained apron across his wide middle and set a pewter pitcher of lemonade on the counter. "I jus' mixed this up. Travelers stoppin' in will need something cool."

Meg knew he must be wondering about her abrupt arrival and the way she'd dashed up the stairs without a word. He had to be very curious about how things went at the Logans, and why she came back alone.

"Lemonade sounds good. Thank you," Meg replied. "Did Joseph get off for home early yesterday morning?"

"Yep. Took off right at dawn. Seemed real anxious to get going. Good fella, that one."

"Yes, Joseph and his wife are the nicest people," Meg answered, and took a deep breath. "Ruben, I have something to ask you. I know you're wondering about all this with the Logans. I'll tell you all about it. But first I need to know if there's a chance you could use some help around here. I need a place to stay for me and my son. I could cook and clean and help with travelers. Whatever needs doing I'll work hard and do my best. Is there any chance I could work for room and board?"

Ruben looked at her, eyebrows lifted in surprise. "You need to work? What about your kinfolk? I better hear your story before I even think of answering you." He settled on his stool behind the counter and looked expectantly at Meg.

Meg took a sip of lemonade and began. Ruben mopped his brow when she'd finished, then sat unmoving and silent for a moment.

He met her eyes. "Well. That's quite the tale. That there is Stu Logan's boy? I can see it now. The resemblance. Them two Logan boys started comin' in with their father when they were just knee high to a grasshopper. I watched 'em grow up and now both are daddies! Time goes by so durn fast."

He wiped the drops of perspiration that dotted his upper lip and paused in contemplation, "Come to think of it, I noticed I been runnin' out of steam by nightfall most days, now that the weather is gettin' hotter. Seems like I can't take it like I used to."

He gave a quick laugh, "Shucks, I used to be able to shut this place down after the last customers left at night and then git right up at dawn and make breakfast for those needin' it. Guess during the war years, when it wasn't so busy—hardly anybody was travelin' but the soldiers, an' not many of them stopped in here at that, I didn't notice so much. But things shore have picked up lately, and I git so blamed tired sometimes I kin hardly keep moving. Maybe some help would be a good idea."

His eyes lit up. "You could move to the room at the end of the hall upstairs. It has two windows and two beds. It'd be a lot cooler than the one you're in and it's bigger, too. We'd hafta work it out what all you'd do. But I don't see why we can't give it a try. I ain't makin' no promises, you unnerstand. Jus' sayin' it's worth a try. If it don't work out, you gotta go back home. Deal?"

Meg's heart leaped. She wanted to jump up and hug him. "Yes, I understand. I'll work hard. Oh, thank you for the chance! You won't regret it," she responded, feeling her heart lighten. "I can start right now. What do you want me to do?"

Ruben chuckled. "Well, first, why don't you and the youngun git moved into the bigger room upstairs? Needs a good cleanin' first, I reckon. I gotta think on this a spell. How it's all gonna work. Come back down when yer done. I got some catfish and taters to fry up for supper and I need to make enough for travelers later. I'll kinda show you around the place. Bring down the sheets from both them rooms while you're at it. The washin' is what I really need help with. I hate it—all that heatin' the water and swishin' in the tub an' rinsin' and hangin' on the line. Ugh. That I know ya can do for me right away. Ya done washin' before?"

Meg spoke, her voice eager. "Sure. I've helped with the washing lots at home. I'll do it! I'll start right away!"

She almost danced back up the stairs. Stephen responded to her mood, and "helped" carry their belongings to the end room. This room was much larger, with a breeze that ruffled the ragged, dusty curtains when she opened the windows to air it out. She pushed the beds together so Stephen's was between the wall and hers, arranged their clothing in the scarred tin wardrobe, and decided to come back up and scrub the floor and wash the curtains as soon as she could. She'd wash everything in this room, and then do the same for the other three rooms down the hall as soon as she had time.

THE following days passed quickly. Ruben's relief at the arrangement became more obvious every day, as he showed Meg the workings of the tavern. By the end of the first week, he began disappearing into his room behind the kitchen for a nap every afternoon. Meg tucked Stephen in upstairs at the same time, and then spent the next few hours of each day preparing food for the evening meal, doing laundry outside in the big tub in the shed, and cleaning.

Ruben always shooed her away as soon as the evening meal was finished. "You don't need to be down here at night. I kin handle it jes' fine after supper," he said while escorting her to the stairs. His voice left no room for protest.

So Meg took Stephen out the back door and down to the creek to wade and splash as twilight deepened every evening. She kept a bar of soap in the crook of an oak tree and brought along a towel and his little nightshirt so he came back clean and ready for bed. She often waded in while bathing him, sinking into the gently rushing water herself to wash her hair and bathe. That way, she seldom had to haul and heat water for baths in the zinc tub in the shed. These evenings at the creek became rare moments of privacy and peace.

Ruben talked one of the regular customers into bringing in a carved oak highchair, worn smooth by many years of use, and set it up at the end of the bar for Stephen. The boy thrived on attention from customers, spent many hours playing on the front porch with Ruben's gentle old dog, and interacted easily with children who came in on mail day or were traveling through with their parents.

After the first time a woman asked "How old is she?" Ruben helped Meg trim off most of the curls that hung on Stephen's neck. Ruben turned the scissors to Meg's waist-length hair, too, taking enough off so she could easily brush through it again.

Stephen's legs quickly lost their baby fat while he scrambled through his busy days. He caught on to using the privy during the first few days at the tavern. It seemed he'd suddenly outgrown almost every piece of clothing they'd brought along. So on Ruben's weekly trip to Springfield for supplies, he brought back fabric for new curtains for all the rooms and cotton and denim for little shirts and pants.

Meg spent her nights sewing by the upstairs window until darkness fell. Then, as voices and the tinkling of the piano wafted from below, she climbed into bed and let her thoughts drift toward slumber. Her mind wandered at that time of day, when thoughts of home came strong. By the end of the first three weeks, she was suffering pangs of homesickness every night. She longed to hear her mother's voice, longed to see Louie, and missed Pa. She hoped they'd received her second letter by now and realized she better write again before too many more days passed. She imagined seeing Elsie again, and tasting her molasses cookies and warm cornbread with butter dripping down the sides.

Meg wondered how Jeb was doing, and imagined him back home with Charles and Sam and Cassie. And, at the thought of her little cabin now empty, tears came and she felt even sadder, not for Jeb, but for the life that could have been and was now lost to them all. Memories of life with Jeb caused her great melancholy and she wondered what had happened to their dreams. Then she would acknowledge that it was the kidnapping that had changed life for all the people she loved. That always led to thoughts of Stu. Her dreams were filled with him.

On a warm Saturday morning, a month after Meg had started at Griffin's, she was behind the counter, washing cups from the night before while she waited for a traveling couple to finish breakfast. They looked prosperous, had complimented her on the fluffy biscuits and rich sausage gravy, and might be the kind who would leave her a tip. It had been a pleasant surprise to be able to slip small amounts of change into her apron pocket from tips in the tavern. She had a sock half full of coins under her mattress, and planned to go along with Ruben the next time he went to Springfield. She thought of what she wanted to buy—more thread, a bar of store-bought scented soap, and calico for a new dress, if there was enough money. She wanted to look at bonnets, too. She hadn't brought her old one along, and now wished for one after seeing the stylish ones some of the traveling women wore. There most likely wouldn't be enough money, but it would be fun to look, anyway.

At the sound of the door opening, she looked up from the cups and was stunned to see her father.

"Pa! Pa!" she cried, and rushed for his arms. He grabbed her in a hug, and swung her around while she squealed in delight.

"Hey! How's my angel? Where's Stephen?"

"Here he is, Pa! Over here!"

Meg pointed to where Stephen sat in his highchair. His eyes grew big as he looked from Pa to Meg. His grandfather reached down to pick him up and recognition dawned on Stephen's little face. He broke into a huge smile and reached out for Jim, who hoisted him into a bear hug of love. Stephen pulled away after a minute and patted his grandfather's cheek as if to test that he was real. Meg and Jim laughed in delight.

"Here, Pa. Keep him a minute. I'll tell Ruben you're here so he can come out and finish washing these cups. Oh, Pa! I can't believe you're here!"

Meg tore away and called for Ruben. Within minutes, she and Pa were seated at a table. A beaming Ruben, after being introduced, brought Jim a steaming mug of coffee. Stephen squirmed out of his grandfather's lap after a few minutes and hopped excitedly around the table.

"Look at him!" Jim exclaimed. "You're gone a little over only a month and he's running and wearing new pants. He's had a hair cut. He looks like a boy instead of a baby. He's grown so much!"

He turned his attention back to Meg. "So here you are. After Ma and I got your last letter, we decided to give you a few more weeks, and then come and find you if you weren't back by then. Joseph and Tillie sent a long letter to us, telling us that Joseph had seen to it that you were settled and safe, so that relieved us, too."

His tone grew solemn and his eyes darkened. "You've got some answering to do to Elsie and your mother about the way you just up and left without a word. They had a mighty hard time until we heard from you. Ma was planning to come with me now, but Louie came down with some sort of fever and she didn't feel right leaving him. He's been feeling poorly for a few days, so she said just come and make sure you and Stephen are all right. I'm supposed to tell you to come home with me. Ma sends her love, so do Elsie and Moses. Louie says get back because there's toads in the pond and he wants to show Stephen. We want you to come home. We worry about you all the time. Ma said to tell you she misses you every day. Louie asks for you and Stephen every day."

Meg looked into her father's loving eyes. She noticed faint wrinkles at their corners that she didn't remember. His reddish-gold beard had streaks of silver that stood out in this light. It was such a relief to see him that she had to fight back tears.

"Oh, Pa. I miss you all, too, every day. What's the matter with Louie?"

"We don't know. When I get back, if he's not better, we'll get Doc. Someone at church last Sunday said measles were reported in Memphis. Said... well, never mind." His eyes betrayed his concern.

Meg's heart filled with guilt. *Here Pa had to come all this way to find me while Louie was sick.* She fretted, "I so hope he's all better when you get back there. I miss him, and all of you very, very much."

"Well, then. Come back with me. Let's pack the two of you up and head right out today. Come home, Angel. You wrote that you had twelve dollars. But that can't be lasting you for everything you need for you and the baby."

"I'm working here, Pa. And I have more than twelve dollars now. I help Ruben out for room and board and I get tips. I have enough money. What about Jeb? I can't go back to him. He was miserable and drinking all the time. That's not the life I want. I'm waiting for Stephen's father to get back here. We're managing fine. Ruben is so good to us, and I keep busy."

"You're waiting for Stephen's father? What do you mean? You didn't find him?" Jim interrupted.

After Meg explained, Jim shook his head. "You don't need to stay here. We can leave word for him. You belong home with us. You can come back and live at home, and maybe you and Jeb will work it out in time. He's around every night asking about you. Looks awful. Doesn't say much. Just sort of slinks away. I have a mind to talk to him. Ask him what in Sam Hill got into him. He's not the Jeb we knew, either. But he doesn't stay long enough to really talk to."

He spread his hands. "Your mother and I told everyone you went north to visit relatives. Not exactly a lie, I guess," he gave a small chuckle. "Jeb must be backing up that story. Will you come home now, Angel? Ma's melancholy since you left, and everyone misses you. If the trouble with Jeb was that bad, you could have told us. We would've helped you, you know. That's what parents are for. We weren't blind to it, by the way. We saw how he was, but we didn't want to interfere."

As Ruben approached to refill Jim's cup, Meg looked up. "Ruben, I think I'll go back home for a visit. Can you get along without me for a while? My little brother's sick, and my Ma misses Stephen and me. I think we'd better go. I'm sorry."

Ruben's face fell. He turned to Jim. "I been takin' real good care of these two. I send her upstairs every night 'fore the rowdy crowd even knows she's here. She's been a mighty big help to me. Things are cleaner than they have been for years. Even the windows, by gosh. She sewed new curtains and the wash is always caught up. She helps with the food, too. She knows how to work and shur e'nuf earns her keep."

He paused for a minute. "Your little brother is sick, you say? What is it?"

Jim answered, "A fever. He was feeling poorly the few days before I left, so my wife stayed with him. He broke out in a kind of rash the day before yesterday. We put him right to bed. If he's not better when I get back, the doc will come out. We hear there's measles around. The boy's never been sick a day in his life."

Ruben looked alarmed. "Oh, no. Last few days, travelers been talkin' 'bout a measles epidemic down in Memphis. There's been more'n a dozen younguns buried already, they say. A fella last night said the newspapers as far away as Washington are telling folks to keep their younguns close to home. Guess schools are even shuttin' down to keep it from spreadin'."

Just then, Stephen dashed up and crawled under Jim's leg after a ball. Everyone looked down at the boy, then back at each other.

Jim's eyes reflected sudden anxiety and he pushed back his chair. He stepped back away from Stephen on the floor.

"My God! Louie might have measles! I better get back! Meg, stay here until you get word from us. Keep Stephen completely away from any children who come through. I'll send a telegraph as soon as I know how Louie is." He turned to Ruben. "Where do I send a telegraph to get to you here?"

"Ruben Ward. General Store. Springfield. They know me. They'll send it along with any travelers headin' this way. We'll know about it the day after it gits there, for sure." Ruben held up his beefy hands to Jim. "Wait a minute. I'm sendin' along a roast beef sandwich. Ya gotta have something to eat before you hit the road."

"Thanks. And thank you for taking care of my daughter and grandson. I'll entrust them to your care until I can get back for them. My wife and I will be back for them as soon as we can." Jim's voice betrayed growing anxiety.

Jim turned to Meg, his face ashen with worry, and gathered her into his arms. His words were clipped. "Oh, Angel. You better stay here. You can't come with me. You stay right here with Stephen. Don't go out to that Logan place again. Don't go anywhere. We'll come back and get you. Your Ma and I will help you. But I have to get back to Ma and Louie." He took a step toward the door. "Keep Stephen away from everybody. Goodbye for now, Angel."

Jim released Meg, stuffed the sandwich Ruben handed him into his coat pocket, took a last, long look at Stephen on the floor, and hurried out the door. Meg ran to watch him as he charged down the road, riding hard. He turned back and gave a quick wave before he disappeared from sight.

"He's right, Missy. We need to keep the boy away from everbody 'til this measles thing gits over. Whenever somebody comes through, we'll have to git him back to your room right away. As soon as the supper crowd starts comin' now, you take him up. I'll do the servin' for now. That little guy wouldn't have a chance at his age."

Meg's heart pounded with fear, not only for Stephen, but for dear Louie. She yearned to be home and see Louie's mischievous little face again. Then she realized that if she and Stephen had still been there, Stephen might be sick now, too. It seemed a miracle that she had taken her baby out of Tennessee just before a measles outbreak. She hoped that wasn't what was wrong with Louie. She looked up at Ruben and their eyes met in mute fear and sympathy. Anxiety settled like a heavy blanket around Meg. She picked up Pa's coffee mug and headed for the kitchen.

CHAPTER EIGHTEEN

Consumed with worry the next day, Meg barely heard Ruben greet a new arrival. But the voice that answered him caused her to stop in her tracks.

She whirled around to face Jeb, who stood just inside the swinging entry doors, hat in his hand, hair disheveled. Despite the shock of the moment, Meg noticed that his hat was the one she had sent away for and given him for Christmas. She stared at him, speechless.

Jeb strode past Ruben. "Meg. I'm sorry. I'm so sorry for everything. I've come for you. Please come home with me." His hazel eyes burned with intensity and his voice rang strong and sure. Pale and tired and thin, he still sounded determined.

"How... how did you find me?" Meg stammered.

"I followed your Pa. When I went to your place, your Ma said Louie was sicker than ever and I should ride hard to try to catch your Pa. She sent for the Doc. I met your Pa on the road heading south and told him. I asked him where to find you."

Gripping terror overcame Meg at the news about Louie.

She gasped to Ruben, who stood watching, apron twisted in his hands, face twisted with curiosity and concern. "Ruben, this is Jeb. We need to go upstairs for a few minutes."

She grabbed Stephen out of his highchair and rushed up the stairs, Jeb close behind. She pushed open the door of her room and hurriedly tucked Stephen into the bed.

"Night, night, Sweetie. Night, night?" she breathlessly asked her son.

He looked back at her with big eyes, then obediently turned over, grabbing the corner of his blanket to rub against his cheek like he always did just before falling asleep.

She turned to Jeb, who stood inside the door, feet at an awkward angle half in and half out. "Shut the door," she whispered. He stepped in and closed the door behind him with quiet, careful movements.

Meg could only croak. "What's this about Louie? What's the matter with him?" Tears began to leak down her cheeks. *My little brother that sick.* Her stomach clenched.

Jeb leaned over, set his hat on the chair and stepped closer to Meg. His words came low and fast and his eyes never left hers. "Louie's very sick. They couldn't even wake him up the day I left. They think it's measles. My Pa is keeping Sam and Cassie in the house 'cuz the Millers have it, too. All five of the little ones there. Everybody's pretty scared. But your Ma says you're not to worry. She won't leave Louie's side and she knows she can see him through it. She sends her love." He paused, "So do I."

The impassioned look in Jeb's eyes didn't look like it belonged to the same man she'd last seen crumpled beneath the covers in drunken slumber. In front of her now was the Jeb she'd imagined all her life as her husband. He was strong and tan; the contours of his lean body almost as familiar to her as her own. His face seemed more manly now that it was free of freckles, and his nose looked like it had thickened since she saw him. One of the blue cotton shirts she'd sewn for him showed wear. His familiar hazel eyes remained locked into hers. His words had been spoken with sincerity and vigor, in a voice that had settled into a deeper and huskier tone than she remembered.

Meg realized with amazement that she was very glad to see Jeb, very glad to have him here. It was as if her old friend had returned from a long journey and was finally back at her side. He reached for her and she collapsed into his arms. It was a good fit. He held her tightly, as if he'd never let her go.

"Oh, Meg," he whispered with a sidelong look at the tiny hump under the covers that was Stephen. "I've missed you so much. I'm so sorry for what I put you through. Elsie and Moses talked to me the other night, after I left your place. They were waiting on the path. They told me I was a fool. Said I might have lost you forever. Elsie said to think about it—how I was holding it over you about another man when it wasn't your fault at all. And what I should have been doing was helping you get over it. Moses said I was thinking only about myself. They said I was letting the most special and beautiful girl in the world get away from me. By the time I got done walking back to Pa's, I knew they were right."

He crushed her to him and hurried on, "I don't know what was wrong with me all that time. I'm so sorry, my love. My wife. My best friend. Can you forgive me? Can we start over? Can we try again?" Jeb's voice rose with hope. "This time it'll be like it shoulda been. Like we always planned. I promise to be the best husband. I won't drink, I promise. It can be like we always dreamed. Will you come home? Please, Meg? Will you?" He tucked his head into her shoulder to hide brimming tears.

The warm, comforting cloud of his words settled over Meg. Relief flooded over her. *This is the Jeb I know.* He cradled her to him, rocking her back and forth as if to comfort them both after a long, hard struggle. Meg swayed in his arms, becoming soothed and calmed.

After long moments, she raised her head and sought Jeb's eyes. There was no doubting the sincerity and passion she saw there. Her Jeb was back.

"What about...?" Meg began. But Jeb interrupted her.

"Stephen?" he asked.

Meg nodded.

"From this moment on, he is my son. I will love him as much as any of the children I want us to have. He's already missed out on a year of having a father. I'll make it up to him. Is he old enough to go squirrel hunting with me yet?" he asked with an eager, playful grin. He brushed away the streaks of his tears and gave a self-conscious half smile.

Meg laughed back at him, "Not quite!"

Their smiles dwindled as they stared at each other. Jeb moved his arms under her and lifted her to the edge of her bed, then lay her down with tender hands. They looked over at Stephen, who slept soundly beneath his covers against the wall, oblivious to any activity in the room.

Jeb lifted the blankets around them into a cocoon, then proved his love to her with a passion like never before.

In the morning, they clung to each other, unwilling to part before Jeb mounted up for the long ride back. They'd brought Stephen down for supper the night before, and explained to Ruben that Meg and Stephen would stay only until the measles epidemic was over. Jeb kept his word—willingly carrying Stephen down the stairs, helping with his cup of milk, and playing hide and seek with him after the meal.

Again after Stephen had been tucked in for the night, Jeb came to Meg with burning passion. They finally fell into exhausted sleep in each other's arms, as if that was where they belonged, until the crowing of a neighboring rooster forced them to consciousness.

The long hug at parting felt natural and good, and Meg had a hard time letting go of her Jeb.

The dust of Jeb's horse had faded in the distance, when Meg turned to go back up the porch steps, feet as light as balls of cotton. She couldn't keep a smile off her face. *We're going home, we're going home,* she sang to herself. *Soon we'll see Ma and Elsie and Louie and everyone.* The relief was nearly overwhelming. She hadn't realized how homesick she was. *It won't be long. Going home.* It sounded so good. *My Jeb is back.*

She drifted into the tavern with a smile, almost dancing, lost in memories and dreams. Ruben was helping Stephen finish the last bites of a hotcake. Stephen's face was smeared with syrup, and he teased Ruben by shutting his mouth every time just as Ruben brought the fork up. They were laughing together, and Meg's heart nearly burst with happiness as she realized how lucky she was. She ran to Ruben and gave him an impulsive hug from behind.

"Ruben. Thank you so much for all you've done. It was so lucky that Joseph and I stopped at Griffin's Tavern!"

"Right you are, Missy," Ruben grinned back. He pushed himself away from Stephen and handed the fork to Meg. "Better finish up the boy's breakfast. I still have some mail to sort before folks start comin' in. Mail day, ya know."

He turned to go, then paused. "Say. What ya gonna do about the Logans? I spose we'll see Bill soon. They've let their mail pile up here ever since you ran out on 'em, come to think of it. Maybe they heard you're stayin' here. One o' these days, one of 'em'll be in. If they ask about you, I better have an answer ready."

Meg's heart felt light. There was no struggle with her answer. "Tell them I'm sorry I bothered them. That's all. They don't need to know where I am or anything. I want to go home. I want to forget them. I have to go back where I belong. I just have to go home and be with Ma and Pa and Louie and Jeb. Back home. That's the life I'm supposed to have. It'll work now. I'll be so happy to be going home."

That afternoon, while Ruben and Stephen napped, Meg handed out mail to a steady stream of locals. She didn't glance up as she said, "Name?" to the next man in line.

"Logan," he replied.

Meg looked up in surprise.

"How are you, Meg?" Bill asked. His smile was cautious, as if he was unsure how she would react and his eyes narrowed with unspoken questions.

"Fine, Bill. And you?" Meg replied. She returned his look boldly, surprised at the flash of animosity that swept over her. The sting of Ruth's snub and the arrogance of William's little speech to her came back vividly as she faced him.

"Virginia sends her greetings. We still hope you'll consider coming back. My parents haven't spoken a word of you to us since you left, but Virginia and me, well, we think they should change their minds." Bill faltered. He looked behind at the two men in line. "Why don't you help them first? I'll wait." He stepped aside.

As soon as the other men left with their mail, Bill returned to the counter and continued, "Virginia and me, we got these six notices ready for Stu." He laid six envelopes on the counter, each addressed in bold letters to STUART LOGAN OF ILLINOIS. PLEASE POST.

"We wrote in them for him to come home as soon as he can because Meg is here with his son. Do you want to add anything?"

Meg sighed, and gave Bill a tight smile. "No, that sounds fine. It's very kind of you and Virginia. Give her my greeting, too, please."

Bill's lips twisted. "Meg, you're being stubborn. You should come back to the ranch with me. Come on, don't be like this."

"No," Meg said. "Your mother never even really looked at me. They think I trapped Stu. That I'm a... well, a..."

"No they don't," Bill answered.

"I'm not going back there until Stu is with me. I will not go back where we're not wanted."

There was no more to be said. They averted their eyes from each other during the awkward silence that followed. Finally, Bill gathered up the stack of mail Meg slid across the counter to him. He stared into her eyes for a long moment, gave a disgusted shake of his head and spun to the door. He looked back at her over his shoulder, anger filling his eyes before stomping out the door.

Meg stood for a moment, fighting the feelings that tried to squirm their way past her resolve. Flashes of the

Logan ranch, Virginia's face, and then of Stu, caught her before she could shake them away. For a moment, she wavered. She looked up at the empty doorway.

Then, with firm footsteps, she crossed to the fireplace and dropped all six white envelopes with their bold lettering onto the embers. In a few seconds, flames leapt across the paper. She watched until the ashes were indistinguishable from those of the night before.

CHAPTER NINETEEN

MEG couldn't believe her eyes when Jeb stepped through the door again only six days later. She dropped the broom and ran for his arms, but the look on his face stopped her in her tracks.

Pale and haggard, eyes shadowed by dark hollows, expression stricken, his face crumpled as he croaked, "Oh, Meg. They sent me... I'm so sorry... It's Louie. He didn't make it. It was measles. Neither did Sam. They're dead, Meg. They're both dead."

Great sobs escaped, and he stumbled toward her. They fell into each other's arms, weeping, as they clutched each other in agony.

Meg fought the too bright whiteness that swirled through her head. Louie dead! It couldn't be! She knew it was true, though. Never had she seen such agony and grief on anyone's face as she was seeing on Jeb's. Stabs of intense pain knifed through her. Oh, Louie! She'd never see him again. Never hear his voice or his laugh. He died. Her little brother was dead. *Oh, poor Ma! Poor Pa! They must be out of their minds with grief. And Sam, too. Little Sam. He was only five. What about Cassie?*

"Cassie? What about Cassie?" Meg cried, pulling back from Jeb's arms.

"It looks like she's gonna make it. Her fever finally broke. She was better when I left, even sitting up. She asked for you. So did Louie, every day before... before... Oh, God, Meg, they're dead. I had to come and tell you.

The funerals are gonna be as soon as I bring you back. They're gonna be buried together. Pa says they'll keep each other company that way. Your Ma said she couldn't bury her child with her other one gone, too."

Stephen called "Mama? Mama?" from his highchair, but his puzzled little voice barely penetrated Meg's consciousness.

Jeb collapsed into the nearest chair, looking up through tears and a face furrowed by pain.

Meg moved to him and cradled his head to her waist. "I have to go home. Are you too tired to leave right now? Do you need to rest?"

"I don't know. I don't know," Jeb wept.

"Come upstairs with me.," Meg managed, reeling with shock. "Stephen, you stay in your chair until I come back. Sit there like a good boy."

She led Jeb up to her room, steered him to the bed, slid his boots off, pulled the covers over him and ordered, "Rest. Rest while I get ready." She knelt and tenderly kissed his tear-filled eyes. He turned onto his side and gathered the blanket to his shoulders with a quiet moan.

Meg dashed back downstairs and shouted for Ruben. "Ruben! Ruben! Where are you?"

He emerged from his room, sleepy-eyed, looking alarmed. "What is it, Missy?"

"I have to go! I have to leave right away! Jeb's here. My little brother died. So did Jeb's little brother. It was the measles. Jeb came to get me. I made him lay down upstairs while I get ready. I have to pack and go right now!" Meg cried out. The light in the room danced before her eyes. She gasped for each breath.

Ruben crossed the room with heavy strides. He grabbed Meg's shaking hands in his beefy ones. "Sit down. Sit down right now," he ordered, and pushed her firmly into a chair. He pulled a chair over next to her, and captured her hands in his warm, strong ones.

"Now stop and think a minute, Meg," he said in a firm, commanding voice she'd never heard from him before.

He reached up, grabbed her chin and forced her to look at him. Meg tried to quiet her breathing and listen to him.

The room spun, but she heard his words. "You can't take the little fella back with you. There's still measles there, most likely. He could get exposed. He's only a year old. You gotta think about him. I'll saddle one of my horses for you right away. And I'll feed and water Jeb's while I'm out there. But you both gotta stop and think a minute. You jest sit here and think while I tend the horses. I'll bring you some water. I want you to drink it all, real slow, every drop. Now you jest sit here and do as I say."

Ruben returned, set a glass of water in front of Meg and hurried out the front door to unhitch Jeb's horse. Meg sipped the water, soothed by the coolness as it slid down her throat. Her breathing slowed. She glanced at Stephen who was sitting very still, his eyes solemn.

"Mama?" he called, his voice soft and scared. "Mama?"

Meg rushed to him and pulled him into her arms. She buried her face in his sweet smelling hair and felt sobs well up and spill over. She crushed him to her. *What am I going to do? I can't take him back home. But I have to go to Ma and Pa right away. As fast as I can. Will Ruben keep Stephen?*

He struggled in her arms and pulled back, trying to look at her. She knew she was upsetting him, but she couldn't stop her tears.

She gulped them back as best she could, brushed a hand over her eyes, and smiled down at him. "Mama's alright, Sweetie. It's alright."

She set him on the floor, covered her face and tried to stifle fresh sobs.

Stephen clung to her leg, patting it, saying, "Awight, Mama. Awight, Mama," over and over.

Ruben found them that way and again helped her back to her chair. "His horse was near wore out. I saddled my two best and I'll keep his 'til you come back. We gotta figger out what to do with this young'un. I could keep him, but, ya know, with runnin' the place all by myself and all, I jest don't know how I'd manage. An' all the travelers that stop by now. How'd I keep him away from the younguns who might be carryin' the measles, too? What about Bill? At the Logan place? They're his kin. Do ya think they'd keep him while you're gone?"

"No. I can't leave him where he's not wanted. Bill and Virginia would do it, I'm sure, but it would cause trouble there, I know. And you can't do it. Let me think. Maybe... maybe... I could drop him off at Tillie and Joseph's on the way, don't you think?"

"Well, yup. Good thinking. You let that young man up there rest a few more hours, then you could get to Joseph's by mornin'. You two can ride right on home then, and be to yer Ma's by nightfall the next day if ya ride hard. Be sure to water them horses good every few hours, and let 'em git their breath and eat good while you're at Joseph's. I'm gonna pack ya up some jerky and biscuits. You eat some of that chicken pot pie right now. Eat lots. You'll need your strength." Ruben patted Meg's hand and shuffled out the door.

In a daze, Meg picked up Stephen and carried him upstairs. Jeb lay in exactly the same position she'd left him. His breath was even and his face, softened by sleep, had lost some of it distress. She shushed Stephen as she held him on her hip and gathered clothing. She crept back downstairs and out the swinging doors and packed her things into the saddlebags of the two horses that stood ready at the hitching rail. She took Stephen to the privy, helped him drink another cup of milk, and then slumped into a chair in the dining room.

A few travelers wandered in, but Meg took no notice of them. While Ruben served them their meals, he passed Meg and left a fresh glass of water and more tender morsels of chicken pie to tempt her. She had no notion of time passing.

Soon, Ruben announced, "It's time ya got goin'. Go up and wake him now. You gotta git on the road."

Jeb woke with a start at Meg's touch. His face froze into anguish when he realized where he was. He followed Meg downstairs and managed to swallow a few bites of the pot pie that Ruben set before him with a stern admonition to eat. Jeb agreed that leaving Stephen with Joseph and Tillie was a good idea, and before long, they were on the road south.

The old couple welcomed Stephen, comforted Meg as best they could, and insisted that Jeb and Meg rest until morning.

All Meg was aware of on the ride the next day was the relentless pounding of the horses' hooves. When they finally thundered down the lane in the twilight, Meg burst into fresh sobs. She tumbled off the horse into her mother's embrace, reached over her shoulder for Pa, and they wept together for their Louie.

THE funeral was held the next day under a bright spring sky, the kind the two little boys used to spend in the tree house and down at the pond. They were buried next to Jeb's mother in the graveyard on the hill behind the church.

Jeb's father, Charles, a gray shadow of himself, held Cassie's hand and leaned into Jeb at the gravesite. Meg stood with her mother and father, swaying with dizziness when the first shovel of dirt hit the coffin. She hadn't been able to say goodbye to Louie. She would never again wake to see his skinny arms and legs flung every which way in his tangled bedding across the room. Her mother and father looked and moved like skeletons. Elsie and Moses clung to each other, moaning softly. The crowd around the grave stood hushed in empathy. Meg knew the minister was speaking, but the words didn't penetrate her mind.

When it was over, Jeb left his father's side, walked over to Meg, and wrapped her in his arms. "I'll be over tonight. I love you," he whispered.

During the following days, everyone went through the motions of daily life. Food was prepared and served, but seldom eaten. Jeb came over every night. He and Meg went for long walks, always stopping in at their empty cabin. Stephen's crib stood forlornly by the stove. Jeb's ax remained buried deep in the stump where he had left it.

Meg's friends Zona and Zelda came over in their father's fancy new tasseled buggy, but their offer of a ride and friendly chatter failed to draw Meg out of her grief. They were full of news about John Brink's upcoming wedding to a Philadelphia girl, and tried hard to cheer Meg up, but nothing could penetrate her wall of mourning. Her heart ached for Louie, and her arms for Stephen. She knew she had to leave soon to be with her baby.

Jeb told her his father wanted them to move in over at the big house, and that Charles had offered to give them the main bedroom and move into the one Cassie was in now. Cassie and Stephen could move up into the loft if Jeb helped fix it up. Charles planned to sign the deed to the house over to them so it would be theirs. Jeb promised his love and devotion over and over, and treated Meg with great tenderness. She was comforted, and so was he, by their togetherness.

Ma and Pa improved a little more each day. On the third day, Elsie and Meg gathered eggs, and then made Pa's favorite twisted dough cinnamon rolls. Moses had the mules hitched up early every morning and insisted that Jim go with him to keep up with the planting. By the fifth day, even Ma came out of her room for morning coffee. She and Meg and Elsie spent hours at the kitchen table, remembering Louie. They wept together until there were no tears left.

At supper on the sixth night, Jeb and Meg announced that they would leave in the morning to get Stephen and go back to Ruben's to pick up the belongings that were left there since everyone felt the measles outbreak was ending. Pa agreed to send a telegram as soon as Doc gave the all clear for Stephen to be brought back to Crockett

County. Ma's eyes brightened for the first time at the mention of Stephen coming home.

Over at Jeb's father's house, Meg hugged Cassie goodbye, and promised the sad-faced little girl that she and Jeb and Stephen would be back soon and move into the house with her.

Jeb accompanied Meg back to Tillie and Joseph's, and then on to Ruben's. He spent the nights holding her close and roused against her for the first time since the funeral. When he left the tavern to go home, they parted as lovers and companions, eager to begin their new life together.

By the time Jeb returned for them three weeks later, Meg suspected that another baby was on the way. It was as if fate had played a helping hand in her decision to go home. She hoped Stu's hold on her would lessen now. But her intuition told her that it wouldn't go away that easily. She didn't wonder if she would ever see Stu again, just when. She knew in her heart that they would meet again. Her heart quickened at the thought, despite her best efforts to quell the memory of his loving blue eyes. She knew he would continue to come to her in her dreams, no matter how hard she fought to erase him.

CHAPTER TWENTY

ELIZABETH, named after Jeb's mother, was born in March, only three days after Stephen turned two. From the first, that name seemed too big for the dainty child, and she quickly became known as "Lizzie". She captivated her father with her delicate features, hazel eyes and the halo of reddish curls that matched his own. Meg was delighted with the petite daughter whose solemn gaze while nursing seemed to study her mother's face with wise eyes.

The year following Lizzie's birth flew past as Meg managed the bustling household. Jeb and his father had fixed up the house's loft for Stephen and Cassie, and converted part of the big main room into a small bedroom for Lizzie. By the time they were through, a large shady porch also wrapped the front of the house. Jeb doted on his daughter, and made a better effort than before to pay attention to Stephen. Meg and Jeb often sat on the porch swing after everyone went to bed, talking as they listened to the crickets, enjoyed the cool night breezes, and settled into the life they'd always dreamed about.

Both ignored the occasional times Jeb still drank, as if talking about it would make it real. Meg fumed when he failed to show up for supper and hated having to make up excuses to the children and Charles to explain his absences. When Jeb had to pay for repair on the wagon's broken axle that he drove into a tree while drunk, she absorbed the cost into the general store money so Charles wouldn't know. She fought feelings of repulsion at the times she woke up beside him to the odor of stale alcohol.

It didn't happen often, but it wore on Meg to never be able to predict when the next time would be. She could anticipate it sometimes, when she noticed him becoming restless and impatient at things that shouldn't have bothered him. When it had been awhile since he drank, there was a subtle change in his personality that didn't seem apparent to anyone other than Meg. He refused to acknowledge it, and barked at her if she dared mention it. Always after a drinking episode, he was contrite and subdued, promising earnestly that he wouldn't be tempted again, and that the drinking was over. It was the only cloud in their lives, and it troubled Meg greatly. She confided in no one and hoped that Charles, her parents, and Elsie and Moses weren't noticing.

But it was a heavy burden for Meg—the deception, the worry, and especially the times he was drunk. On mornings after, he didn't seem to remember how he'd acted toward her, the rudeness and derision that occurred only when they were alone. It was like living with two different men. Meg unfailingly hoped that each time was the last time, like he always promised. She felt frustrated that she couldn't get him over it, no matter how hard she tried.

It became an undiscussed secret, ignored while they pretended it didn't exist. Jeb was able to go for weeks at a time as a devoted and happy husband and father, and Meg would then wonder if he was right that she was making it into more of a problem than it really was. She was reluctant to bring turmoil to the life they'd created after such a rough beginning. They had many good times, many good things about their life. The real Jeb was truly the interesting and affectionate companion she'd grown up loving. She clung to the good things. When thoughts of Stu popped up, she pushed him out of her mind as best she could.

An early and unseasonably warm spring came to Tennessee that year. Leaves and plants drooped in the thick, muggy air, and animals sought shade until the relentless sun finally set at night. Meg began taking Cassie and Stephen and Lizzie, now a toddler, to the pond every day after lunch. It was on such an afternoon while the children splashed and squealed, "Momma! Momma, look at me!" that Meg's tenuous life came undone.

Meg was taken completely by surprise, as she sat contentedly on the grassy bank, her light cotton skirt wound up around her knees, feet bare, hair braided loosely down her back, looking almost like a child herself. She basked in the warm sun, enjoying the sound of the children's voices.

"Meg! Meg!" The loud whisper from behind startled her. She turned toward it in surprise. There, barely visible in the bushes at the edge of the woods, a man beckoned to her. She started in fright and scrambled to her feet.

"Meg. It's me, Stu," she heard whispered.

Her heart skittered. Stu! She stared, hardly breathing. She quickly checked the children. Stephen squealed while Cassie splashed water on his chubby legs. Absorbed in their activity, the children were paying no attention to Meg.

Stu had been far from her mind during the recent bustling months. He had become a pleasant memory, occasionally recalled as a personal indulgence, no longer a significant part of the life she was building. His appearance now was completely unexpected. Meg stepped toward him in shock, unable to stop herself.

He whispered, "Come back out here tonight. Can you come back out here?"

His voice brought memories flooding back. She strained for the sight of his face, but he pulled back further into the shadow of the trees.

"Will you? And... bring the boy?" he pleaded.

Instinctively, Meg nodded. With a rustle, he was gone. Meg turned back toward the children, swallowing the constriction in her throat.

Cassie noticed her movement and called up to her, "Meg! Meg! Look at me!", and flung herself head-first into the pond. Laughing and sputtering, she looked back and wiped the water from her eyes.

"Good, Cassie. Very good," Meg responded automatically, and clapped her hands.

She made it through the afternoon and then the evening meal in a fog, hoping nobody would notice her distraction and agitation. She decided to tell Jeb that she wanted to walk over to her mother's after supper. Although it was unusual behavior for her, she could think of no other way to get out to the pond. She planned the deception, amazed at herself for even considering such reckless action. She wondered why she couldn't simply stay home. It wasn't right to sneak out to meet another man. But some part of her argued that this wasn't just some man, this was Stu. His pull was strong, too strong to deny. Maybe she would have been able to fight it if only Jeb's drinking hadn't dismayed her so many times.

She justified her plan, figuring that she owed it to herself to see Stu, maybe if only to finally put an end to it all. Maybe to feel good again, like she was still the smart and strong and beautiful woman she felt like when she was with Stu. She needed to see him. She was going.

"You're going to your Mom's by yourself?" Jeb asked, his eyebrows knit in confusion. "Are you taking the children?"

"Just Stephen. Lizzie and Cassie can stay here with you." Meg replied, fighting off a burning shame that crept up her neck.

With another puzzled look, Jeb shrugged his shoulders. "Well, fine, then. Are you sure you don't want me to come? Pa can stay here with the girls."

"No. I won't be gone long. You're sweet to offer. Save me a place on the swing. Ma and Elsie have a new embroidery stitch they want to show me. I didn't have time today while I was there. The little ones kept me hopping the whole time."

She grabbed Stephen, hoping her face wouldn't betray the lie. She walked out the door and hurried down the path to the pond, heart throbbing in her throat. Stu was there, waiting in the shadows, as she knew he would be.

He met her eyes, reached out without a word, and drew her and Stephen into his embrace. "Oh, Meg! You're more beautiful than ever. They said you came to Illinois! I couldn't believe it when I got home and found out you'd been there and we have a baby. We have a son! When I saw you both there on the bank this afternoon, I almost lost my mind." His eyes burned with emotion.

Stephen wiggled in her arms and turned wide eyes toward this stranger.

Stu reached out and tenderly cupped Stephen's head. "Hello, son," he murmured. His voice cracked. "God, Meg. He's a fine, fine boy." He lowered his head. "What I've put you through. I am so sorry."

Stephen remained completely still in her arms, staring. Stu's words and ruggedly handsome face took Meg's breath away. His tenderness toward Stephen warmed her soul.

"Can I hold him?" Stu asked, his tone quiet and tentative.

Meg held Stephen out toward his father. Stu gathered the boy into his arms with awkward and careful movements. Stephen, as if sensing the love that surrounded him, leaned into his father's arms without protest. Stu cradled Stephen's head, gravely studying the boy's face. Meg's eyes brimmed with tears of happiness at the sight.

Stu was deeply tanned. His dark hair shone in the faint light from the stars. He smelled of horses and wood smoke and fresh air, exactly like she remembered. The arms that just released her had been strong, yet tender. Drawn into his spell, she fought to keep her senses. It was hard to speak. She couldn't pull her gaze from him and Stephen. He returned her look with admiration, curiosity, and love covering his face. He remained silent now, waiting.

"He's three now. He's a good boy," Meg managed through a dry throat.

"I saw him here with you this afternoon," Stu choked out. "And I couldn't believe it. He's perfect. A fine boy." He gave a proud smile. "He has my eyebrows."

Meg nodded. She faltered, trying hard to remain calm and rational. Words wouldn't come. Stu studied her for a minute, then pulled her against Stephen into his arms and covered her lips with his. Meg floated into the passionate kiss, feeling contentment seep deep into her being. This was wrong, but it felt so right, so very satisfying. When the kiss finally ended, both were gasping for breath.

Meg regained her composure first and stepped away, reaching for Stephen. When she set him down, Stu pulled her back to him and gently lowered them to the ground.

"Go ahead," he said, his voice low and tender. "Tell me everything."

Stephen climbed into Meg's lap and she hugged him to her. "I suppose Bill told you how it went with your parents when I was in Illinois? And about Stephen?"

Stu nodded.

"Well, my little brother Louie died from measles right after that, and I had to come home. I planned to wait there and keep working at Griffin's Tavern until you got back. But I had to come home after Louie died, for Ma and Pa, you know. Jeb, that's my husband, wanted us to try again. I left him to go to you because he was miserable and mean and drinking, and I couldn't live like that, and I wasn't going to let Stephen grow up with it. But since I came back, Jeb's been trying real hard." She hesitated. "And, we have a daughter. Lizzie. That's the little girl with the curly hair you saw here with us today. The older girl is Jeb's little sister. We live with Jeb's father and the sister now."

"You had another baby?" Stu asked in surprise, a touch of hurt in his voice. He pulled away slightly.

Meg nodded. Stu sighed, and turned almost imperceptibly away a bit more. Silence stretched between them.

"You're still with him, then? You had another child? You had his baby?" he finally asked.

Meg nodded again, not knowing what to say. Awkward moments passed agonizingly.

"What did you think of the ranch?" Stu asked abruptly, his voice strained and unnatural.

"I loved it," Meg answered. "But I don't have very good memories of it."

Stu didn't reply to that, but continued with stilted, fragmented conversation, as if it was difficult for him to concentrate. "I'm sorry about your brother. That's the little guy who tripped on the veranda that day? The day I took you?"

"Yes," Meg replied, surprised. Louie had tripped that day on the porch? Then Stu hadn't hurt him.

She turned toward Stu to tell him how glad she was to learn he hadn't hurt Louie, but he was already continuing. "I was out West. Got as far as western Kansas..." his voice trailed off. "But I..." His voice had grown cool and quiet, almost devoid of emotion.

It became a struggle to keep the conversation going. Important words that weren't being said formed a barrier between them. Meg nestled Stephen to her and desperately wanted to hear that Stu had cleared things up with his parents. Or that he had a plan to fit her into his life. She longed for the right words from him. She wasn't going to ask to be a part of his life. She wasn't going to complain about the problem with Jeb's drinking. *Stu has to want me and Stephen enough to make it happen.* But the words didn't come.

An awkward silence grew and stretched until the strain forced Meg to fight back tears of frustration. Both became restless on the hard ground. When Stu abruptly rose and held out his hand to help her and Stephen up, she felt relief. He continued to hold her hand when she was standing, and looked intently into her eyes. But she couldn't read his eyes in the darkness.

"Is he, this Jeb, your husband, is he good to you? Do you love him?"

"Yes," Meg lied, and dropped her eyes. Then, as if the devil controlled her tongue, she added, "I'm not where I belong, though."

She lifted her face boldly to his and felt hot tears slip down her cheeks, waiting for him to respond. Her heart cried out. *Why doesn't he say he loves me? Why can't he see how it really is? Why doesn't he say the hell with all this, I'm taking you and our son with me?* Where were the words she needed to hear?

He held her hand for another long moment, his skin burning hers. She waited for the right words from him, desperate for his commitment. But there was only silence. Deep, intense silence, heavy with emotion. Pride kept her from speaking. She wouldn't beg. She wouldn't ask to be a part of his life. If he loved her as much as she loved him, he should know. He should make it happen.

After a lingering look at Stephen, Stu abruptly dropped her hand, turned and strode swiftly off into the woods without a word. Without a look back.

Meg stood rooted to the spot until the sound of his footsteps faded. She felt too devastated, confused, and frustrated to get her thoughts together. Finally, fury overcame her. *Damn him! Damn him for making me feel that passion and love again! For luring me out here! For not taking me and his son with him! For not fixing things with his family in Illinois! For having the power to revive our love again. For making me want him so much. For making it impossible to forget him. For filling my dreams. For coming back into my life now like this and then just walking away!*

The fury slowly drained away into the moonlight as she stood there hugging Stephen to her chest in the cool night air. A deep sadness overcame her. She knew in the depths of her being that Stu loved her with a passion as strong as hers was for him. Maybe he believed it was a life that couldn't be. It was clear that she'd have to hurt others, break apart a family, for them to be together. And maybe so would he. They might grow to hate and resent each other if they took that path. The price they'd have to pay to be together might be so high it would destroy their love. Maybe Stu was wise and caring in disappearing, so the choice had been made for her. Better to hold onto the precious memories she cherished in her heart. Maybe the sacrifice would allow them both to hold on to the little they were able to have of each other.

With a heavy heart, she turned and began the walk back home, certain Stu would remain in her heart for the rest of her life.

CHAPTER TWENTY ONE

MEG forced the encounter with Stu to the back of her mind, rarely allowing herself to think of it, trying to convince herself that it didn't matter anymore. Her place was here with her family. This was her world now; the children needed a stable life. Whatever wasn't right with Jeb, she'd work on.

But she sensed a strange, new elusive remoteness in Jeb, as if he was lost in his own distant thoughts. He worked hard with Charles and the farm thrived. He was home almost every night, doted on his little Lizzie, rough-housed with Stephen, and fell asleep with his arm wrapped around Meg like always. A subtle difference in his demeanor remained, though.

As it went on, Meg found herself not caring as much as she would have a few months ago. This behavior and his erratic bouts of drinking dimmed her desire to excuse him. In an effort to fix it and overcome her misgivings, Meg redoubled her efforts to be a good wife and mother. She spoiled Jeb with attention and affection, hoping his edginess and moodiness would disappear.

Over a Sunday supper, when Jeb asked her mother if she and Elsie had learned any more new embroidery stitches, it all came undone. At Ma's confusion over the question, Jeb backed off, shrugging his shoulders like the question was a misunderstanding on his part.

While they walked home that night with the little ones between them, he murmured over their heads, "You were with him that night you told me you went walking over to your mother's by yourself, weren't you?"

Meg couldn't answer. She didn't have to. They knew each other well enough to understand what wasn't said. The resulting coldness between them wasn't from the night's chill, and it lingered through the following days.

Meg's twenty first birthday dawned with a light drizzle. While she helped Ma and Elsie prepare ham and greens and fresh bread, they turned toward a sound from the front yard to see Pa returning early from his trip to town. He drove the wagon right up to the front porch, two unfamiliar horses trailing on a lead behind. Meg stepped out onto the porch, but couldn't read the look on his face as he dismounted in the muddy yard and turned to her.

"Pa! What are you doing back so early?" she greeted him.

He gave her a long look, eyes clouded with questions. "Well, at the general store this morning Isaiah said this mare and yearling were delivered there three days ago. He was directed to give the horses to whoever from our family showed up first, and make sure Meg got them."

"Me?" Meg squeaked in surprise.

She studied the beautiful red sorrel mare that stood placidly. A long-legged colt at her heels pawed the ground and tossed his head. The beautiful, strong animals with white socks and blond manes brought a flash of memory. These were horses from the Logan's corral in Illinois.

She turned to her father in amazement. "Who left them for me? What else did he say?"

"Only that these horses were to be delivered to you. The man who left them paid Isaiah ten dollars to care for them until one of us showed up. Then, I guess he just high-tailed it off down the road. Nobody ever saw him before or since. It's quite the talk of the town."

He and Meg stared at each other. He raised his eyebrows and waited for Meg to speak.

"Oh, Pa! They have to be from the soldier. Stephen's father. They're from his place in Illinois. I'm sure of it. They look exactly like the horses I saw there."

The mare held its head up to look at her curiously. It was one of the most beautiful horses Meg had ever laid eyes on.

Pa shook his head, worry creasing his face. "Well, this puts you in a quandary, young lady. If you keep 'em, Jeb will have to know where they came from. We could take 'em back, I suppose, but then you'd have to deal with the Logans again. The man who dropped them off didn't leave any word at all. Just up and left. You'd think if things were different with his family, he would've left word for you. Maybe... well, I don't know... we better decide something here."

"Could you just take them and keep them here at your place, Pa? We could make up a story... no, that wouldn't be right."

"You're right, Angel. We don't want to lie about this. Let's go talk it over with Ma. See what she thinks."

When Miriam heard the story, she peered out at the horses. "Land sakes! They are just beautiful! Those came from the soldier's farm? Are you sure, Meg?"

"I can't think of any other way to explain it, Ma," Meg replied. "The Logans have a huge horse farm with horses just like these. I told the soldier I lost Sugar in the war and wished I'd get another horse someday. They have to be from him."

"Well, we know what has to be done if you keep the horses," Pa said. His tone left no room for argument.

"Yeah, I know. I have to tell Jeb." Meg looked from one to the other. "Even if I sent them back, it would be something I'd hidden from Jeb. So he has to know. He won't be happy. But I don't want to lie to him or hide it from him."

"Oh, Honey, I don't know," Ma said. "You know Jeb best."

Pa added, "Just tell him the truth. Don't wait. Do it right away, tonight." He paused and shook his head.

"It'll be a tough thing to do. I'm trying to think how I'd want my wife to tell me about a valuable, unexpected gift from another man. It's hard to know how I'd feel!" Pa turned to his wife. "I guess I'd want to hear how much she loves me and that she did nothing to encourage the gift. And I hope I'd have the heart to understand. I'd want the subject to be closed then, though. It's sure not something I'd want to keep talking about."

Ma smiled at her husband and nodded her agreement.

As Meg struggled with the words she'd need to say to Jeb, anger grew within her. *How could Stu do this? Just drop something into my life and disappear, leaving me to deal with whatever trouble it might cause?* Compassion fought for her emotions. After all, he'd been trying to stay out of her life. The horses were a valuable and thoughtful gift that proved he remembered her words that night long ago when she told him about losing Sugar. Maybe he was sure she'd be able to explain the horses somehow. At least he hadn't shown up and forced a confrontation with Jeb.

That night when supper ended, Meg asked Charles to take the children for a walk so she and Jeb could talk alone.

She dropped her eyes after the first few quiet moments on the back-porch swing, faltered, stopped, and turned to her husband. "Jeb, there's something I have to tell you."

He turned to face her, brows scrunched. "What?"

"There are two new horses in Pa's barn. They were delivered to the general store in town for me three days ago. I think they came from Stephen's father." She spread her hands. "I didn't know anything about it."

Jeb swung away, making no response or acknowledgement. After a moment of silence, he bolted down the path ahead of her. The bedroom latch had been dropped by the time she made it to the house and tried to enter the bedroom.

With a heavy heart, Meg gathered the quilt from the rocking chair and prepared to slip in beside Lizzie for the night. But a strange, faint sound drew her to her bedroom door. Guilt overwhelmed her when she recognized the sound as muffled sobs. Her heart had never felt so heavy. The night in Lizzie's bed was unbearably long. She lay sleepless, overcome with sadness and guilt.

The next morning, a subdued and quiet Jeb ate breakfast with everyone as usual. He and Charles left for the fields like always, and Meg dragged through the longest day of her life. Jeb avoided her eyes during the evening meal, and hurried out to the barn while she put the children to bed instead of waiting for her on the porch swing.

She followed him out as soon as she could. At the squeak of the barn door, he took quick steps away from her toward the rear door.

"Jeb, wait!" Meg called. "Please wait. We need to talk. I didn't know anything about those horses. We don't have to keep them. We can give them away if you want."

Jeb turned a resentful and accusing stare in her direction, but stood where he was, glaring at her. He shook his head, face contorted in disgust, lips pursed into a hard white line. His refusal to communicate sparked a surprising rage in Meg.

She shouted across the barn, "I don't know why he sent the horses! I knew nothing about it! I don't know why you're so mad. Maybe it's because we never got over all of this in the first place!" She stomped a few steps toward him in fury. "Why do you think you can react to what happened to me by drinking and acting cold to me? I'm just supposed to live with it? Or isn't that it? Are you just a drunk? Because I won't spend my life with a drunk! And my children won't grow up with one, either!"

She kicked at the hay on the floor, causing puffs of dust to rise, and took another step toward him. Fists clenched, feeling heat rise in her face, she raged on. "Why do I have to spend my life trying to be the perfect wife, making up for what happened, and you act like you expect it? I wouldn't even think about him if you were the way you used to be. I don't know how to have the life we always planned, because I have to live with your drinking and the way you treat me! Don't blame this all on me!" Livid with fury, Meg tried to quiet her heaving breath.

Jeb took a step toward her, then halted, threw up his arms and yelled. "Yeah, well maybe I have to live with it the rest of my life! Some other man who was with my wife. With her! Who's still in my wife's thoughts! How would you like it if I was in love with someone else and you knew it? How would you like it if she sent me presents?" He swung around and kicked hard at the pile of hay at his side. A cloud of dust and hay blasted into the air between them.

Meg raged back. "Well, I can't get over it until you do! Don't you get it? We both have to get over it! We can't let it keep eating away at us!"

Jeb stared at her in surprise, as if finally realizing the depth of rage her uncharacteristic words and manner expressed. He jerked away and dashed out the rear door.

Meg stood shaking, infuriated, and very surprised at the words that had sprung spontaneously from her lips. She turned back toward the house, stomped out of the barn, and slammed the heavy wooden door behind her as hard as she could.

A full week of strained silence between them followed. The horses stayed at Pa's. No mention of them was made by anyone. Charles and the children, puzzled and wary, seemed to sense a serious and private matter in the air that had nothing to do with them. Lizzie and Stephen fussed more than usual, needy of Meg's attention. Cassie slipped over to her father's lap frequently and Charles uncharacteristically drew all three little ones to him for a story or a walk after supper each night. Meg and Jeb slept untouching in bitter silence in the cold bed night after night.

Meg woke every morning with a fury that wouldn't fade. She went through the motions of each day, eyes burning, throat dry, moving automatically through her tasks. She and Jeb did not look at each other, touch, or speak. Meg had never felt so vexed and resentful, and was surprised at the stubborn, bitter anger that wouldn't subside. She felt a growing resentment toward both Jeb and Stu.

But when she awoke on Sunday morning to Jeb's tentative hand on her back, a deep breath of relief escaped before she could catch it. The strain of the last week had taken a toll and she was glad at this sign of communication. She rolled back over her pillow to face him, searching his eyes for a sign of what he was feeling.

"Meg? Will you talk to me?" Jeb whispered in the early light. His earnest eyes met hers.

Meg still felt irate and stormy, unwilling to go back to feeling that it was up to her to make everything right. She lay rigid on her side of the bed and waited for Jeb to continue.

"You're right. I've been wrong all this time. But I'm over it now," Jeb announced, as if he had practiced the words. It wasn't enough for Meg, and she waited without answering.

"You won't have to put up with it anymore," Jeb continued, his words now tinged with hesitation.

Meg was surprised to feel no tenderness for him "You're right, I don't have to put up with it anymore. And I won't."

She stared at him, fighting the bitterness she'd kept buried for too long. "I don't need you. I don't need him. I don't need anyone else. I think I can be happier by myself with Lizzie and Stephen. I'll go back to Ruben's and work. I liked it there. I was busy and made enough money to live just fine, and Ruben was good to us. Nobody caused trouble in my life. I can make it there if I have to."

She whirled her body away from him and sat up. "That's what I want to do. It's my life. I don't want to stay here and worry the rest of my life over what you'll be brooding about. Or when you'll go drown your self-pity in liquor again. I don't want to have to fix it for you, or for anybody. I don't want to share my life with anybody, anymore."

Jeb's eyes grew wide. He rose to support his arm on the pillow and stared at her. "You don't mean that!" he exclaimed, voice rising.

"Yes, I do," Meg retorted, feeling powerful and finally in control. "I do mean it. I'll make it on my own just fine. It's too bad the dream of our life together has been ruined. But that's what's happened. And it's not all my fault."

She stared back at him, fuming, surprised at the strength of her conviction. She'd done nothing but think about it during this long and difficult week, and hadn't realized until this moment how definite her feelings were. She'd never in her life been so sure of anything.

Jeb stared at her in astonishment. "You really mean it, don't you? You'd leave me?" He sat upright and reached for her.

Meg pulled away, swung her legs off the bed and stood. "Yes, I do mean it.'

She gulped, "I feel really sad about it, though. You know I always loved you and looked forward to our life together. But it isn't like I hoped. I can't live with it the way it is."

She slid her nightgown off and reached for her housedress, slipping it over her head. "You can see Lizzie whenever you want and I'll never say a bad word about you to her. I don't want to hurt you or punish you. But this isn't going to be the life I lead. I don't want another man. I think I'll be better off by myself, even if it's for the rest of my life. It breaks my heart to leave all that could have been."

Jeb fell back onto his pillow, dazed. He put his arm across his eyes and lay very still. Meg sat back down on the edge of the bed, breathing hard from the effort and emotion of the words she'd just spoken. She pulled her socks on, feeling no compassion for Jeb, only relief and a growing elation. She felt strong, as if a burden had been lifted and she was free to fly. Her heart felt light and her movements were vigorous. Jeb lay unmoving. She stormed out of the room and banged the door behind her.

Morning sunlight streamed into the kitchen. A forlorn Cassie sat alone at the kitchen table, her blue flowered nightie wrapped tightly around the thin legs she clutched to her chest.

"Why, Cassie. What are you doing out here all alone?" Meg asked in surprise.

"Meg? Are you better?" Cassie asked. Her earnest eyes searched Meg's. "Pa said you weren't well so we should be leaving you alone. I was worried. You aren't sick like Mama was, are you? Are you better today?"

Meg's heart melted at the sight of those vulnerable brown eyes. Memories of Cassie's mother, and then Sam and Louie, flashed through her mind. She stepped over to the table and gathered Cassie to her. "Oh, Honey. I am better now. And it's not like your Mama's sickness at all. In fact, I'm over it and just fine. "

Cassie sank against Meg with relief.

Meg continued, "And how are you? Have you eaten any breakfast? Where are Lizzie and Stephen? Don't tell me they're not up yet!'

With a relieved grin, Cassie replied, "Everybody's still sleeping 'cept me. Lizzie cried in the night so I brought her in bed with me. Then I snuck out a little while ago. I peeked in at Stephen and at Pa, but they're sleeping hard." She wiggled and looked up at Meg. "Will you make hotcakes?"

Meg felt like she was waking from a dream and noticing Cassie for the first time in days. Lizzie had cried in the night and she hadn't even heard her. What had she been thinking? Her arms hungered for her babies.

She smiled at Cassie. "Hotcakes it will be. Wanna help?"

The kitchen was bustling with the aroma of bacon and hotcakes and the chatter of the little ones when Jeb finally emerged from the bedroom.

Charles had Lizzie on his lap, and was cutting up hotcakes for Stephen. His coffee cup steamed in front of him and relief at Meg's cheerfulness lit his expression. He looked up at Jeb. "Morning, son. Coffee?"

"No thanks, Pa," Jeb answered, with a forced smile in his father's direction. "Can you finish with breakfast so I can take Meg outside for a while?"

Meg twirled away from the stove in surprise.

Charles tipped his chin, a question in his eyes.

"C'mon," Jeb caught Meg's eye, and motioned toward the door. Meg untied her apron and followed him out. With faces full of curiosity, the children and Charles watched them leave.

"Mama?" Stephen called behind them.

"Mama? Mama?" Lizzie's little voice echoed.

"I'll be right back!" Meg called over her shoulder, giving the children a bright smile. "Eat those hotcakes now. Let Grandpa help you." She closed the door behind her and followed Jeb down the path.

After enough steps to get them out of earshot of the house, Jeb turned to her. "Meg. Please don't leave. I need you. I need our family. God, I've been a fool. I swear to you that the problems are over. I vow to be the best husband any wife ever had from this moment on."

Jeb breathed hard as he faced Meg. Sincerity shone from his eyes. "I don't know all the right words to say. I can't talk about it anymore. I just want to show you. Please, let me show you."

Meg gulped. Before she could fight it back, hope sprung into her heart. She stood wordless, battered by the emotions of the morning and the past week. A long sigh escaped. How she wanted it to be true! Did she dare once again become vulnerable? *Do I dare believe him this time? Is there a chance?* She looked at Jeb standing on the path between her and their house, hope shining from his eyes. She pictured the little ones and Charles waiting inside.

"No more, Jeb. Not even once. No more drinking at any time for any reason. You turn into someone I don't know when you drink. And I never know when that'll be. And no more brooding about Stu. That's his name. He isn't anything to us. Don't ever bring him up to me again. Don't ever use him as an excuse. Can you do it? Because if you can't, there'll be no more chances." She leaned toward him. "We'll go riding this afternoon on the new horses. And we'll never speak again about where those horses came from. We'll just enjoy them, like they're our reward for the hardship we've been put through. And if there's ever more contact from Stephen's father, we'll deal with it together. I will never keep anything from you. You'll help me and I'll help you. That's how it has to be. We have to be past it as of this moment."

Jeb swallowed hard, struggling for words. He hesitated. "I'll try. I think I can do it...," his voice trailed off as he searched her face, eager for approval of his words.

Meg's heart turned to stone as he spoke. She saw clearly and suddenly that Jeb didn't have the will to commit to a life without drinking or blaming her for what had happened. He was only saying he'd try. Try! *He won't get over the kidnapping, ever. He doesn't really want to. He needs excuses.* And now that she was removing every possible excuse, he was looking for a way to pardon his behavior when it happened again. She could see it so clearly now.

Rage was quickly replaced by determination. "No, Jeb. Trying won't be good enough." She turned away from his stricken face, stomped back and pushed open the door to the kitchen.

CHAPTER TWENTY TWO

It took only a few days until the wagon was loaded and she was ready to go. Ma and Pa had taken the news very well. To Meg's surprise, Pa explained how Ma had been talking about going back to Massachusetts ever since Louie died. She hadn't been able to shake her melancholy since burying their son, and he thought a trip back home to see all their kinfolk would do her good. They'd go now.

"Are you sure you won't come with us, Angel?" Pa asked again the night before they were all going to set out. "I know Ruben wrote that he'd be happy to get you back any time, but you could put it off until we all got back from out East if you go with us. The folks there would be so happy to see you and meet Stephen and Lizzie. You don't have to go back to Ruben's yet."

"Oh, Pa. I've never been out East and I know how nice it would be to meet all the relatives and see where you grew up. But now doesn't feel like the right time to me. It isn't easy to make this break from Jeb. I have the chance now to settle in at Ruben's tavern with a place to live for me and Stephen and Lizzie. It's the only way I know of to make enough to keep us. I better take this chance to make it in a life on my own."

She fought back the temptation to go with them. "If I travel with you and Ma, Ruben might find somebody else and I'll lose my chance. He needs help now. I better grab this chance. I'm afraid if I stay with you and Ma, it will just be harder later on all of us. It might give Jeb hope that I'll come back with you, too. Don't you agree, this is best?"

"Well, yeah, it does make sense. I guess we've talked it through enough these past few days. We'll miss you lots, though, Angel. It'll be hard to say goodbye when we go in different directions from Joseph and Tillie's. But you're probably right. A lot of the folks around here don't think it's right for a wife to leave her husband, especially with little ones, so a clean break and a new start somewhere else may be best. But remember we could work it out so you could just stay here with us. We'll make room, and the farm can support us all, and Elsie and Moses would be so happy to have..."

Meg interrupted. "Pa, we've been all through this. I have to go. And it has to be now."

Pa dropped his chin in resignation. He reached out and drew her to him. Their hug was long and intense. Both realized that life as they knew it would be forever left behind when they set off in opposite directions.

"My Angel," he murmured. "Stay safe. Write if ever you need us. We'll be right there as soon as we can."

"I know, Pa. I know. "Meg treasured the feel of his arms around her. It would be a long time until she felt so secure again. But her reservation was overcome by a definite desire to start life on her own.

It was bittersweet, traveling the next day beside Ma and Pa and knowing they would soon be heading so far in the other direction. They all stayed with Joseph and Tillie that night and there were long, loving hugs all around in the morning when it was time to part. But Meg had no reservations about her plan.

She rode back to Ruben's, filled with confidence, Lizzie and Stephen tucked before her in the saddle of the horse Stu had sent. The colt trailed on a lead behind, carrying their belongings. Meg was ready to begin life on her own.

The days at Griffins Tavern fell quickly into a routine. Meg rose early with the children and spent mornings preparing breakfast for travelers. The rich smell of cooking encompassed Stephen and Lizzie while they dawdled over hotcakes or oatmeal or eggs and grits. They became comfortable with people who welcomed the opportunity to share morning coffee with two little ones who scampered underfoot. By the times things became really busy, Ruben had done the milking and came in to help through the lunch time.

Later, after he sorted and distributed the mail, he retreated to his room for a nap. While he slept and the children had their naps upstairs, Meg laundered bedding and clothing, hung many loads on the clothesline, prepared food for the evening meal, gathered eggs, caught up on cleaning, and distributed mail to afternoon callers. Suppertime found Lizzie and Stephen completely tired out after busy days tagging after Ruben and Meg, playing, and romping with the dog.

Ruben always shooed all three of them away from the tavern as soon as the supper crowd thinned. He was very protective, allowing no contact between Meg, Stephen and Lizzie and the crowds that filled the tavern when night began to fall.

So Meg spent early evenings down at the creek like before, watching her little ones splash away the dust of the day. Many bars of soap were replaced in the crook of the big oak on the bank. Meg read or sewed or wrote to Ma and Pa after tucking Stephen and Lizzie in for the night, soothed by the now familiar sounds from downstairs. She pushed thoughts of Jeb away, sure she was doing the right thing. She tried unsuccessfully to avoid indulging in memories and dreams of Stu, certain they would meet again if only she waited long enough. She didn't know when or how, but a deep instinct told her that he was out there somewhere thinking of her. She welcomed the unexplainable sense of peace it brought her. *Let him come to me when he's ready. I'll wait, no matter how long it takes.*

Stephen and Lizzie celebrated their birthdays before Ma and Pa returned from Massachusetts. The letters from back East had been frequent, and full of details about life with the kinfolk. Ma seemed to be taking great comfort in being there. Her letters, more cheerful each time, warmed Meg's heart. Pa wrote a few lines of his own at the end of each letter, always to his "Angel", and sounded more eager than Ma to get back to the farm.

Meg and the children accompanied Ruben to Springfield every two weeks to pick up supplies. She enjoyed casual chats with young women her age who were also buying notions and provisions in the big general store. It was great fun observing the fashions and studying advertising posters for entertainment and new products. Stephen and Lizzie trailed after their mother, wide-eyed and obedient, eager for the promised treat for the ride home. Stephen amazed Meg—he picked a different thing to try every time—a huge dill pickle or a rope of black licorice or a pickled pig's foot. Lizzie would carefully study his choice, then be drawn to the candy case where she inevitably ended up with a handful of lemon drops or root beer barrels.

On the way home, the children fell asleep in the back of the wagon, sprawled among the goods, their sticky hands and satisfied little faces bobbing along with the ruts in the road. Ruben enjoyed the trips as much as the rest of them, chatting amiably all the way, helping Meg become knowledgeable about the news, the latest gossip, and upcoming plans for the tavern. She began to hear the story of his life, as well.

Their camaraderie grew as the months passed. They worked well together and soon became known as "Ruben and Meg from Griffin's". The stunning young mother and the pudgy old man, eagerly discussing purchases, finishing sentences for each other, comfortably side-by-side, were a puzzling combination to those who didn't know them. But their ease with each other, their cheerful manner, and their obvious delight in the youngsters who accompanied them, quickly won over all who met them.

It was on one of those long rides homes, in the mesmerizing twilight as the wagon rolled steadily along, that Meg brought up what was beginning to bother her. "Ruben, what do you think? Sometimes I've wonder what it would be like to be one of those women who have husbands and homes of their own. Do you think Stephen and Lizzie are missing out by not having a father and a normal upbringing? Stephen will be five his next birthday and Lizzie's almost three now."

Ruben looked sideways at her, but didn't speak.

Meg continued, "Well, I guess I'm asking for myself, kind of, too. I notice how that clerk, Johnny, always looks at me so long. He sort of trails after me as soon as we get in the store. Like he doesn't have anything else to do. He's real nice and always asks about the children. And when I wait outside the bank for you, gentlemen tip their hats to me. Sometimes, even the ones in the fancy carriages. I wonder what it would be like to have a life like other women. Not that I think about going back to Jeb, for sure. But sometimes I feel kind of lonesome, you know what I mean?"

Ruben swallowed hard. "Yup. I know what ya mean. I know the feelin' well. It's somethin' only you can decide, though. Guess I never wanted to hitch up with anyone else after Sarah died. I just couldn't put any other woman in her place in my heart or my life. She was the one for me. Sometimes the loneliness got so bad I almost broke down in them early days after she passed, but I've managed to git along all these years. Bein' by yourself ain't so bad, really."

He flipped the reins and glanced over at her. "Well, Meg, do whatever your feelings tell you. You'll know if it's ever time ta smile back at one of those gents. But never you worry 'til then. You and them younguns have a place at Griffin's as long as ya wanna stay. To tell ya the truth, I never had it so good. All the help ya give me. And, I git heaps of pleasure having the younguns around. Makes me kinda wish, ever now and agin, that I hadn't a' been a widower so soon after we married. Maybe I woulda had a family, too..." His voice trailed off.

"Oh, Ruben, we're just like family, aren't we?"

"Sure nuf you are! So what're we squawkin' about anyway?"

He and Meg grinned at each other, he slapped the reins across the team's back, and they rolled home with lightened hearts. During the following months, Meg was too busy to dwell on the loneliness that nudged into her thoughts.

She allowed thoughts of Stu to become an indulgence she enjoyed before falling asleep, and in daydreams over the laundry tub or stove. The details of their time together were still clear after all the years because she returned to the memories so often. She could recall at will every nuance of his voice and posture. His face was etched into her mind. She took great comfort in reliving all they had shared, and was sometimes pleasantly surprised by an unexpected detail that would pop up and enrich a memory. Usually, that was enough, but sometimes in the darkness of her room when a night breeze stirred the curtains and a net of stars sparkled in the black sky beyond, longing for him overcame her. She couldn't fight the pain in her heart. *Where is he and why doesn't he come back to me?*

THE months flew by, until one afternoon Stephen cried out from the front porch. "Mama! Mama! Somebody's coming. They're waving at me! Who is it? Look! Look!"

Meg rushed from behind the counter and followed the direction of Stephen's pointing finger. A wagon rolled toward them. A familiar wagon. In a minute, she was dashing wildly down the road to meet it.

"Ma! Ma! Pa!" She ran as fast as she could toward the approaching wagon.

That night Meg and the children stayed late at a big wooden table down in the tavern, catching up with the news from Massachusetts, and drinking in the sight of the familiar faces. They laughed and talked, and the little ones had never been hugged so much or stayed up so late.

"Yeah, we had to come back," Pa explained. "It's been half a year, you know, since we left. We got a telegram from George at the store in town. He said Moses came in about two weeks ago, something about three men showing up at the farm with a claim or deed or something for our land and telling Moses and Elsie they had to get off the property. George wrote it all down for Moses and they sent it right off to me. The newspapers back East are full of stories about these carpetbagger swindlers cheating Southern folk out of their homesteads with fake papers, so I figured we better get right back and take care of this. Did you hear anything about it?"

"No, Pa. I've had no word from anybody at home," Meg replied.

Her words were met with silence as everyone realized that meant there had been no words between her and Jeb, either. Nobody had mentioned Jeb's name, but the subject put a damper on the reunion, and soon everyone headed up to bed.

In the morning, Miriam and Jim gave final hugs all around and made plans for Jim to come back as soon as everything was settled with the homestead. He planned to accompany Meg and the children back for a visit, so parting wasn't hard since all knew they would see each other again soon. Lizzie waved and called "Bye-bye, Gamma. Bye-bye, Gamma" until Ma and Pa's wagon was out of sight. She was delighted with the new "Gamma" word and practiced it for days while following Stephen around.

Stephen was a much admired big brother. The two were inseparable, looking first for each other as soon as their eyes opened in the morning. Lizzie's reddish blond hair now hung in thick ringlets that framed her freckled, elfin face. She was thin and tough, usually barefoot, and didn't stay clean long. Stephen was growing out of his baby looks, handsome with striking golden hair and deep blue eyes beneath definite dark brows like his father. They were busy children, not at all shy, and delighted Meg and Ruben every day with their antics and company.

Meg retained her girlish slimness due to the constant activity required to keep the tavern going. She was unaware of how men studied her as she bustled around. Her lush hair always escaped from attempts to pin it up, falling in golden waves around her shoulders. Male customers often became tongue-tied or stammered when she turned her attention to them. Many became lost in her unique sapphire eyes and had to ask her to repeat what she just said. A number of them became steady customers, always appearing when they knew Meg would be on duty. But Meg's heart belonged so completely to another that she saw none of the signals of interest that came her way. She remained cheerful, pleasant, efficient at her work, and took great pride in her ability to provide for herself and her children.

THE years flew by, and by the time Stephen turned ten, Meg realized that he soon would be wanting to know about his father. He deserved to know. Her heart belonged to Stu, and she wished stubborn pride hadn't prevented her from telling him how she felt and what she needed so long ago. She began mentioning his name to travelers, always hoping for a sign of recognition. She scanned every newspaper that came through the mail, checking for his name.

Every June, Pa drove the wagon to Griffin's for Meg and the children to ride back with him. The week at home always soothed Meg. She avoided Jeb completely, letting Ma or Pa accompany Lizzie to see her father and grandfather and Cassie.

Elsie and Moses, their salt and pepper curls becoming whiter each year, were a comforting part of every visit. It surprised nobody that they had chosen to remain on the farm at the time of emancipation since they'd long been like family to the Bensons. Pa and Moses enlarged their cabin with a wide front porch and a separate bedroom. Elsie took great pleasure in accompanying Miriam to town and being able to buy such things as her own new frying pan and bright flowered material for curtains.

Jeb's visits to see Lizzie became ever more infrequent as the years passed, relieving Meg of the anxiety of facing him. When she knew he was due to arrive, she retreated to the laundry shed or to other tasks, which kept her away from him. The times they did see each other were awkward, and Meg fled as soon as she could politely get away. When, after one visit, Lizzie told her mother that Jeb had a new "Mama" at his house, Meg felt relief, and hoped little Cassie would benefit from finally having a woman around the house again.

Meg sent letters several times a year to let Cassie know she was not forgotten, and had only a mild curiosity about Jeb's new partner.

Letters to Cassie weren't the only ones that went in and out from Griffin's Tavern.

Deeply regretful now about the notices from Bill and Virginia that she had burned in the fireplace, Meg sent out many letters addressed to "Stuart Logan of Illinois". Each was labelled "PLEASE POST" and directed to every fort or settlement that she learned of from travelers. Twice a year, she sent to all addresses again. Her hope of a reply never materialized, but every batch of mail Griffins received caused a tiny flutter of hope in her heart.

One day, a thick, cream-colored envelope arrived bearing her name, it's return address a law firm back in Crockett County. She willingly signed the papers, freeing Jeb and herself. *"I'm a divorced woman. With children to raise on my own. What will people think now?"*

She directed that question to Ruben, who turned to her with earnest eyes. "Meg, don't fret. We won't talk about it. Then nobody else will. It's not so good, bein' divorced. But it's not yer fault. Ya did the right thing, freein' yourself from him."

"Well..." Meg answered.

"I mean it," Ruben said. "Be proud of how you're handling your life. You're a good woman, doin' yer best. Let's not talk about it anymore. Nothin's really changed."

"Thank you, Ruben. You're a big part of why I am who I am. I'll always be grateful to you."

A long hug followed their conversation.

Meg accepted her loneliness and longing for Stu as the price that must be paid to follow her heart. She no longer fought it. Her devotion never faltered; she knew the day would come when she would again find herself in Stu's arms. Her instinct about this was so strong that dreams of that day fortified her as the years passed.

CHAPTER TWENTY THREE

Six more years had passed the morning Stephen leaned over the bed, his face creased with anxiety. "Ma? Ma? How are you this morning? Did you cough much in the night?"

Meg opened her eyes and made a futile attempt to raise her head. Stephen was alarmed by this weakness, her pale face, and the deep shadows beneath her eyes that weren't there yesterday.

"Stephen," she whispered. "I had trouble breathing all night. You better get Doc again."

"I'll send Lizzie," Stephen replied, "but I'm staying with you."

He called for his sister and sent her off to town for Doc Williams. Morning sun burning through the lace curtains allowed Stephen to see how frail his mother looked.

He was suddenly very afraid. "Ma? Ma? I sent Lizzie for Doc."

Meg lifted her head weakly and whispered, "There's something I want to tell you, Son. Something I should have told you long ago."

"No, Ma. You shouldn't talk. Wait 'til Doc gets here."

Meg shook her head. She motioned Stephen over and patted a space on the side of the bed. "Sit here. I can't talk too well, but I have to tell you." She broke off and took several raspy breaths.

"What is it, Ma?" Stephen asked. "Would it help if I prop the pillows up?"

Meg coughed weakly as Stephen arranged the pillows beneath her head.

"Now, Ma, what is so important that it can't wait 'til you're better?"

"In case I don't get better, I have to tell you now."

"No, Ma. Don't talk like that!" Stephen cried.

But Meg shook her head in that stubborn way she had. Her voice was weak, but determined. "Maybe I will get through this. But Doc said he's done all he can. This consumption has to break on its own. So please, Son, hear me out."

Stephen settled himself on the edge of her bed, reluctant, and more afraid than he'd ever felt. It wasn't like Ma to talk this way.

"It's about your father, Stephen. When you asked about him I know I told you he disappeared at Appomattox, but it isn't true." She clutched his hand with her cool, small fingers. "I planned to tell you, but it was never the right time. You deserve to know this. He didn't die in the war. His name is Stuart Logan, like I always told you. But... but, well... he's not dead. At least, I don't think so." She paused, and struggled for breath.

Stephen drew back, his expression incredulous.

"Here's how it was, Stephen. Here's what happened. I know he loved us... but... here's how it was..."

The fragile voice whispered on, carrying Stephen back in time. He listened in fascination and disbelief to the story she told.

Finally, Meg paused, and took a deep breath. "My, I've gone on and on..."

"Yes, Ma. But you've been breathing easier and easier as you went along. Do you feel better?" Stephen asked, still reeling from his mother's words. He was shocked at the news and wondered how his mother could have kept this from him for so long.

"Well, yes. I guess you're right. I can breathe easier. Thank goodness. Finally."

She and Stephen turned toward a small sound by door. Lizzie stood there, solemnly meeting their gazes.

"Lizzie! How long have you been back? What did Doc say? Is he coming?" Stephen asked. "How long have you been listening?"

"I got back real quick. I ran fast," Lizzie replied. "I heard most of what Ma told you." Her cheeks reddened and she looked away. "Well then. Doc's gone out to the Rickets' for their new baby. Nurse isn't sure when he'll be back cuz their babies always take a long time." She moved over to stand beside the bed. "Ma, you look better. You were even talking easier toward the end. Is it easier to breathe?" Lizzie leaned down and took her mother's hand, her eyebrows lifted. "Why didn't you ever tell us before, Ma? Why did you keep it a secret about Stephen's Pa?"

Meg tried to gather her thoughts. "I don't know, Honey. We'll talk about it later when I'm not feeling so tired. And, yes. I do feel better. My breathing's easier, for sure. I'm a little hungry, too, I guess."

She smiled and patted Lizzie's hand. "Now that you both know the story, I feel easier without having to keep the secret about Stephen's father anymore. But I do feel tuckered out. We'll talk some more later. Some of that soup from last night sounds real good all of a sudden. Maybe I could have a little?"

She reached for Stephen and Lizzie and gathered them into her arms. "I love you both. Can you understand now why we've stayed here all this time?"

Lizzie nodded, and Stephen's heart leapt at this change in Ma. Maybe she wasn't so bad off after all. She did seem better. He returned her hug, then scrambled off the bed and headed for the kitchen on flying feet. He'd think more about what she told him later, up in his room, when he had time to absorb it.

When Doc appeared in the late afternoon, he was pleased to have to wake his patient from a deep, restful sleep. Encouraged by the pink in her cheeks, he reported to the children after finishing in her room. "I'm not sure why your Ma overcame the consumption all of a sudden. But she's definitely better. Another day or two like this, and she'll be up and around. But, she has to take it easy for quite a while or she'll relapse," he began repacking his bag.

"You hear me, Meg?" he called toward her room. "I mean it. I don't want to have to come back here for a long time. You're a healthy young woman, but you can only get over this completely if you take it easy for the next few weeks. Promise me you won't be up and at it tomorrow? I know you. You go like blazes all the time and you just won't slow down a bit."

His voice was stern, but his eyes twinkled with affection as he winked at Stephen and Lizzie. "You take good care of your mother, you two. She should be fine soon. Be good and help her all you can."

Stephen and Lizzie answered eagerly, "We will! We will!" Relief blazed from their eyes, and they scrambled back to their mother's room as soon as Doc was out the door.

That night Stephen and Lizzie swam late down at the creek while Meg slept. Afterwards, they sat on the bank in the warm June darkness, contented, and relived every detail of the story Ma had told them earlier in the day. It was very late by the time they began their walk back to the tavern, still marveling at the news of Stephen's father and immensely relieved to know that Ma was better and life would return to normal.

"So, Stephen, don't you think we should try to find your father for Ma?" Lizzie asked, turning her face to him in the moonlight.

"Yeah. I've been thinking the same thing," Stephen replied. "It sounds like she still loves him so much. I can't believe she's been waiting for him all these years and never said a word to us." He turned hopeful eyes to his sister, "I want to find him, too. My father might still be alive. I can't believe it! All this time, she just took care of us, and worked, and dreamed of seeing him again." He leaped ahead on the path in excitement. "I bet Ruben will help us talk her into letting me go try to find him. Shoot, that Logan place is only an hour from here. I could go there. I will go there. Nobody can stop me. They're my people. If I'm going to find my father, I should start with them. Maybe they know something. I have to do it now that I know about him!"

The next day, they convinced Ruben that the search for Stuart Logan should begin right away, for Ma. All three of them spent the day popping in at Meg's bedside whenever she was awake, trying to convince her to let Stephen ride over to the Logan ranch.

By suppertime, she'd agreed to let Stephen make the trip the next day. Despite her worry at how he might be treated there, she couldn't hide her hope that they might finally have had word of Stu by now.

Letting go of the secret she had kept from her children for so long freed her to finally acknowledge the longing for the man who still consumed her dreams. And it was a great relief to see that Stephen harbored no resentment at her lie. *He's such a good son. I've worried for years that he wouldn't understand why I've kept the secret.*

Meg felt good enough the next morning to get out of bed for the first time in two weeks, and shuffled out to the porch as Stephen prepared to leave. With surprising vigor, she instructed, "Ask for Bill when you get there, Honey. Or Virginia, if he's not there," she hesitated. "I really should go with you."

"No, Ma. You can't be traveling. Doc said you have to take it easy for a few weeks. We shouldn't wait any longer to start searching. I can do it. I'm sixteen. I can ride that far easily. That ranch should be easy to find and it's not that far. Bill sounds like a nice enough man. I'll be fine. I want to find my father. For you, and for me. Don't worry. I'll be back tonight," Stephen's words tumbled with excitement and purpose.

Ruben added, "Stephen's right. If anyone goes with him, it will be me. You won't be going out anywhere,

Meg. Doc said it'll be a while 'til you're well." He looked at Meg with a stern face and put his hands on his broad hips. "You're staying here and resting. I mean it!"

"But he's only sixteen. He shouldn't go alone," Meg protested. "Even if you go along, he's the one who has to face them. I should go along."

"Ma, I'm sixteen. And, how old were you when you and my father met?" Stephen asked.

Her eyes skittered away from his and her cheeks reddened. "Well, I was seventeen, just having my birthday, turning eighteen." With a resigned shrug, she acquiesced, "I suppose you have to go then. Alright, you can go." She was unable to hide the hint of hope in her voice.

CHAPTER TWENTY FOUR

MEG'S directions were easy to follow, and the hour's ride passed in no time. Stephen rode tall in the saddle, proud to be riding the stallion he now knew had been sent to him by his father as a colt so many years ago. His heart began to thud when he turned off the main road to follow the lane between the low brick walls and tall trees that were just as Ma had described.

When he came within sight of the big house, he pulled up on the reins and sat staring at the place where his father grew up. These were his people. His father had spent his childhood in that house. Stephen felt no fear about what his visit might be like, only a determination to meet these people, gather what knowledge he could about his father's whereabouts, and move ahead with his search. He took a determined, deep breath, spurred his horse forward and reined to a stop at the front steps.

A young man opened the door at once, as if he'd been watching Stephen approach and called out, "Hello? You looking for someone?"

Stephen guessed this would be little Robbie, now grown up. "Yup. Bill Logan. Is he here?" Stephen asked.

"Yeah, he's over at the corral... C'mon, I'll take you," the young man answered. He gave a tentative grin, closed the door behind him, and started down the steps toward Stephen. His eyes betrayed curiosity and his eyebrows lifted when he noticed Stephen's horse. Stephen smiled back, relieved to meet this young man with the dark curls and smiling eyes. Stephen dismounted, tied his horse to the rail, and followed Robbie around the corner of the house.

"Nice horse," Robbie commented with a backward glance at the stallion, unable to hide obvious curiosity.

Stephen nodded in acknowledgement, and wondered what Robbie would say if he knew the horse had come from this very place fourteen years ago. Although Robbie couldn't hide his curiosity, he refrained from further questions, and pointed toward a man leading a horse through its paces in the huge corral behind the house.

"There he is. That's Bill. He's my father. I'm Robbie," Robbie said.

Fighting the urge to say "I know", Stephen extended his hand and responded, "I'm Stephen."

Robbie's eyes flickered with curiosity at the name. He reached over and the boys shook hands, shy and tentative at first, then with a stronger grip as their eyes met. Stephen felt a surprising and encouraging connection.

"Want me to come over there with you?" Robbie asked. "I was just coming out to help him now, anyway." He, too, seemed reassured by the handshake and looked more comfortable.

"No, thanks. I need to talk to him myself first. Personal business," Stephen answered.

Robbie's curiosity was obvious, but he slowed, and hung back. Stephen approached the corral, studying the man who ran beside a muscular red stallion, training it to turn with the bridle. Stephen felt overcome with emotion at this first sight of his uncle and his throat tightened. Here was a blood relative, his father's brother, the first person he'd ever known from his father's side of the family. He gave a brief touch to his own black eyebrows that were duplicates of the ones on the man in front of him. He tried to draw a steadying breath, but felt very shaky, and found himself breathing hard as he reached the fence.

Suddenly, a boy's voice rang out from the open hayloft in the barn next to the corral. "Papa! Look! Somebody's here!"

Stephen turned to see a freckle-faced boy perched in the hayloft above. Bill's eyes followed the boy's pointing arm, and then locked onto Stephen as he pulled the stallion to a halt. Bill started toward Stephen, then hesitated. He stood, staring hard, for a long moment.

"My God!... are you? It can't be..." he exclaimed and began to rush toward the fence.

Stephen was taken aback. He hadn't expected to be recognized. But it was apparent that Bill had already figured out who he was.

"Son, are you... are you Stephen?" Bill called out as he drew near, his face lit with eagerness and surprise.

Stephen managed a dip of his chin.

Bill bounded over the fence and reached for Stephen's hand. "I always knew you'd show up one day! Is your mother with you? My God! I don't believe it! Robbie, come on over here and meet Stephen. This is Stuart's son. The one we told you about! This is him! You two are cousins."

He still held Stephen's hand in a hearty grip, then called to the boy in the loft, "Tad, get down here and meet your cousin!"

Stephen soon found himself on the ground, enveloped in friendly exclamations and vigorous handshakes.

"Tad, this is your cousin, Stephen. The one we talked about who lives over at Griffin's Tavern. Uncle Stuart's boy. He's finally come!"

The boy stared, tongue-tied. His eyes were bright blue, set in a mass of freckles beneath fiery red hair that curled wildly, willy-nilly around his head. Bits of straw clung to his shoulders and faded cotton britches.

"Well, Stephen, what brings you?" Bill asked. "Your mother must have sent you. Is she all right?" He pulled back to study Stephen's face. "Durn! You look just like Stu! So much like him! I'll be damned!" He gave his head a shake. "Last time I saw you, you were just a baby. Damn!"

"My mother told me, just yesterday, about my father and all of you here," Stephen replied. "She was sick with the consumption and was afraid she might not get another chance." At Bill's frown of concern, he added, "But she's better. Doc says she'll be good as new in a few weeks. After she told me about all of you and my father, we talked it through and decided it was time to try to find him. I've come because we hope you have word of his whereabouts."

Bill frowned. "Wish we did. He took off right after he got back from seein' your mother in Tennessee the second time. He was afraid if he told our folks here the whole story, they'd be furious at him. For taking a young girl like that. For disgracing the family. So he didn't explain anything to them, just up and left one day."

He looked toward the house. "And my folks, well, your grandparents, have been mighty embarrassed about how they treated your Ma when she brought you here. You were just a wee one. They were so shocked to have a girl and a baby show up claiming to be Stu's family." He grimaced. "At the time, they said they were so shocked that they didn't treat your mother well. It wasn't long after she left, they realized they might have been wrong, that Stu got into the trouble because he was suffering, in his mind, from the war. I talked to them a lot about how Stu was just so damn sick of the war that he wasn't himself."

Bill reached out and put an arm around Stephen's shoulders and went on, "Stu was feelin' so damn bad before he left, and then one morning he just left. We haven't had a word from him since. God, I've been so worried about him. I miss my brother!" Bill paused. A look of concern flashed across his face. "I suppose you know the whole story, right?"

Stephen nodded. Robbie and Tad stood to the side, listening, eyes wide.

Bill continued, "Well, we've kept trying to find him all these years. We still send word with everyone we know who's heading West. I'm pretty sure that's where he would've headed, since he ran that way the first time. We send along a batch of notices with anyone we know who's heading out West, and ask them to post them wherever they can. Never got a word back, though. Nobody's ever heard of him. It's been fourteen years. Makes you sixteen, right?"

Stephen nodded again, fascinated, loving the sound of his uncle's voice, marveling at the resemblance to his own face.

Bill went on, "Mother and Father changed our mail route so we didn't have to pick up our mail at Griffin's. Embarrassed, I guess. Ashamed of how they treated Stu, and your Ma, too. They've been too proud to go to your Ma and ask her to come back. But we've kept track of you. You've been at Griffin's all this time, haven't you?"

When Stephen nodded, Bill said, "Well, I wanted to go see you, but they convinced me we better leave well enough alone until we heard from Stu. They thought if we couldn't bring any good news to your Ma, it was best to stay out of the way. So they wouldn't risk making it worse with your mother, you know? We never dreamed it would go on this long, though."

He grinned at Stephen. "Meg was plenty mad when she left that morning. She has spunk, your mother. I've never agreed with my folks about waiting to go see her and try to make amends. I thought we should go right away and apologize, but they've been pretty strong about letting it lie until Stuart shows up. But nobody ever thought it would go on this long. Not nearly this long." He spread his hands with an apologetic look. "I wonder where that brother of mine is. God, I'd give anything to see him again! We all figured if he'd contacted your mother, we'd have heard about it. Has he? Has there been any word at all?"

In a voice filled with regret, Stephen answered, "No. That's why I'm here. Ma kept trying to find him, too, all these years. She sent letters and notices, too. Lots of them. But not a word ever came back. I didn't even know about all this until yesterday. Even Ruben never let on what he knew."

"Ruben! That old... still as fat and sassy as always?" Bill grinned.

"Yeah, he's good. He and Ma run that place like clockwork. He's been sorta like a father to me... well... the closest thing I had, I guess," Stephen's voice broke a bit, surprising him.

"Hey," Bill responded. "C'mere." He settled his arm more firmly across Stephen's shoulders. "Come on up to the house. We have some introducing to do." He guided Stephen toward the house.

Stephen readily followed, relieved at how things were going. Robbie strode at his side with Tad scampering along underfoot. Stephen swallowed bitter disappointment at the realization that his father's whereabouts were unknown to the Logans, too. But hope surfaced as he realized that his fear of being met with hostility at this house was groundless. Maybe they would help. He felt empowered by the Bill and Robbie striding beside him, and the hope of finding his father deepened. Tad danced alongside in excitement, his face upturned to Stephen in open curiosity.

Bill threw open the kitchen door and motioned Stephen in behind him. Stephen was momentarily stunned—the room was just like Ma had described. There were the two long walls of windows and the pump where his grandfather William had filled the coffeepot that morning long ago. Flowered curtains and chair cushions were just as Ma had told him, although a bit faded. A small woman turned from her reading in a rocking chair by the window. She looked questioningly at Bill, then Stephen.

"Mother! Look! He's here! He's finally here! It's Stephen! Last time you saw him, he was just a baby!" Bill exclaimed, and pulled Stephen forward.

The old woman tried to rise, but Bill rushed to her side. "It's all right, Mother. Stay there. Here, Stephen. Come on over."

Hesitantly, Stephen approached his grandmother. She studied his face, intent dark eyes locked into his. "Your mother? Is she well?" she asked in a soft voice.

It was the loveliest, most refined voice Stephen had ever heard. He choked. This was his grandmother. This was the woman who had raised his father. She was as lovely as Ma said. Her face was nearly unlined, her white hair sprinkled with traces of its original shining darkness, and she wore a dress of rich, dark brown fabric that looked very soft.

He fought the tightness in his throat and swallowed hard. "Ma has had the consumption. But she's getting better. She just told me all about everything... about... about my father... about all of you... when she was so sick," he faltered, unable to continue.

"Robbie, Go get your grandfather. He should be in the stable. Tell him to come right away," his grandmother ordered.

Robbie ran out the back door, then burst back in. "Hey! Your horse. It looks like one of ours. Is it one...?"

"Yeah. It came from my father. It's one of yours that he sent down to us years ago," Stephen replied. "No wonder it caught your eye. It's your stock. From here."

They grinned at each other before Robbie tore out, letting the door slam behind him. Tad scampered after him.

"You have a horse from our stock?" his grandmother asked.

"Yes, Ma'am. My... my... Stuart sent my mother a mare and me a colt, when I was just little. Sort of a farewell, I guess. Ma's horse died a year ago, but I've had Spartacus ever since I can remember. We've refused a lot of offers for him. I bet I've ridden a thousand miles on him. He's the best! And I'll never sell him," Stephen explained.

She again sought Stephen's eyes. "And son. Are you well?"

Bill and Todd rushed in the door, breathing hard.

"Yes, Ma'am," Stephen answered, touched.

"Has your mother had word of Stuart?"

Stephen shook his head. His grandmother lowered her head in a vain effort to hide the tears that began to slip down her cheeks. Swiping at them, she raised her head. "Bill, will you help me? I want to see this horse."

Bill rushed to her side, and supported her as she painfully rose to her feet. She leaned on his arm and glanced toward Stephen. "Come along then, Stephen," she instructed him.

They walked through the kitchen door into the hall Stephen recalled from his mother's description. To the left, he saw the sitting room with the huge stone fireplace. Brass plates still shone from the mantel. Stephen felt odd, like being in a dream. They opened the front door, and his grandmother moved to where she could see Spartacus tethered at the rail.

"Yes, I remember that line. So the two of them weren't sold after all?" She turned to Bill. "And you knew?"

"Yes, Ma. I knew."

"Stuart gave them horses before he left?" she murmured to herself. With a heavy sigh, she clutched Bill's arm tighter. "Take me to the sitting room for when your father gets here."

Soon Stephen found himself standing in the room Ma had described. When Virginia appeared and helped Bill seat his mother, voices could be heard from the kitchen. In a moment, Robbie and Tad rushed in, followed by a tall, white-haired man, whose straight black brows stood out sharply in his lean, lined face. He stared at Stephen. Their eyes met, and the room fell silent. Stephen remembered his mother's courage in facing this man, and, emboldened by the memory, brazenly matched the old man's stare. A flicker of surprise, then amusement, lit the old man's eyes, before he succumbed to a smile. He stepped toward Stephen and extended a hand.

"Welcome, Stephen," his voice cracked, and he swallowed hard. "Been too long."

With those words, he moved closer and gathered Stephen to him. Stephen found himself gripped in the strongest hug he had ever experienced. The strength of those arms surprised him. He smelled his grandfather for the first time—a strong, horsey, outdoors aroma, with a subtle hint of tobacco. He felt his grandfather trembling, and instinctively hugged hard back to steady them both.

When they separated, his grandfather asked, "Your mother...?"

"She's fine. She told me the story of my father and all of you just yesterday. She's been sick. We weren't sure how I'd be met here, but we decided we had to do something. Coming here is a first step. We want to find my father. We're going to try our best to find him. Ma has waited for him all these years, but..."

"You haven't heard from Stuart at all then?" William interrupted.

When Stephen shook his head, nobody spoke for a long moment.

Then William continued, "Well, it's about time we all worked together to find him. This has gone on too long. We need to do everything we can to bring him home." He paused, "Stu's not the only one who's been stubborn. Your grandmother and I regret our actions toward your mother. We should have gone to see her and make this right years ago. We miss our son. We never dreamed he would stay away so long. Without a word. We always hoped he'd get in touch with your mother and they'd try coming back to see us. But there's never been a word. Does your mother have any clues for us?"

He walked over to stand beside his wife's chair, and put his hand on her shoulder. She reached up and covered his hand tenderly with her tiny, gnarled one.

All eyes turned to Stephen. "No, she's heard nothing. Nothing at all. She's waited for him all these years, hoping and praying every day, she says. And she sent out lots of notices and always asked strangers who passed through. She's tired of waiting, too. No matter what I found here, we decided we're going to search for him now, track down every clue, with or without anybody else's help. I'm going to find him. I'll never quit. I will find my father!" Stephen declared.

Robbie stepped forward. "Well, you won't be going alone. I'll go with you. I've heard about him all my life. He's my uncle. I'm going, too." He turned to his father, "Stephen shouldn't go by himself. He's sixteen, but I'm twenty. We'll be a good team. I'm sure you can spare me here for a while. We're going, right away, and that's it!"

He strode to Stephen's side, ignoring the looks of amazement on everyone's faces. He looked at his father, chin thrust out in defiance, eyes blazing. Bill stared back in astonishment. Stephen couldn't believe his ears.

Three hours later, filled with beef stew, biscuits and raspberry pie, they rode off side-by-side for Griffin's. Virginia and Sissy had joined the group as soon as they heard the commotion. Virginia, as warm and welcoming as Meg had described, had helped her son pack. Her face had paled at the news of the trip, but she said not a word against it. Sissy, now a long-legged thirteen-year-old with dark curls that matched her mother's, blushed every time she met Stephen's eyes.

Bill and Virginia with Sissy between them and Tad alongside, stood beside William and Ruth on the front steps, waving. Stephen's heart felt warmed by the love and acceptance that had made him part of his father's family during the past few hours. He couldn't wait to tell Ma. She'd be so surprised at the apology he was instructed to relay, and the invitation to visit, if she could find it in her heart to see the Logans again. Before he and Robbie turned out of the lane onto the main road, Stephen turned back over his shoulder for a final look at the group on the steps. Family. That was his family. He choked back a tightness in his throat. He had to bring his father back home.

MEG and Ruben and Lizzie were astounded when Stephen rode up to the tavern with Robbie at his side.

They listened in amazement as Stephen and Robbie explained how the Logans felt. Stephen saw a hardness melt from Ma's face when she realized what this meant.

Meg, Lizzie, and Ruben joined in the excitement of the plans for the boys to leave on the search first thing in the morning. Bright hope burned in Meg's eyes while Stephen and Robbie added to their provisions, pored over maps with Ruben, counted and recounted the thick wad of bills their grandfather had insisted on giving them. Stephen was determined to replace the hope in Ma's eyes with joy. He was determined to find out what happened to Stuart Logan.

CHAPTER TWENTY FIVE

EVERYONE agreed the two young men should head first for St. Louis. That bustling city, the "Gateway to the West", would most likely be the best place to leave new postings and begin asking questions. Early June days would allow long hours in the saddle, and even if they were gone for several months, the weather wouldn't be a hardship. Ruben added to their provisions until their bulging saddlebags could hold no more. Meg and Robbie had liked each other from the moment they met, and Lizzie's face turned bright pink every time Robbie affectionately tugged her long, curly pigtails.

The night before they left, Ma motioned Stephen out to the back steps while everyone else bustled around. "Here, this is the only letter I ever got from your father," she said, pulling an envelope from her apron pocket and handing it to Stephen. "He wrote only once, right after he left the horses for us back in Tennessee. He wanted to make sure I knew the horses were to be mine and yours. Pa brought me the letter from the post office and we never told anyone else about it except Jeb. There was no return address so I couldn't write back. I suppose Stu did it that way so I wouldn't be drawn into something that would complicate my life... that would be just like him..." Her voice trailed off.

Stephen tucked the fragile, faded envelope into his shirt pocket, not daring to look at it. His father's handwriting.

His father had touched this envelope. Stephen's heart skittered at the thought.

"Son, please take good care of that letter. It's the only one I have from him. You can read it. It will show you what kind of man your father is. If you find him, he'll recognize it, I'm sure, and know you are truly his Stephen. Maybe you want to save it for one night on the trail, when you'll feel ready to read it?" She paused, then continued, "Be careful, Son. It's going to be hard to see you ride off in the morning. Don't stay away longer than summer. When the leaves show their first signs of yellow, when the days hold the first whiff of cold, I'll need you home. I couldn't bear not having you back safe and sound." She fought back tears. "Promise me. If you don't find him, we'll try again, another way, another time. You have to promise to be back by early fall."

His mother's earnest face turned to him for acknowledgement of her words. She captured his hands between hers.

Stephen wound his fingers around hers. "Well sure, Ma. I promise to be back, way before that if I can. I won't cause you worry. I'll send those envelopes that you and Ruben got ready every two weeks from wherever we are." With a reassuring laugh, he continued, "I'll be fine. Robbie is perfect to have along with me. We haven't known each other that long, but he seems like he could be my brother. He's easy to be with and good on a horse. We'll be fine. And I'll do my best to find... St... my father."

Their long hug was the kind that only a mother and child could share. Stephen grew even more inspired by the light of hope that lit his mother's eyes. He hardly slept at all that night, consumed with excitement and determination. Shortly after dawn, the two young men rode out, filled with hotcakes and hope.

By noon that first day, Stephen was very glad for Robbie's presence beside him. The unfamiliar roads that challenged them as soon as they passed through Carbondale would have been tough to face alone. A cheerful Robbie rode beside him, just as eager as he was to get started with the search.

Stephen let his mind wander as he guided Spartacus along the sunny country roads. He marveled that, only a week ago, he hadn't even known his father might be alive. Now he had a whole new family, his mother was happier than he had ever seen her, and he was beginning a journey that might lead him to the father he had never known. Feeling impatient, he welcomed the challenge that lay before him.

Robbie proved to be an easygoing, capable companion. They chatted occasionally during the first day's ride, then settled beside the campfire for the night after enjoying Ma's ham sandwiches and molasses cookies. Stephen slept well in his bedroll, secure in the knowledge that he was well on his way to finding his father.

Stephen thought hard during the long hours of the second day in the saddle. Although he was distracted by the increasing number of riders, buggies, wagons, and roadside establishments as they neared St. Louis, he was sure of his decision by the time they pulled up at the outskirts of the city as the sun began to slip toward the horizon.

They stopped early that evening, camping beneath a huge oak near railroad tracks. Robbie proved adept with a fire and a frying pan, so the care of the horses fell to Stephen. They wolfed down a hearty supper of beans and bacon cooked over the campfire, settled the horses and bedded down for the night while darkness dropped around them like a silent black curtain.

In the light of the dying embers, Stephen called across the campfire, "Rob. You awake?"

"Mmmm. Hmmmm." Robbie mumbled, his voice muffled. "What?"

"Well, I did a lot of thinking on the ride. I'm not sure heading West out of St. Louis is the way to go."

Robbie stirred, and leaned up on his elbow to peer at Stephen through the firelight. "What do you mean?"

"Well. Just think about all the notices and messages

that everybody has sent West all these years. Nobody ever heard anything back. We never heard from anyone who even had the slightest clue. Not one word, ever. Not a hint of him. Seems like somebody would have heard of him, don't you think? A man can't just disappear. Wagon trains leave logs of the names of the people in their parties. The Army keeps records, and Ruben said everyone checks those notice boards at the post offices. So many travelers passed through Griffin's during all those years, and Ma says she asked all the time about Stuart Logan. It just seems like there should have been some word by now. Unless he died. But even then, deaths are recorded. His kinfolk would have been notified, don't you think?"

Robbie listened, eyes reflecting the dying orange of the campfire. "Yeah. It does seem funny that there's never been a single word about him." He sat up and hugged his knees to his chest.

Stephen continued. "So, I figure, maybe my father didn't head West. It sounds like he was pretty upset, to just leave the ranch without even saying goodbye to Bill. He must have been real sad about my Ma and me, and about everything. So, if I was really serious about getting away, I wouldn't go where I'd gone before. Because people would know me. Or know of me. Know what I mean?"

"Well, yeah, that does make sense. What do you figure he did then?" Robbie asked, now intrigued.

"Well, I think I would go the opposite way. When Ruben was going over the maps with us, he showed us those vast wilderness regions in Indiana and western Ohio. He heard the forests are so tall and thick, you can't see daylight through the leaves. And he said there's even more uncharted area if you go north toward Canada. Remember when he told about bears and wolves and cougars, and how nobody wants to settle there because it's still so dangerous and uninhabited?"

Robbie nodded. "I see what you're getting at. It would be a good place if you wanted to disappear. But Ruben said Canada is huge and pretty wild, too. Maybe he went there. We can't search all that. It would take years!"

"We don't have to search all of it. We just have to think things through. What if he chose Canada or Ohio or Indiana? How would he have gone? What were the main roads back then? We could just start asking on the main roads that would have been used fifteen years ago. All we can do is start asking. And show his picture. Even if it's the one from when he joined the Army, somebody still might recognize him. After all, there weren't very many people traveling that long ago, except for the wagon trains. I really don't think we should go West. There just hasn't been anything coming back from there. Ever."

"When did you think of this? Shouldn't we have asked your Ma and Ruben and Bill and everyone? They all think we're heading West."

Stephen shrugged. "Yeah. I only started wondering about it today. I remembered what Ruben said about the forests in Ohio and Indiana, and it just came to me. It's what I'd do if I really wanted to hide."

By the time the embers had died to white ashes, the young men had decided to spend the next couple of days in St. Louis, checking at the post office and cemeteries, examining military records and wagon train rosters, asking hotel and rooming house proprietors, showing Stu's picture, and leaving notices everywhere. If they still had no results by the end of the second day, they would change direction and head for Indiana and Ohio. The change in plans was exciting, but also a bit unsettling, and neither slept well.

Both young men were fascinated by the city that greeted them the next morning. Wagons careened along muddy, rutted roads, splashing pedestrians on the boardwalks. Signs proclaimed the wonders of Dr. Denton's Elixir, Union Jack Whiskey, Missouri Flour, and Long John's Tobacco. People darted among the horses and wagons, voices shouted, doors slammed, blacksmiths clanged in their fiery huts.

The commotion, the smells, and the sights nearly overwhelmed the young men. They looked at each other in embarrassed wonder as they passed through a section of town where red-lipped women called lewd remarks to them from windows and doorways. They stopped to watch thousands of cattle that milled in the stockyards, then plugged their noses and raced off, laughing. Robbie's dark eyes sparkled, and he shouted to Stephen frequently.

"Look at that! Hey, look over here! What's that?"

They stopped at military headquarters and left a formal inquiry on record, even though Stuart's name didn't show up in any of the rosters. They talked to postmasters at the main post office and the two branch offices at the city's outskirts, posted their notices, and divided bulletin boards in half, carefully scrutinizing them for any mention of a Stuart Logan.

At dark, they made their way back to their campsite, glad for the respite from the turmoil of the city. They talked of what they had seen until both dropped into exhausted sleep. After a second day spent the same way, in addition to showing Stuart's picture at the front desk of every hotel in town, it was clear that St. Louis would produce no clues for them. They peeled a few bills from William's money to pay for a chicken supper at an inn on the edge of town, then bought flour, hardtack, fresh eggs, and a side of salt pork at a bustling general store before heading back to their campsite.

Again Stephen asked across the embers, "Are you game to head East tomorrow? What do you think?" He continued, "I think if he went West from here, we would have found a trace. Maybe he just rode out on his own, but I don't think he was that foolish. But he could have hitched up with a group of other travelers on the trail and just blended in. Or used another name. If he really wanted to stay hidden, he could have done just about anything. But I really think there would have been some trace of him. In those old hotel registers. Or at a post office. He had to get supplies somewhere. He still has to. Salt and flour and essentials like that. Somebody should know of him. I hope nothing happened to him. We didn't check the cemeteries, you know."

The silence that followed his words grew until both had fallen asleep, each lost in his own thoughts of the man they knew only from pictures and words.

Stephen woke to Robbie stirring the fire and tossing on a few branches. Robbie wore a worried expression, his movements heavy. He turned to Stephen when he heard him getting out of his bedroll.

"What you said yesterday about checking cemeteries. We better do that. Why didn't we think of that before?"

The young men stared at each other.

"You're right, we have to," Stephen replied.

They broke camp in somber silence, then headed for St. Louis proper.

After solemnly walking the dewy grass between the rows of gravestones and wooden crosses at the St. Louis cemetery by early morning light, they entered the limestone caretaker's hut. There, the three two bound record books yielded nobody by the name of Logan. Stephen and Robbie headed out, their spirits lightened.

By the end of the first day heading East, they'd ridden far enough to reach a tiny town in central Indiana called Salem. Robbie's face had grown ruddy from their days in the sun and wind. He wore his black hat tipped back jauntily, and reveled in being on horseback in unfamiliar territory. His lanky frame sat comfortably on his horse, and his head bobbed every which way as he tried to absorb everything he saw. Again, Stephen realized what a perfect companion Robbie was, and he once more felt grateful for his cousin's company.

He also felt a strange and strong sense of melancholy throughout the day. The thoughts about searching cemeteries had touched on something Stephen hadn't allowed himself to think about before. What if they found only a headstone at the end of their quest? What if he had to bring back that news to Ma? Suddenly, the seriousness of this whole thing overcame him. In desperation, he pushed Robbie on until darkness made it too hard to see.

"Hey! Are we ever going to stop? It's been a long time since that pitiful lunch stop. I hardly had time to eat and I'm starved now. What's pushing us today like this?" Robbie called ahead, as Stephen reluctantly pulled up a weary Spartacus and turned back in the saddle.

"We won't make it to the border tonight, if that's what you're trying to do. It's another couple 'a hours, I reckon. Let's stop. These horses are winded. C'mon, let's stop," Robbie called out.

Spartacus dropped his head in fatigue, and Stephen chided himself for pushing him so hard all day.

"Yup. You're right." Stephen responded as he dismounted, pulled the saddle and blanket off and led Spartacus to a stream along the road. "Here ya go, boy. Sorry it's been such a long hard day," Stephen caressed his horse's shoulder and gave him a pat before turning to Robbie.

"Sorry. Guess I can't get the picture of a cemetery out of my mind. God, I hope that's not what we find." He sank to the ground by the saddlebags, but made no move to open them.

Robbie strode over and crouched beside him. "It's not what we'll find. Don't you even think like that. I bet we're on the right track. It makes sense that he would come this way. I was thinking about it all day. He liked to be on his own, my father says. Maybe Uncle Stu just found himself a place buried in the forests and there he stayed. He was a top notch shot with a rifle—brought back game all the time for Grandma, ever since he was young."

Robbie stood up and brushed the dirt from his knees. "We'll just start asking at every single place from now on. And show his picture. And leave notices. He was too tough to die. He made it through the war. All the years of it—never got wounded, even. And he must think of your Ma. He musta really loved her to stay out of her life all this time. He didn't want to make more trouble for her, the way my Pa sees it. Most men would have just gone after what they wanted. He must'a really cared. That would'a kept a tough man like him alive!"

Stephen grinned at this picture of his father and felt his spirits rise. Robbie was the best. He nodded at Robbie. "Thanks. Let me know if I push too hard again, hey? Just holler at me. Guess I got caught up in worrying."

Robbie smiled, "Sure. Let's eat. I'm starved! What do we have tonight?"

Too tired to make a campfire, they tethered the horses in a nearby meadow filled with lush clover, then unwrapped smoked fish and hardtack. With few words, they wrapped in their bedrolls as the night air cooled them to sleep.

BACK at Griffin's Tavern, Meg eagerly searched through each day's mail for a letter from her son. When one finally arrived on the mail wagon, she drank in the words Stephen had written, and wondered if his feeling about heading East was right. She was relieved that the two young men seemed to be handling life on the trail well enough, and took great comfort in the details Stephen wrote about their trip. She imagined them riding side by side, and marveled at the strength her son possessed. Ruben and Lizzie pored over the letter with her, exclaiming at the picture of faraway life that Stephen painted with his words.

Every night, Meg slept with Stephen's letters under her pillow. Somehow, this search brought Stu as much to life as if she had just been with him. Explaining all this to Stephen triggered feelings she thought had faded with the years. She felt in her heart that Stephen would find his father. She knew Stu would be coming back to her.

She wondered at the power he still held over her. After all these years, she could still see his eyes clearly and feel his lips on hers. She wished she could have known years ago how much she would miss him. She couldn't get him out of her heart. She longed for him.

CHAPTER TWENTY SIX

THE morning sun had risen high by the time they stirred. Both horses were busy munching meadow grass, and appeared well rested. Robbie fried eggs and salt pork while Stephen saddled up the horses and made sure they drank again from the stream. With determined hearts, they started off refreshed and ready to begin the search again.

This day, Robbie's mood matched Stephen's. They solemnly inquired at the next town's three boarding houses and the tiny log post office. The postmaster listened to their tale, shook his head in sympathy, and suggested they also check church records. He thought a marriage or death might be in the records that preachers always kept. Or maybe if a child had been born to this Logan, the name would be recorded.

Encouraged by this new idea, the young men checked at the town's only church. The elderly pastor, bent and white haired, listened to their eager questions with an ear cocked their way. He led them to his record book, where they scanned the names he had listed in his squiggled handwriting during the last twenty years. When they finished and had found nothing, he waved to them as they turned their horses out of town.

"Wish I could'a helped!" he called after them with a long face.

But Stephen and Robbie were encouraged by this new idea. It meant that they would be leaving no stone unturned if they checked churches along with post offices, cemeteries, and lodgings. They rode ahead, eager and anxious to reach the next town or settlement.

For the next two weeks, they worked their way east through central Indiana. It was slow going, with all the stops, and time spent asking questions, reading records, and tromping through old graveyards. Every third or fourth night, they used William's money to pay for lodging, meals, and a bath, as well as feed and a stable for the horses. They were surprised at the wilderness that surrounded them, and that settlements were so few and far between. They learned from friendly townsfolk that most settlers had eventually headed further out West, or turned south toward the more populated areas of the Virginias and Kentucky. Most had avoided the thick, unpopulated forests that stretched unbroken northward toward the Great Lakes and Canada. But because of the sparse population, memories were sharp. Old timers, grateful for new listeners, loved to tell their tales to the young men.

In this way, the history of the area came alive for Stephen and Robbie and each day brought new knowledge and adventure. They were taken by surprise on a July morning when a hunched old postmaster in a tiny town called Belle Fontaine studied Stuart's picture much longer than anyone else ever had.

"Can't be sure. No... well... Naw. Wouldn't be him... Well...," the old man croaked, peering at them over his crooked spectacles.

"What? What!" Stephen and Robbie yelled together, lurching toward him across the post office counter.

The old man leapt back, startled by their response, then regained his composure when he recognized their eagerness. "Well, this sort of looks like a young Arthur. Arthur's been around these parts, oh, must be ten years. Well, must be longer than that. Can't rightly recall. He don't look a thing like this now, mind ya. I could be dead wrong but I remember when he first came around these parts. This picture carries a resemblance. It surely does."

Stephen felt the breath leave his body in a huge gasp. He and Robbie looked at each other incredulously. Finally, a break! Finally, somebody might have a clue! They turned back to the old man.

"Where is he now?" Robbie asked.

"Yeah, is he still around?" Stephen added at the same time.

"Well, you two young bucks, jest settle down a second here. You'll git me all riled up. All I said was it has a bit of the same look. Round the eyes, there. I ain't seen him for a couple a' years now, three maybe. He never comes around since it happened."

Feeling as if he would burst with impatience, Stephen took a deep breath. "This man is my father. We've been searching for him for years. We need to know where the man you speak of is. We need to hear all you know about him. We need to find him." He paused to gulp some air.

Robbie put a restraining arm on Stephen's shoulder. He spoke to the old man, his voice slow and calm. "This could be very important information to us. Do you have time to sit down with us and tell us about it?"

The old man leaned toward Robbie. "Well, sure. You kin come around in the back here. I sit by the stove in the back room most times, 'lessen folks come in for their mail. I got time. But I gotta do my job if someone comes in, ya know."

"Sure, that's fine," Robbie replied kindly.

He pulled Stephen with him toward the end of the counter and then around behind it with him. The old man settled into what was obviously his favorite place, a wooden rocking chair worn shiny on the arms. He sat close to the heat of the orange embers that glowed in a pot-bellied stove, drew a patched quilt over his knees, and settled in. Robbie perched on the round cover of a nearby barrel, and indicated to Stephen that he should take the log bench near the stove. He nodded at the old man to begin.

"Well, ya see," the old man began. "If this is the feller yer lookin' fer, he came by first 'bout ten, fifteen years ago, like I said. Well, maybe not quite that long. Hard to remember exactly. Anyways... he first wanted a post box, fer an address, ya know. Said he was gonna homestead up north a ways. An' I reckon he did. Came to town 'bout once a month in them days, gettin' loads of supplies and lumber. But them times got fewer and fewer soon's he got a place built up there, ya know. Pretty soon, he didn't need no more nails or them things. Guess he got his cabin built. Not many's ever seen it. Too far out. Nobody hardly ever goes that far into the forest. No reason to, ya know. Maybe some hunters now and agin. That's 'bout the only news we ever hear of him. 'Fore too long, he jest never came round no more, 'cept maybe once a year. Never had no mail to speak of, either."

The old man rocked, relishing the telling of his tale. Stephen and Robbie sat mesmerized, their senses on alert. They bit back their frustration at the slow pace of the man's words. Both realized that silence would allow the fastest transfer of information. Any interruption they made would only interfere with the train of the old man's thoughts.

But Stephen couldn't help himself. He blurted out, "But what happened? Why doesn't he come in anymore? Where is he now?!"

The old man turned rheumy eyes to him. "Well, yeah, he's still out there, far's I know. It was terrible. Folks round here talked about it for quite a spell, I'll tell ya!"

His chair began to rock harder as he continued. "Well, he got hisself a woman. Now this is all jest what I heard. I didn't get it right from him, ya know."

Stephen and Robbie nodded, more impatient than ever.

"So he got the woman. I did see her, the one time. She was passin' through the same day he happened to be in town. Jest a beautiful young thing, she was. Long, shining black hair all the way down her back. Face as pretty as any woman I ever saw, big blue eyes, color of the ocean. She was with a pack of them gypsies. Pretty rough bunch, just passin' through town. On the main road, same one you been on. Arthur, he had to step aside to let them pass. Right then, her horse stumbled and she started to fall right off. He jumped in real quick and broke her fall, and she went an' fell right into his arms! They say their eyes met before he even set her down, and they never stopped lookin' at each other after that. She went with him. Jest like that. By nightfall, they were long gone. Left together on his horse with his supplies. She rode behind him in the saddle, holdin' on. Such a thing we never did see before or since!"

Stephen gasped. If this man was his father, he had taken up with another woman! A gypsy! Never had he thought that another woman might be in the picture. He listened hard as the old man continued.

"They was out there together a lot 'a years. Never had no young'uns. Anyone who passed by said the place was kep' up real well. Flowers along the side of the house. And good solid fences. They never made no trouble. Jest kept to themselves. But, oh, what happened! Can't blame the man for goin' crazy. Since it happened, he never once came to town. God, what a story!"

Stephen and Robbie held their breath. After pausing for a huge sigh, the old man went on.

"He told it to a boy who jest happened out there one day, got too far from home huntin' coon. Boy asked where the woman was. Man jest broke down and cried while he told. Guess any man would've. See, she got real sick. An' he couldn't get her better. Finally, he rode all the way to Fort Wayne, three days away, for the doc. We don't got a doc, ya know. The doc wouldn't go back with him. Said he couldn't ride three days there and three days back for one patient. Couldn't be away that long. Well, by the time Arthur got back, she was gone. Left all alone there, ya know. So, he wrapped her all nice in her best dress, fixed her hair real nice. But he couldn't bury her yet. He sat with her for two days, mournin'. Couldn't bring himself to put her in the ground. Long 'bout the second night, he fell asleep sittin' there by her, leanin' his head on the table. Musta been real tuckered out after all that ridin' and tendin' to her and then losin' her."

He paused with a faraway look in his eye. Stephen and Robbie sat, spellbound. Suddenly, there was a call from the front.

"Marvin? Marvin? You around? I need my mail."

The old man started, then struggled stiffly from the rocking chair. Stephen and Robbie could hear the murmur of voices as the old man passed the mail on to the man in the front room. They stared at each other, wide-eyed, not daring to speak.

Marvin returned, sank into his chair, and continued as if there had been no interruption. "He musta been sleepin' pretty hard. Cuz the first thing he heard was the crash. It was one a' them pitch black nights. Even with the window open, no moon shinin' in. One of those black as hell nights, ya know the kind I mean? Well, he grabbed the gun that was settin' right by his chair and fired off at a shape that was leapin' out the window. Then he lit up the lantern. God, it must'a been awful! She was layin' on the bed where he left her, but her hands and arms were bloody and grabbin' onto sumpin'. She had wolf fur in her hands and under her fingernails. Her neck was chewed up somethin' fierce."

He stopped. Stephen and Robbie had gasped in unison. No one spoke. They stared at the old man.

"Guess she wasn't altogether dead, after all. 'Til then, anyways. Folks say she was in one of them spells. Might'a come out'a it had a doc come. Or jest with time, ya know, some folks do."

The silence lengthened. Finally, Robbie shook his head. "My God! What a story! Is it true?!"

The old man nodded. "They say so. I ain't seen Arthur since then."

Through the sick feeling in his stomach, Stephen asked, "So, if it's true, how do you know he's still out there?"

"Folks have seen him. He always melts away. Doesn't wanna talk. They say them flowers along the house are something to see. Jest brilliant. And he put up a cross for her in the middle of all them blooms. She's prob'ly buried there, ya know."

Stephen swallowed and tried to regain his composure. "Do you have the records back from when this Arthur registered for a post office box? Anything?"

"Well, sure. I keep all them records. Gotta, ya know. This is a United States Post Office," he announced puffing his bony chest with pride. "I'm the only postmaster ever been at this station. I got all of 'em right in the metal boxes here. Gov'ment sends these boxes out every year for the records to be stored in."

He rose, and walked across the room to a stack of dust-covered gray metal boxes along the wall. "What year did ya say again?"

"It would have been '67 or '68, I think," Stephen replied.

"Here we go. Not many papers in this one. It was way back when I first started. I remember most folks who come along in those early days. Still remember most ever'body, to tell ya the truth."

Stephen and Robbie moved over to the stained, scarred wooden counter, and watched the old man blow the dust off a dented box and work the latch open. The box contained a small stack of ledger sheets that Martin scooped out with a practiced hand.

"What name we lookin' for agin now?" he asked with a quizzical look at Stephen as he began scanning the top page.

"Logan. Stuart Logan," Stephen replied, unable to tear his eyes from the scrawled lists the man held.

"Don't sound familiar. Nope, not at all. Don't remember a Logan," the man muttered.

He tossed the top page onto the desk. Stephen immediately snatched it. Robbie grabbed the next one. Five minutes later, they were done. There was no "Logan" on any of the pages. Stephen's heart fell as he met Robbie's stricken gaze. It had felt so right; like they were near.

"So, tell me his full name. Maybe we missed somethin' here," the old man said, sympathy in his voice as he noticed their distress.

"I don't know his middle name. Just Stuart Logan," Stephen answered misery etching his voice. "Robbie, do you know?"

Robbie shook his head.

In the silence that followed, the old man stroked his beard, deep in thought. "Ya know, that picture jest bothers me. I could'a swore it's Arthur. Looks jest like him when he first got here. Anybody else named Arthur in the family? Sometimes folks jest use another name they know. Maybe it's one of them other names here."

Robbie's head snapped up. "Yeah! My grandfather's name is William Arthur Logan! I didn't even think of it 'til now!" He looked at the postmaster, eyes shining.

All three bent their heads over the lists, which were now spread out on the desk. There it was. "W. Arthur. June, 1868. No previous address".

"W. Arthur! That could be it!" Stephen shouted. "W. Arthur! After Grandfather!" He swung an arm around Robbie's shoulder and almost danced. "I think it's him!"

Robbie nodded eagerly in assent. The old man held the ledger up. "Yep. That's his, alright. That's Arthur's. Nobody ever called him anything cept' Arthur. That's the feller in your picture!" He smiled a broad toothless grin and beamed at the young men.

"So, where is he? How do we get to him?" Stephen and Robbie shouted together.

"Well, here's how to git to his place. It's a long way, mind ya. It's hard travel out there in them forests. Not no roads like you've been travelin' on. It'll be tough goin'."

As soon as he finished giving directions, Stephen and Robbie sprinted for their horses, calling thanks back over their shoulders. They rode hard in their excitement, until the horses began to slow.

"Robbie, we have to take it easier!" Stephen finally shouted.

Robbie reined in and waited for Stephen to pull up alongside of him. "I know. I just can't go slow! My God! I think we found him!" His eyes sparkled, and he waved his arms wildly with excitement as he spoke. "This is it! God! I'm so... so... scared. What if it is him? What will we do?"

"What if it isn't him? What if he hides...?" Stephen stammered, the words tumbling out.

Robbie paused a second, and then replied, his words firm. "Well, let's just settle down here for a minute. I think it's most likely him. I think we've found him. That old man said one hard day's ride, then watch for a big, black, tepee-shaped rock on the left. That's where the trail's supposed to cut off to his place. I hope it isn't too overgrown to see the rock. We have to slow down and be real careful so we don't miss the turn. Let's just take it easy here for a minute and make a plan."

Stephen nodded. "Let's water the horses at that brook over there. You're right. It shouldn't be that hard to find, especially with the two of us watching real hard. But if we ride fast, by late afternoon we should be near the big rock. We can camp there and then we can follow the trail it marks in the morning."

CHAPTER TWENTY SEVEN

THEY rode at a steady slow pace until afternoon shadows hung dark beneath the surrounding trees. Huge oaks and elms lifted massive, leafy branches high above the trail, blocking much of the waning light. Thick brush crowded the sides, sending hungry tendrils and vines hopefully across the overgrown path. Thick, fragrant evergreens struggled upward through the dappled light.

The young men felt the power of this mighty forest, and became eager to set up camp before complete darkness overcame them. They grew subdued by the dense growth that surrounded them, muffling even the sounds of the birds. They became anxious about staying on the trail, which had begun to diminish with every mile as daylight faded. They were sure they were getting close, and watched intently for the black tepee-shaped rock the old postmaster had described.

Robbie, riding ahead, spotted it first. "There!" he called back over his shoulder. "There it is! That's gotta be it!"

Stephen galloped up beside him. There could be no mistaking the huge, pointed black rock that towered alongside the trail. They knew they would have to only follow the barely visible side trail for an hour or so from here. And, then, they'd be there. Stephen's heart beat fast as he imagined what lay ahead. He met Robbie's huge eyes. Both were breathing hard.

"It's getting too dark already with all these trees," Robbie said, glancing around, his face scrunched with nervousness. "We better call it a day like we planned. I don't want to be caught out here in the dark with panthers and wolves and bears and who knows what else out there. We could camp here until there's light in the morning. The horses are pretty tired. And we really don't want to get there in the dark, surprise him, do we?"

Stephen nodded in agreement. "Yeah, it would be stupid to approach someone so far back in the woods at night. I feel weird, anyway. The bird calls are muffled. Even the horses' steps don't sound normal in here. This is really deep forest. I'm all for setting up camp before it gets darker. I feel kind of spooked, don't you?"

"Yup. I sure do. This is heavy forest, all right. Remember what we heard about all the wolves and bears and cougars? We better make a big fire. There's plenty of wood and branches. Maybe two fires. And maybe we should sleep between the fires and the rock. Let's tether the horses close, too, don't you think?"

Both young men looked over their shoulders often while gathering wood and setting up camp, unsettled by the eerie atmosphere deep in the heavy woods, and feeling the strain of what lay ahead in the morning. Few words were spoken as they boiled a stew with the steak, potatoes, and carrots they had picked up in the last little town. By the time they finished eating, deep black shadows lay thickly around them. The natural sounds of the forest were so deadened by the dense vegetation that when an owl hooted nearby, men and horses alike jumped. Even the horses seemed to sense the eerie atmosphere and huddled as close as they could to the men, stretching their tether ropes.

Neither Stephen nor Robbie slept well, awakening in fits and starts throughout the night, in response to this unfamiliar and chilling atmosphere. They awakened with the earliest hint of gray dawn, and bolted down a breakfast of cold ham and biscuits before breaking camp.

While they saddled the horses, Robbie broke the uneasy silence, "Well, are you ready? This will be a big morning. I wonder if he's still there? I wonder what he will be like? Are you scared?" He turned from tightening his horse's cinch, his face worried.

Stephen responded, feeling an odd and unexpected bravery overcome him. This is what he had set out to do. "Yeah, I thought a lot about it during the night. Woke up a lot. Did you, too?"

Robbie nodded.

"Well, I thought about it," Stephen continued. "I shouldn't be afraid. I need to do this for my Ma. When I thought about how much she's counting on me, and all the years she's waited for him, I vowed to myself that I'd do the best that I can. I need to find my father. I just hope he's there. If all we find is an empty cabin, I don't know what I'll do."

With a firm shake of his head, he went on, "I think it'll be him. That old postmaster said our picture looked so much like him. I think we found out where he's been all this time. If he's there, I really don't know what I'll do. Depends a lot on what he's like. I'm damn scared if you wanna know the truth, but I'm not gonna stop now. I have to do this."

Robbie settled his hat further onto his forehead and tipped his head toward Stephen in agreement. "Well, I'm staying right beside you. If it's him, everyone back in Illinois will be so happy. Let's get to it!"

THAT same July morning, Meg fought a nagging, vague uneasiness. Stephen's last letter had been a little over two weeks ago, and she was anxious to hear from him again. The tasks that usually distracted her and helped the hours go by felt like annoyances today. An odd discomfort dominated her emotions, making it difficult to concentrate. Her heart felt pulled toward her son, and a strong feeling of disquiet claimed her. Thoughts of Stu were stronger than usual today. She puzzled, wondering what these feelings meant. *Is Stephen all right? Is he close to Stu?* She couldn't shake the strange mood, which overpowered her while the long day dragged on.

THE young men's early morning ride through fading mist along the faint path seemed to take forever. Neither spoke while the horses nervously picked their way along the overgrown, nearly invisible path.

Suddenly, without warning, the trees parted to reveal a large clearing. A sturdy, weathered log cabin stood centered among a profusion of blooming flowers, which rioted along all sides of the structure. Tall hollyhock stalks heavy with red and pink blossoms with scalloped edges thrust upward behind a glorious assortment of purple and yellow pansies. Bright yellow daisies, bluebells, brilliant marigolds in yellow and orange, and a border of intense white lilies-of-the-valley formed a barrier against the encroaching meadow grass. They gasped with delight at the sight, and knew without a doubt they had reached Arthur's cabin.

They sat spellbound until a sound behind them caught their attention.

Before they could turn toward it, a gruff voice commanded, "Don't turn around. I have a gun on your backs. I can shoot both of you before you know what's hit you." The voice was deep and chillingly cold.

Stephen gasped in surprise and terror. But Robbie, startled for only a moment, replied in a firm voice, "Uncle Stu? Is that you? I recognize your voice, I think. Is that you?"

There was only silence behind them until, finally, Robbie asked again, "Uncle Stu?"

The voice answered, its tone different, lower, changed. "Who are you?"

"Uncle Stu? It's me, Robbie. From home. This is Stephen with me. Stephen, your son."

Stephen was awed by Robbie's courage, and glanced sideways at him. As he did, Robbie twisted around in the saddle to look behind. Stephen followed suit, overcome by curiosity.

They saw a man dressed in worn buckskin breeches and shirt and moccasins. A thick black beard flowed over his shoulders and halfway down his chest. Stephen's attention was caught immediately by the thick, straight, dark eyebrows exactly like his own. In that instant, he knew. This man was his father.

Filled with excitement and sudden courage, he met the man's gaze and spoke, "I came to find you for my mother, Meg. We came to find you." As the words left his mouth, his voice broke and his throat tightened with unexpected, powerful emotion.

The man lowered his rifle. His mouth dropped open in astonishment. He stared at Stephen. Their eyes locked. Stephen had never been surer of anything in his life. He was looking into his father's eyes. He'd found his father! He gulped and took a deep breath. His father stood before him. Remembering his vow to his mother, and the precious letter in his pocket, he continued to meet the man's incredulous stare.

A long time passed without further movement or words.

Finally, Robbie spoke again, "Uncle Stu?"

The man shook his head. He dropped his chin and mumbled, "I can't believe it! My God!"

Stephen reached into his pocket for the letter he'd carried over his heart since the day his mother gave it to him. He thrust it toward his father. "Here, Ma sent this. She said I could read it. But I didn't. She said to give it to you when I first found you so you'll know how much she wants you to come back to her. She's waited all these years."

The man stepped forward and took the letter from Stephen with a trembling hand. He stepped back and studied the envelope. His gruff voice shook with emotion, "I don't have to read it. I remember every word. She saved it all this time?"

At Stephen's nod, the man turned away, his shoulders heaving. He kept his face averted for long moments while his shoulders trembled. Mutely, Robbie and Stephen looked at each other.

Finally, the man turned back to them and whispered broken words. "Boys, you took me by surprise here.

Get on down. Give those horses a rest. How long've you been traveling? I can't believe you're here. I can't believe you're really here!"

His face regained a bit of color as he spoke, and he bent to retrieve his rifle from where it leaned against a tree. "C'mon. C'mon with me... My God..."

With his rifle in one hand and the letter in the other, he led the way toward his cabin.

Stephen and Robbie dismounted and followed him, leading their horses. They glanced at each other once, beaming, excited, grinning, stunned by what was happening.

The inside of the cabin was dark, its only window on the back wall boarded up. Seeing them glance at the window, Stu asked, "Did you hear... about it?"

Stephen and Robbie lowered their eyes. All three stood in silence for a long moment.

Then Stu shook his head hard, as if to clear it. "I can't talk about it even now. Understand? I thought I was just meant to be unhappy. My luck is bad... I guess things just went wrong for me ever since the war..." his voice faded off.

Neither young man knew what to say. They looked around the cabin, noting the neatly made bed along one wall, and the pegs holding clothing on one wall, traps on another. A wooden counter that ran half the length of the closest wall abutted a black iron cook stove. A pile of logs rose in a neat triangle beside the door. Tin cooking utensils, cups, and plates sat on a slab counter beside glass canisters of flour, coffee, sugar, and cornmeal. A large cast iron frying pan lay atop the stove. It was a tidy and cozy room, despite the shadows, which lurked in the corners. Their eyes were drawn to a jug at the center of the counter that was filled to overflowing with blossoms from the garden

"She liked flowers," Stu offered sadly.

Stephen, overcome by empathy for his father, turned to him and reached out his arms. Stu was in them in a second, his shoulders again heaving. He returned Stephen's hug desperately and strongly. When they finally parted, both had to wipe their eyes. Robbie stood back watching, a goofy grin across his face.

He spoke, "Grandma sends her love to you, Uncle Stu. Grandfather, too. They said to tell you right off how sorry they are and how hard they've been searching for you. They want you to come home real bad. Grandmother is really crippled up now in her hands and hips. She wants you to bring Meg back with you to them so she can make peace with you both. Grandfather said to tell you he sure does miss your hand with the horses. We have thirteen palominos now, and twenty sorrels, and we started selling to the race tracks..." his voice faded as he realized he might be babbling.

But Stu's eyes lit up at the words. "Ma is still doing fine, then? Pa is good? What about that baby that was due for Bill and Virginia? Was it a boy or girl? Are there any more young'uns there...? The horses? You have twenty sorrels now? The ranch must be doing well!"

The words tumbled from his mouth too fast for Robbie and Stephen to answer.

Before they knew it, hours of excited discussion had taken place. When they finally became aware of the slant of afternoon light in the cabin, Stu declared, "Oh, your horses! We have to water them and get them some feed. Let's go. Then I'll fry us up some lunch. You must be starved!"

He turned to go outside. Robbie followed, but Stephen remained standing inside for a minute. He looked around again at his father's home and marveled that he was here. He breathed in the aroma of the cabin. This was his father's home. He'd done it. Found his father. How he longed to tell his mother right now.

Then he noticed the letter lying on the counter where Stu had laid it when they came in. All those nights it had lay buried in his pocket, calling to him to read it. But he hadn't been able to take the pages out of the envelope.

Somehow it seemed too private, too much between two lovers, not his business. But, now that he knew what his father was like, a burning curiosity made him reach for it. He slid the slim pages out and began to read.

> "My dearest Meg,
>
> By the time you read this, you should have received the mare and colt I delivered to the general store for you and our son. May the horses live long healthy lives and carry you both many miles in safety and comfort. May they remind you every day of my enduring love.
>
> I cannot, in good conscience, remain a part of your life. It looks like there would be nothing in Illinois for us except hardship. I leave you to the life you have made with your husband and new daughter. I dare not dwell on thoughts of you in the arms of another, or I will go crazy. I can only get as far away from memories of you and what I did to you as possible. I will never be able to overcome the wrong I did you or make it up to you. I'm sure I can't make it right without causing you more hardship.
>
> There is no return address on this envelope because I do not want to be found. There will never be a night that I don't fall asleep to thoughts of you. I'll carry our love in my heart until the day I die. May the sun shine upon you and yours for all the days to come. With this letter, I set you free.
>
> All my love forever,
>
> Stu.

Stephen absorbed the words. What a love his father had for his mother! His heart melted for the man outside.

Just then he heard Stu call, "Stephen. Come out. Don't tell me! This is the colt I sent?"

His father and Robbie were leading the horses toward

a small corral and lean-to shelter at the edge of the clearing, where three other horses nudged the fence curiously. Stephen quickly stuffed the letter back into the envelope and stepped out into the daylight. He nodded at them. Stu's face broke into the first smile Stephen had ever seen on his father's face. White teeth split the heavy beard, and he turned to stroke Spartacus with loving swipes of his hand.

"He's a beauty, just like I remembered," he called. "Did your mother like hers? She told me she hoped to own a horse again after losing hers to the war."

Stephen nodded again. "I named him Spartacus. Ma called hers Sugar Two."

With a satisfied grin, Stu led the horses toward the corral.

Later, Stephen and Robbie brought their saddlebags into the cabin where Stu put together a meal of leftover cornbread, dandelion greens cooked to tenderness in salt water, and crisp fried trout. They sat late around the small wooden table in front of the stove, laughing and talking and catching up on lost years, until their voices became hoarse and the blackness outside signaled deep night. Stu insisted they take his bed, while he rolled up in their bedrolls by the door.

They spent the next day packing up Stu's belongings, and the following morning headed out. As they left the clearing, Stephen tried not to notice his father turning back in the saddle for one last long look at the cabin in the clearing, his face betraying a poignant sadness.

CHAPTER TWENTY EIGHT

By the time they reached Bellefontaine, a bustling town, two days later, Stu's spirits had lifted. They spent the night at an old hotel, enjoying a supper of pork chops, gravy, boiled red potatoes, and blueberry pie. The next morning, Stephen and Robbie were astounded at the change in Stu. He'd shaved, his dark hair was neatly cut, and he wore a new white shirt, black twill britches, and shining leather boots. But most surprising of all, was the look of expectancy on his face, where before there had been only sadness. He grinned at them, and motioned them to join him in the dining room. They filled up on eggs, bacon, toast, and cold buttermilk, and set out for home.

The trip went much faster this time as they rode steadily back through the towns and settlements they had searched so painstakingly on the way. What was left of William's money bought meals, hotel rooms, and stables for the horses. By the end of the fourth day, all three were completely at ease with each other, and became ever more excited at beginning to see familiar landscape.

Their last night on the road was spent in the little town of Perrysville, where careful baths and shaving were attended to in the big wooden, hotel bath tub. They lingered long at the table after supper was finished, talking excitedly about reaching home the next day. Stu's eyes sparkled as even more details of life at the ranch and Griffin's Tavern were shared. Stephen was giddy with anticipation at bringing his mother her wish.

Robbie joked and laughed, and even sang along with the tune from the piano player in the bar adjoining the dining room.

When the dining room closed down, they reluctantly called it a night and headed to their rooms upstairs. Stephen slept only in spurts, filled with dreams of his mother and home, waking often to check the window for signs of daylight. When it finally lightened outside the window, he heard movement from Stu in the next room, and realized he wasn't the only one anxious for this day to begin.

They slipped away from the hotel early, too eager to be on their way to wait for breakfast. They rode through the steaming mist of the summer morning, heading ever further into southern Illinois. The sun promised another long hot day as it rose, already brilliant, over the pastures and farmland that bordered the road. Although they had skipped breakfast, nobody felt hungry. The horses sensed home, and moved with spirit. A quick midday stop at a stream to rest the horses and share biscuits from the saddlebags was a frustrating delay. They barely spoke, as if words, too, might slow them down.

Finally, as afternoon drew to a close, there it was—Griffin's Tavern. Stephen felt surprised by the emotion that gripped him at the sight of the familiar building. By now, it was nearly supper time, and the old brown and white dog staggered to his feet at the bottom of the steps where he'd been snoozing away another day. He sniffed the air, and began barking vigorously when the riders approached.

Lizzie ran out the front door, stopped in her tracks, then shrieked back over her shoulder, "Ma! Ruben! Come quick! It's Stephen! He's home! He has somebody with him! Oh! Come quick!" She jumped up and down in excitement, her voice high pitched and squeaking with joy, "Stephen! Stephen!"

Stephen spurred his horse forward, fighting sudden, surprising tears that blocked his vision. He was home.

He'd done it. He'd brought his mother her wish! His heart felt like it would burst with joy.

He leaped off Spartacus and charged up the steps into a waiting mass of arms. Ma's voice, and Ruben's, had never sounded so good. How much he had missed them! After the frenzy of the first few seconds, he pulled away, and looked at all three of them. Meg's glowing eyes met his for a moment, and then shifted to the other two riders who were just pulling up. She stared at the tall, dark man beside Robbie, and Stephen heard her gasp. Ruben and Lizzie moved close in beside Stephen as Meg started haltingly toward the steps. Time froze for a long moment. Meg and Stu's eyes met and locked. Nobody breathed or moved.

"Meg?" Stu finally called down, his voice low and gentle. When she didn't answer, he slipped off his horse and took a step toward her. "Meg? It's me."

A second later, they were rushing toward each other and fell together in an embrace of such intensity and natural intimacy that everyone looked away self-consciously. Meg buried her face in Stu's shirt, and her shoulders shook with silent sobs. Stu pressed her to him and bent his head to her golden hair as he cradled her to him.

"I'm here. I'm finally here, my darling. My Meg," they heard him murmur.

The words that followed were muffled by their embrace, but the tone left no doubt as to their meaning. Finally, Meg pulled back a little and looked up at the man who held her. They smiled at the same instant, bright, blinding smiles through their tears, and turned together to the others.

Robbie swung down off his horse and joined the excited group. Everyone talked at once in laughing voices as they moved back inside the tavern. Stephen noticed Lizzie hanging back, looking shy, and grabbed his little sister for a whirl until she squealed to be let down. The next hour was chaos, a frenzy of questions and answers. Ruben beamed as he served corn chowder to the hungry riders and kept mugs filled with cider and hot coffee. Robbie left right after eating, after making Stu promise to bring everyone to the ranch bright and early the next morning.

Stephen delighted in the obvious love his parents felt for each other, and knew the days ahead would be only the start of a life of happiness too long denied.

About the Author

BIO—Mary Wasche is the author of two previous mystery/romantic suspense novels, *Escape to Alaska* and *Murder in Wasilla*.

Mary Wasche was first published at age seventeen after winning a state writing contest in Minnesota. She continued to be a contributing writer to national and regional publications while pursuing careers as a dental hygienist, teacher, small business owner, and bank executive. Mary served as President of the Alaska Chapter of Romance Writers of America, Editor of the Chugiak Eagle River Historical Society newsletter, and has held membership in the Alaska Writers Guild, Chugach Writers Group, Pacific Northwest Writers Association, 49Alaska Writers and the Independent Book Publishers' Association. She is currently writing from lake country, Minnesota.

http://marywasche.com